FLIRTING WITH THE CEO

IONA ROSE

AUTHOR'S NOTE

Hey there!

Thank you for choosing my book. I sure hope that you love it. I'd hate to part ways once you're done though. So how about we stay in touch?

My newsletter is a great way to discover more about me and my books. Where you'll find frequent exclusive give-aways, sneak previews of new releases and be first to see new cover reveals.

And as a HUGE thank you for joining, you'll receive a FREE book on me!

With love,

Iona

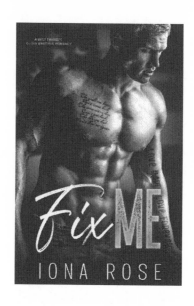

Get Your FREE Book Here:
https://dl.bookfunnel.com/v9yit8b3f7

Flirting With The CEO

Publisher: Some Books

978-1-913990-55-8

1

SUMMER

The club is just starting to get busy.

Rebecca, Jess, Olivia and I have been here for almost an hour now and while I'm glad it's starting to liven up a bit, I'm also already feeling the temperature going up and I know the heat will get to me sooner rather than later. The windows are already starting to steam up. I fan my hand in front of my face and Rebecca nods her head in sympathy with me.

"Should we go and get a drink?" Rebecca shouts over the thump, thump, thump of the music. I nod and follow her through the small groups of people clustered around the place towards the bar. The bar is the most crowded part of the club, but we duck, wiggle, and push our way to the front.

The bartender catches Rebecca's eye.

"Two gin and tonics please," she shouts.

"Four shots of red Aftershock please," I yell.

The bartender returns with our drinks, and since it my turn, I pay for them. Then I pick my shots up, two in each hand and follow Rebecca through the throng. I make my way slowly and carefully, but I still feel little trickles of the sticky liquid running down my fingers. There's not much I can do about it. I wasn't going to ask for a tray for four shots but passing by people dancing, it's hard to avoid little knocks.

We make our way back to the little nook where we were originally standing. We come to this club regularly and this is our spot. It's right on the edge of the dance floor, which means we can rush to the dance floor easily whenever one of our favorite songs comes on. It also has a handy little ledge we can stand our drinks on.

I put the shots down on the ledge and Rebecca looks at me, a questioning frown on her face.

"Four shots? Really?" she asks.

"For the four of us, no?" I reply.

She looks at me with a confused expression.

"Remember Jess and Olivia?" I remind. "They went to the Ladies' room?"

Rebecca bursts out laughing and it's my turn to look confused.

"That was like an hour ago. They are long gone now."

"Oh," I say. I laugh too when I realize how long it's been since I saw either of them and somehow still didn't really register the fact that they had clearly left. I grin at Rebecca. "Oh well. I guess that means two shots each for us then."

Rebecca groans, but she picks up the first of her two shots. I pick mine up and we raise them in the air and down them in unison. Heat floods through me as I swallow. The peppery, cinnamon taste tingles on my tongue. Together we reach for our second shot. I throw mine down my throat and quickly I take a long drink of my gin and tonic to mask the taste of the shot.

I'm starting to feel more than just a little bit tipsy now and I like it since I'm not worried about a hangover. Today is Friday so I have two full days to get over any hangover before I'm back at work on Monday. Tonight, I'm free to do whatever the hell I like, and it feels good knowing that. I smile at that thought. At the moment my favorite song begins to play and I grab Rebecca's hand and pull her onto the dance floor.

We start to dance, our arms up, our hips swaying. Lost to the music.

We dance and drink, and drink and dance for the next couple of hours. Throughout it all, we laugh and feel high on life. Tonight was one of those spur of the moment nights that always ends up being the best nights.

It's getting towards closing time now at Sound Bound. There's only about an hour left before, but the club is still in full swing. We're dancing and my feet are throbbing, but Rebecca loves this song, and we never walk away from each other.

A blonde guy moves towards us and puts his hand on Rebecca's hip from behind, swaying in time with her. Rebecca catches my eye and gives me a look – what's he like? – and I give her a barely perceptible nod back – yeah, he's cute.

She exaggerates the movement of her hips and then she turns around and she smiles at the blonde guy. He says something close to her ear and she laughs and the next moment, she's turned towards him. I'm relieved because that means I can slip away and rest my feet for a moment.

I do just that, moving back towards our spot and plonking myself down on one of the tall stools that line the edges of the club. They're mostly empty except for the odd couple and one poor girl who looks like she's got the weight of the whole world on her thin shoulders.

I massage my feet and look around, content to people watch. The crowd of people seem to move as one, a happy, sweaty undulating mass of dancers. Part of me wants to go and join the mass once more, but part of me, the part with the sore feet, is glad to be free of it. If I'd worn slightly more comfortable shoes, but then I don't feel like my dress would have looked as good.

I check my watch.

There's half an hour to go now before the club starts to kick people out and I hop down off my stool to go towards the ladies' room. I move across the club, going around the dance floor rather than across it. I join the line for a cubicle and wait. The wait time isn't too bad and I'm soon in a cubicle. It's a typical club toilet – there's no lock on the door and no toilet paper and a seat I wouldn't want to sit on if I was paid to. I hover over the seat and then pull some tissues out of my purse. I finish up, go and wash my hands and then I head back out into the main body of the club. The heat hits me as I leave the ladies' room and I decide I've had enough for one night.

I move back across the club, looking for Rebecca and I soon spot her – it wasn't that hard, she hasn't moved from where I left her. She's still on the dance floor with the blonde guy. It's clear they are into each other. Their eyes are locked on each other's faces and their movements are very suggestive.

I smile. It's about time Rebecca let her hair down and had some fun with someone.

Generally speaking, Rebecca is a relationship girl. She doesn't go to clubs to pick up random men and she only dates guys she thinks are in a place where they are ready for something serious. In other words, she's my polar opposite. I'm not interested in a relationship. I'm at a point where I'm finally making a name for myself in my career, and I don't want anything getting in the way of that. That doesn't mean I'm against a hook up if a really, really, really hot guy shows up, but that scenario is as rare as a hen's tooth.

I move through the crowd and touch Rebecca on the shoulder. She looks around and grins when she sees me and then she hugs me tightly.

"Summer," she shouts excitedly. "This is Mark."

The blonde guy gives me a smile and I smile back and do a little wave.

"Listen, I'm going to take off before the line for a cab gets too ridiculous," I say.

"Oh," Rebecca mouth.

She looks deflated looking between me and Mark and I realize she thinks I'm expecting her to come with me. I'm expecting no such thing. The only reason I told her instead of just sneaking off is because I don't want her to worry and spend any time looking for me after I've gone. I would be so mad if she did that to me so I won't do it to her.

Not that getting home is ever a problem for Rebecca. She lives in an apartment above a deli on the next block over from the club. She can literally fall over twice outside of the club and she's as good as home.

I lean towards her and whisper. "Hey, you don't have to come with me. I'll be all right."

"Really?" she asks.

"Really," I confirm. "It's not like we're going in the same direction even if we leave together, is it?"

Rebecca's grin is back, and she hugs me again.

"Thank you," she says in my ear and then she releases me. "See you soon?"

"Yeah definitely," I say. I wink at her. "Enjoy the rest of your night."

"Oh, I will," she laughs.

I give her upper arm a final squeeze and then I give Mark another little wave and head for the exit. The cool night air is refreshing for about a minute and then it makes goosebumps appear on my arms and legs. I start to regret the short dress I'm wearing as I head to the curb to hail a cab.

I reach the line and join it. It's not too bad yet but I know I got here just in time before the massive influx of people at closing time descend on the line at once. I cross my arms and rub my upper arms with the opposite hands. It warms me slightly but not enough to stop me from stamping my feet up and down on the ground.

"Chilly?" an amused sounding male voice asks from behind me.

I half-turn ready to give a cheeky retort, but I find myself speechless when I see the owner of the voice. The voice is sexy – low and husky and I'm expecting someone who is pretty, good looking. What I'm not expecting is the most gorgeous man I have ever seen in my life outside of a movie screen. He's tall, around six feet I'm guessing, and his body is lean and in a nice proportion. No like one of those beefy bodybuilder types but he's no slouch and I can see the defined muscles of his arms beneath his white t-shirt sleeves. I also see what looks like a tattoo of a dragon's head poking out of one sleeve.

I look up at his face for the second time. The first time in my life, I was so taken aback by how good looking a man was, I shamelessly and openly drink him in. He must be a bit older than me – maybe in his mid-thirties to my twenty-nine. His silky black hair is brushed across his forehead and I have to stop myself from reaching out and running my hand through it. He has a strong jawline and well-defined cheekbones that makes him look almost like a Roman statue.

But all that pales into insignificance when I look into his eyes. They are, I suppose, gray, although to me, in the light of the streetlamp, they look silvery and shine like the precious metal. As I stare into those truly mesmerizing eyes, he looks back into mine and I see his irises begin to dilate, and I know he's reacting to me.

Whoa! Somehow, this gorgeous man is attracted to me! And his eyes are betraying his lust for me.

"Go on, speak. I promise I won't bite," he drawls with a wolfish smile.

His smile widens and shows a row of straight, white teeth. I stare at the tiny dimple that appear on his right cheek. To my amazement I feel myself getting wet just looking at him. I give my head a small shake as I remember – I'm being rude. He asked me a question and I can't find the words to answer it.

It wasn't even a difficult question. He only asked me if I'm chilly. The answer is: Yes, I was until I looked into his eyes and heat consumed my body. But I'm not about to say that to him so instead I just give him a half nod.

"I'd give you my jacket but as you can see, I don't have one," he says with an apologetic smile.

"It's okay. You probably wore the fitting T-shirt for the same reason I wore a mini dress," I croak.

He laughs at that, and I feel myself relaxing. Despite the heat between us, he seems like a pretty chilled out guy.

"I don't remember seeing you in Radium," he says. "And I'm damn sure wouldn't have forgotten you if I had."

I smile at his compliment even as I feel my cheeks flushing slightly. I tell myself to stop it. It was just a line and a cheesy as hell one at that. This thought does nothing to stop me from feeling warm inside though.

"That's because I was in Sound Bound," I say, nodding my head in the direction of the club I have just left.

"I sure picked the wrong club tonight," he says.

"You did," I agree. "It was bouncing in there."

"That's not what I..." he starts, then shakes his head slightly and smiles. "You knew exactly what I meant."

I can't help but laugh and he laughs with me.

"So, you had a good night then?" he asks after a moment.

"Yeah," I say. "I really did. What about you?"

"Nothing special, but it wasn't awful or anything." He pauses. "But it's certainly looking up now."

"Is that so?" I murmur with a raised eyebrow.

I'm almost at the front of the cab line and I don't want the time with this man to end. "Shall we share a cab?" I hear myself asking.

"Come home with me," he says, his eyes darkening and his voice intense.

I blink at how confident and forward he is. That wasn't a question or a suggestion. It was a command. He didn't ask if I wanted to go home with him, he just told me that I should. I like that. I like a man who knows what he wants and isn't afraid to say so.

For a few seconds I silently debate playing hard to get, make him work for the yes, but what's the point? He's old enough to have had his share of women and he must know when someone is into him. And I'm definitely into him. He would make the perfect one night stand. Playing hard to get at this point will just make me look like I'm craving attention.

"Ok," I say.

I feel that heat swirl around my body as I agree to his command.

If he is taken aback by my willingness to oblige him, he doesn't show it. He just smiles slowly at me. Fucking hell, look at him I can't imagine he gets many 'no thank yous'.

The couple in front of us get into the cab that pulls up and we're next. We shuffle forward as a large group of men join the back of the line. They are a fair distance away from us, but they're shouting and laughing, and they are so loud it still almost drowns out what he says next, although I do manage to catch it.

"I'm Len by the way," he says.

"Pleasure to meet you Len," I smile.

Then another cab pulls up and he opens the door and gestures for me to get in. I clamber in and shuffle across the seat. Len follows me in and pulls the door closed behind him.

"Ten ninety-three Miller Square please," he says to the driver and the cab pulls away.

I stay quiet, trying to hide my surprise. Miller Square is in one of the most desirable zip codes in the city. It's the home of investment bankers and traders and several B list celebrities. I peer at Len out of the corner of my eye. Is he a model or something that I haven't recognized yet? I'm sure he isn't although he is most definitely hot enough to be.

"What do you do for a living?" I ask after a moment.

"You really want to talk about work right now?"

I shake my head. Truth is I don't. I don't care if Len is some sort of celebrity or if he is a trust fund kid. Tonight is all about finding a hen's tooth. I don't need to spoil it with mundane reality.

"I know what you're doing now," he murmurs softly. "You heard my address and now you're trying to work out if I'm the face of some fancy cologne or something aren't you?"

I debate saying no but he must be able to read the truth on my face and instead I shrug.

"Just wondering if you're not going to be on Oprah or something and tell her about the time you took a girl home that was so clueless she didn't even know who you were?"

Len laughs. "Nope you're definitely safe from that. I have a normal job that pays well."

The cab reaches Len's house and I get out as he pays the cab driver . I look at the house we're stopped outside and my jaw kinda drops. The house isn't just a house. It's more of a mansion. Like something out of a movie. I'm not exactly poor and my apartment is in a nice neighborhood, but this place is in another league altogether.

Len joins me and then he opens the gate and gestures for me to follow him. I follow him up the impressive driveway and to the front door. He pulls out a key, unlocks it and we go inside.

"Would you like a drink or anything?" Len asks, his breath feels warm and close to my head. I feel a shiver go through me.

"No thank you," I whisper.

I've drunk enough already, and I know my limits.

He holds his hand out to me. "Your wish is my command."

I take his hand and he leads me towards a wide staircase. We start to climb it and I feel myself blushing when I realize he took my refusal of a drink to mean I wanted to go straight to bed with him. I debate explaining that's not quite what I meant but what's the point? I do want to get into his bed with him and it's not like I'm going to see him again so what does it matter if I seem a little eager? It's better than having to make awkward small talk.

Lights come on as we walk, lighting up the stairway in front of us. We reach what I think is the top of the stairs, but Len turns and leads me up another flight of stairs. I keep following him and we step off this flight and into a long, cream hallway with deep pile carpet. It's painted cream, a fluffy white carpet finishing it off. Every few feet there is a modern painting displayed.

"So you like modern art?" I ask as I follow Len along the hallway.

"Yes. Do you like them?"

"Yeah," I say. "I'm no art critic but I like the bright colors. They work really well in this space."

He nods, seemingly pleased I like his choice of artwork. Finally, we reach a door. He opens it and pulls me into his bedroom. The room is huge. The wall opposite is all glass. Outside lights show me a stunning view of Len's back yard, including a large swimming pool, and countryside for miles.

I look away from the view and around the room. In the center is a huge bed, the sheets and comforter black satin. The floor is covered in the same plush white carpet as the hallway, and it offsets the black bedding and the black wood furniture perfectly. The wardrobe and chest of drawers and the nightstands are all black wood and although the room is very masculine, it also feels inviting. I suppose this moment should be kind of awkward, it really isn't.

Len moves behind me and closes the bedroom door. He turns to light down so its cast enough of a glow to see by. Then he puts his hand on the small of my back and guides me towards the bed.

"You never did tell me your name," he notes cordially.

We are almost at his bed, and I grin at him over my shoulder.

"No, I didn't," I agree.

"Ohhh little Miss Mysterious, huh," he taunts

I shrug and grin back. He pulls me into his arms, and he looks at me, his face serious, and his gaze so intense that I feel as though he's looking down into my very soul.

"There are more important things to know about you than your name," he says, his voice deep and lust filled. I feel a rush of warmth between my legs. He leans in and brushes his lips against mine, the touch so light it's almost as though I imagined it. His teasing touch sets my body on fire, and I want him so badly it's like a physical ache inside of me.

"More important things like how you taste," he whispers.

He leans in again and this time, when his lips touch mine, he doesn't keep his touch light, and he doesn't pull away. Our lips move together, our tongues colliding and mashing together as we hungrily explore each other's mouths. Len tastes of beer and something kind of spicy and exotic. I love the taste of him.

I want to consume him.

I press my body against his and wrap my arms around him, moving them beneath his t-shirt and over the naked skin of his back. I grab the hem of his t-shirt and lift it up. Our mouths pull apart long enough for the t-shirt to go over Len's head and then they come together again, more hungry than before if that's even possible.

I run my hands over Len's back and up and down his sides. I push my hands into his jeans' pockets and caress his ass through the rough denim. He runs his hands over my body too and one settles on my right breast, rubbing it through the fabric of my dress. I'm not wearing a bra and the friction of the dress rubbing over me brings my nipple to life. It springs up, hard and sensitive, and Len gently pinches it, rolling it between his finger and his thumb and I moan into his mouth.

I press myself even harder against him and I can feel his hard cock pressing against my belly. I want to feel him inside of me and I move my hands from his ass around to the front of his body where I push them between us and open his jeans. I push them down and I run my hand over the outside of his boxer shorts, feeling the length of his cock. I start to push my hand into his boxer shorts, but he grabs my wrist, his mouth coming away from mine.

"Not so fast," he says.

Before I can wonder if I've done something wrong, he pushes me backwards and my legs hit the bed and I tumble down onto it and I realize what he meant – not so fast to touch him because he doesn't want to climax too early and end our fun.

He stands looking down at me on his bed and I look back. His body is every bit as toned as it looked through his clothes and I see now that his dragon tattoo doesn't just sit on his arm – the body of the beast covers part of his chest too. There's something sexy about the tattoo and I keep looking back at it as Len leans down, still looking at me as he takes off his shoes and socks and kicks his jeans off his legs. He reaches down to me and tugs at my dress. It has already worked its way over my hips and so I lift my upper body from the mattress and lift my arms up and Len slips it off over my head and drops it on the ground with his jeans.

He grabs the sides of my panties, I lift my ass and he removes those too, pulling my shoes off while he's down there, his gaze lingering on my glistening slit as he pulls the panties down my legs. When they join the other clothes on the ground, I expect Len to get on top of me, but he doesn't. Instead, he kneels down at the side of the bed. He takes my ankles in his hands and pulls me roughly towards him. He throws my legs over his shoulders and his face comes towards me.

I gasp as his warm, rough tongue finds my slick clit and begins to work it. This is a man who knows how to pleasure a woman and he doesn't mess around. He moves his tongue from side to side, lapping at my clit and pressing down on my most sensitive nerve endings. I writhe beneath him, and I tighten my thighs, bringing them together and holding Len's head in place.

I move my hips in time with his tongue, enjoying the double movement sensation. I can feel my clit tingling deliciously, spreading pleasure outwards and up into my stomach. My pussy aches to be filled and it clenches as another wave of pleasure spreads through my body.

As I hurtle towards a climax, I grab his comforter in both hands, turning them into fists, twisting the cool fabric in my grip. My head goes back and my back arches as he hits the spot one more time and sends me headlong into an orgasm.

I close my eyes and let myself feel the tingling pleasure all the way through my body. My stomach contracts and my pussy tightens. Fireworks explode on my skin sending pleasurable little sparks rolling over me. I call out Len's name as I hit the peak of my orgasm and then I'm silent, gasping for breath as I coast gently back down.

I get no reprieve. The second my muscles turn to jelly, and I lose the hold on Len I had with my thighs, he stands up, my legs falling to either side of him. He smirks at me, a look that is all sex. It's such an intense look that I feel my already desperate pussy clench again.

I start to sit up, but Len has other ideas. He reaches down and takes hold of my knees and then he flips me onto my belly. I don't resist him as he pulls me closer to him by my legs. When I can feel his skin against mine, I push myself up onto all fours.

I hear the rustle of fabric and I figure Len is taking his boxer shorts off. I try to see over my shoulder, but he's standing just out of my line of sight. I'm eagerly awaiting his touch and the anticipation of it is making me crazy with desire.

When his touch finally comes, it comes in the form of a short, sharp slap across my ass cheeks. It's not something I've ever experienced before and I cry out, a mix of, not pain exactly, but surprised indignation and of course, pleasure. I'm not quite sure if I like it but I find myself wanting him to do it again all the same and he doesn't disappoint.

Another sharp slap in the same spot leaves my skin hot and smarting but as the nerve endings register the slight stinging pain of the slap, they send pulses of pleasure through me, and I moan and press my ass backward towards Len.

He slaps me again and I cry out, a sound filled entirely with pleasure now not pain, and I feel myself teetering on the edge of another orgasm, something I would have said was impossible from being spanked.

I wait for the next slap, but it doesn't come. Instead, Len plunges inside of me. There is no warning, no gentle pushing against my opening. He slams in hard and fast, and he fills me right to the top. I cry out again and Len begins to thrust in and out of me. My pussy is wet and slick and Len's huge cock thrusting in and out of me feels absolutely amazing. With each thrust, his tip hits my g-spot on the way back in and that feeling along with the tingling in the skin of my ass sends me over the edge within moments.

I hurtle into an orgasm that seems to consume my full body. Of course, my clit feels it, and it's pulsing with ecstasy, and my pussy tightens around Len's cock as he moves inside of me. But it's more than that. Every nerve in my whole body is thrumming, every bit of me is tingling and when I climax, I climax so hard that I lose consciousness for a second. It's long enough for my elbows to give way and I find myself on my knees, my cheek on the bed.

Len doesn't stop moving inside of me despite the state of me and I love that. I love that he knows I can take this even if my body has betrayed me in the worst possible way. When my orgasm has mostly faded away, I try to push myself back up onto my hands but the muscles in my arms are too weak to move and I stay on my face, but I pump my hips in time with Len's thrusts. His hands are on my hips now, moving me harder and faster as he hurtles towards his own climax.

With one final, hard thrust that makes me scream out, Len climaxes. I feel him spurting inside of me, his cock releasing his pleasure along with his seed. His hands stay on my hips, and he holds me in place as he makes a low, growling sound in the back of his throat.

He holds me until his orgasm is done and then he slips out of me, and he flops down on his back beside me on the mattress. I pull my legs out from under me, staying on my front, my head turned to face Len. He is gasping and panting and it's clear that he felt his own orgasm as strongly as I felt mine.

For a second, I almost regret the fact that I will never see Len again, but I remind myself that it was that knowledge that allowed me to fully let go and enjoy what Len had to offer.

I fold my arms beneath my face and sigh contentedly as I wait for Len to recover. I'm wondering if maybe we're going to do that again and my pussy is aching for Len's cock once more, but a glance at his face tells me it's probably not going to happen. Len's breathing has pretty much reached a normal pace again, but his eyes are already closing. He opens them again and turns his head slightly towards me and gives a sleepy smile and then his eyes close again. He's clearly spent and even if I can keep him awake, I don't think he's going to have it in him to do that again right now.

He reaches across his body, his arm slow and sluggish. He picks my hand up and puts it on his flat stomach and covers it with his own. It's an intimate gesture, something that would normally freak me out, but I tell myself it's only my hand and it's only for a little while. It's not like he's telling me he wants us to fall asleep in each other's arms and wake up together every morning.

I lay beside Len waiting for his breathing to even out. It doesn't take that long, and I'm soon confident that he's asleep but I wait. I need him to be deeply asleep so I can get up and grab my stuff and get out of here without waking him up.

I jerk awake and look around wondering where the hell I am. I see Len beside me, and I remember. I check my watch wondering how long I've been asleep for. I'm shocked to see that it hasn't been more than half an hour. I feel like I've been out for ages. Me falling asleep was never part of the plan but it passed the time quickly and Len must be in a deeper sleep by now.

I push myself up onto my knees and turn so I'm sitting up. He doesn't stir. I take my hand off his stomach, pulling it out from underneath his hand. His hand slides down his side and onto the mattress beside him and he makes a half snoring sound, but he doesn't wake up and I breathe a sigh of relief. Having a conversation at this point would just be awkward.

I scramble off the bed as quietly as I can and grab my panties and slip them on. I pull my dress over my head and pick my purse and shoes up. I creep to the door and open it. I look back once.

Len is still sound asleep and even laid there with his mouth slightly open he is still gorgeous. I'm wondering if I'm making a mistake sneaking away like this, but I know deep down inside of myself that the mistake would be me staying.

I slip out of the bedroom, then run down the corridor, down the stairs, and out of the front door. I wait till I'm out of sight of the house before I pull my cellphone out and call myself a cab.

As I wait for the cab, I can't help but keep thinking of Len.

It's hard not to when I can smell him on my skin and taste him on my lips. It doesn't matter how much I like him though or how good he was in bed. I'm not looking for a relationship right now, not even a casual one. I got what I was looking for; good, no strings sex. I wonder if I should feel bad about sneaking away like this, but I think it's for the best for both of us.

I hate the awkward, morning after conversation where we would both pretend we were going to see each other again, even though we both would know we really had no intentions of it. This way is just easier. Cleaner. More honest. And let's face it, Len was looking for a hookup every bit as much as I was.

You don't just ask someone at the cab line to come home with you if you're looking for more than a one-night stand.

As wonderful as it was, it's over, I told myself, but for some strange reason, I couldn't help feeling slightly sad about it.

2

SUMMER

TWO MONTHS LATER

I pull a small piece of lettuce out of my sandwich and nibble on it absently. There is a meeting coming up after lunch about the future of the company and I have to admit I am nervous.

"So, what do you guys think is going to happen with the new owners then?" Gary says, voicing the thing we were likely all thinking about.

"I don't think it's going to be good news," Suki replies.

"Yeah, but you always look on the bad side. You're such a negative Nelly," Gary says.

"Negative Nelly? Really?" I say with a soft laugh.

"It's something Laura and I are trying with the baby when she has a tantrum," Gary says.

"I'm not having a tantrum. Or being negative. I'm just saying I don't think it's going to be good for us. Surely the new owners will have their own people they will want to bring on board," Suki says.

"Maybe not," I put in. "I mean if they did, then why buy this firm at all? They could just start their own firm."

"Yeah, but they want the client list don't they. That's why they bought the firm," Gary says.

"True," I agree. "I'm not sure they would call us all together for a meeting this way if it was just to tell us to pack our shit and go. Wouldn't they do it by email or something where we couldn't all have a go at them."

"Maybe. Or maybe they think that telling us to our faces is the least they can do seeing as they are getting rid of us," Suki says.

I take a bite of my sandwich and chew it thoughtfully. There are equally good arguments for why we might get kept on by the new firm and why we might be let go by them. We won't know for sure one way or the other until after the meeting. Anything else is just speculation and scare mongering really.

"Seriously though, if the worst does happen do you guys have any plans?" Gary asks. "Because I don't and that's what worries me more than anything else."

"I think I might go out on my own you know," Suki says. "If they get rid of me. It'll probably be the only way I'll ever be brave enough to do it. I can't imagine leaving a secure steady job to go out on my own but if I don't have a secure steady job anyway, then why not?"

They both look at me.

"I'll come and work for you Suki," I joke. I pause and think for a moment. "Seriously I guess I'd have to look for a job at another firm."

And pray I get one before my parents get wind of what happened. I couldn't stand the lecture I would get if I was seen to be unemployed by them. I know the lecture by heart – being a doctor is safe and reliable and you don't get fired without reason. Just because I know it already doesn't mean I want or need to hear it again.

I mean in theory; my parents make all good arguments, but medicine isn't my passion. There's too much ick involved for my liking. And I would miss getting to be creative. And let's face it, as an architect, the chances of being sued for accidentally killing someone are a hell of a lot lower than they are for a doctor and that suits me just fine.

"Maybe they'll keep some staff and not others," Gary is saying. "I don't know whether that will be good for us or not. If they want to keep the best staff, then we're good. But if they want to keep the cheaper staff with less experience and mold them into their way of thinking then it's adios for us."

"Can't we sue them if they let us go for no reason?" Suki says.

"No, because we don't have a contract with them. They technically aren't firing us. Our contract with our old employer ended and this is our new employer deciding whether or not to give us a contract," Gary says.

"You just like the idea of suing someone," I laugh.

"I know," Suki agrees, also laughing. "But it seems so pointless marrying an attorney if you don't get to sue someone at some point. I may as well have married a plumber. At least then I'd have a nice bathroom."

We all laugh at that, and the conversation moves on to Suki's husband's latest case. Of course, she isn't allowed to tell us much – she claims she isn't privy to much, but I'm sure that's a lie – but she tells us a few bits that are public knowledge, and I suspect, one or two that aren't.

"I think we best start making our way to the conference room," Gary says, nodding to the clock above the fridge in the break room.

The meeting with the new owners isn't due to start for another ten minutes yet. I frown at Gary.

"Are you planning on crawling there or something?" I ask. "We've got ten minutes yet and the conference room is like two doors down from here."

"I know but if I'm going to lose my job, I at least want to be seated comfortably for the apology," he says.

Suki and I exchange glances and roll our eyes, but Gary starts packing his things away and we join him. We may as well be sitting in the conference room as here. I pick up my trash and gather Gary and Suki's too and I go and put it all in the garbage can and then I come back to the table and retrieve my cell phone from the table. Suki and I follow Gary to the conference room.

I'm pleased that we are not the first to arrive, but we are far from the last and we get good seats at the table. I put my cell phone on silent in case I forget later on, and I slip it into my pants' pocket.

The room soon starts filling up and it begins to get uncomfortably warm. I debate taking my jacket off, but I decide against it. I purposely wore a pantsuit today because somehow the jacket feels like armor and to take it off will leave me too bare, too exposed, if we are about to get bad news.

Someone opens a window, and the temperature becomes more bearable. The room is a buzz with conversation, and most of it is speculation about what is about to happen and what it will mean for us. I join in with the odd comment here and there, but I mostly stay quiet. I've been through a hundred scenarios in my head, and none seem to be any more or less likely to be the right one than any of the others based purely on what we know about the takeover.

The conference room door opens again and this time, a hush starts to spread out through the room until everyone is quietly watching the man who has entered the room. He stands at the head of the conference room table, a seat that has been left empty for him I now notice. There is something commanding about him, a presence which demands our attention. He is obviously one of the new owners of the firm, although I have no idea which one he is, Jack Wilkinson or Tyler Clark.

He looks younger than I expected him to. Our old partners were both in their seventies and maybe an injection of someone younger might be exactly what this company needs.

The man has dark hair with a few tiny flecks of silver gray which rather than making him look old, make him look worldly and intelligent. His piercing blue eyes scan the room and I feel as though he sees more than he lets on. He's wearing smart black pants and a light blue shirt with a darker blue tie. No jacket.

"Good afternoon, everyone," he says after a moment. He smiles warmly. "I'm Jack Wilkinson. Thank you all for coming. I'm sure you all have some questions, and I'm going to try and address those questions as best I can. Let me start by addressing the biggest worry you likely all have. Everyone's job is safe."

A collective sigh of relief goes up in the room. Jack pauses and gives us a moment to take in the good news. I must admit I am more relieved than I thought I would be, and I'm eager to hear what else he has to say.

"Obviously everyone will be expected to sign new contracts. Our administration team is currently working on that. Your new contracts will be based largely on your existing ones so your salaries and any bonuses or benefits that are in your current contract will be brought over to your new one. The only major change, which I think you will all be pleased to hear, is that we believe that happy employees are more productive than unhappy employees and after some research, we discovered that extra vacation time seemed to be the answer to making employees happy. You will all be getting ten weeks paid vacation time instead of the standard five," Jack explains with a smile.

When he told us our jobs were safe, people held back. There were smiles, quiet sighs of relief, a few exchanged looks of relief between friends. This time, there is no such holding back. The room erupts in a cheer of approval, and I have to hand it to Jack. He knows how to get a group of people on his side. He can say pretty much anything now and people won't care because he has just doubled their paid vacation time.

"We are, or should I say were prior to this buyout, a pretty small firm. There is myself and Tyler, my partner, and then we have a team of about twenty staff. That includes our architects, HR, administration and cleaning staff. We do have a healthy client list though that will be merging with your current client list. One of the most attractive things about this company was the fact that it was large enough to have a fair few junior architects working here," Jack says. "Because of our big client list and small number of staff, we had hit that point where we kind of plateaued as a company – we couldn't take on more work and grow because we didn't have the resources to complete the work and we couldn't take on more staff without the income from the new work – it was a major catch twenty-two and we couldn't get out of it. Now we can, because we have all these extra bodies at our disposal. I would like some of the junior architects to work with my guys on their client lists and allow them to free up some time for acquisitions."

He pauses again and looks around the room. He smiles.

"I'm sorry, obviously at this point I don't know who is

who, but I'm hoping that the ones smiling and nodding their agreement are the junior architects," he said. This got a small laugh and he smiled wider. "We've spent a lot of time going through everyone's portfolios and client lists and seeing what you are working on right now."

Great, I think to myself. If anyone is getting the chop it'll be me because I've just wrapped up a big project and I only have small stuff now, stuff that a junior could easily take care of. But then again, I do have the company's biggest client on my books so that should go in my favor.

"I've arranged for a team of decorators to come in over the weekend and change the décor to one that suits our company, and to hang the new sign. I have also arranged for a team of IT professionals to come in and change the company logo and all of the branding and update it on all of your systems. Do I have admin staff here at this meeting?" Jack says.

He looks around expectantly and a few nervous looking hands go up.

"Good, good," he says. "I need you guys to make sure that any previously printed paperwork which goes out to clients is shredded and ones with the new letterheads are printed off to replace them."

The admin staff nod. That seems like something pretty standard that they were likely expecting to be asked to do.

"Tyler and I would like to get to know you all individually and consequently, we have set up meetings with you all over the next couple of weeks. You will receive an email today detailing the date and time of your meetings with us both. We will then likely have another one-on-one meeting towards the end of the year where we'll talk about your progress with the job and you can discuss how you think the takeover is going," Jack says. "But as I said, we are mostly going to be blending in and getting into our work loads. Nothing will change for you guys on the daily so I would ask that you all do the same until further notice. Does anyone have any questions?"

"What happens if we don't meet your expectations at this second meeting?" someone asks.

"That will depend on how far out of the acceptable box you are and what reason you have for it. If, for example, you seem to have not done enough work, but you can show that you have a needy client who demands all of your time, then you wouldn't be penalized for that. If it's say, a quality issue, we might put you on report for a few months until you get your head back in the game," Jack said. "But I'm sure it won't come to that for any of you otherwise Charles would have gotten rid of you years ago."

He smiles as he says it and a few of my co-workers smile nostalgic little smiles of their own at the mention of Charles, one of the partners from before the takeover.

"Anyone else?" Jack asks.

No one responds and he smiles again.

"Great," he says. "If anything comes to you, both Tyler and I operate an open-door policy so feel free to come and ask us anything you think of. In the meantime, thank you for your cooperation. Meeting adjourned."

Jack's cell phone beeps and he takes it out of his pocket, glances at it, and puts it back away. The conversation had begun to flow almost immediately as he said that the meeting is adjourned and those people who were standing at the back are already leaving the room when Jack speaks up again.

"Sorry, one more thing. Do we have a Summer Malone here?" Jack says.

I tentatively raise my hand. This is it; I think to myself.

I've been chosen as the scapegoat. I'm the one he's going to fire just to show people that he might be a nice enough guy but he's not a soft touch. It will keep everyone on their toes a little bit more.

"Can you hang back please Summer, there's something I want to talk to you about," he says.

I nod mutely as the others head for the doors. It's like a silent scramble to escape made even more essential now that a target has been chosen to be taken out. They all know it could have been them. I certainly haven't had any performance issues, so this must have just been a name chosen at random.

I could threaten him with a lawsuit. Nothing will come of it. This firm owes me nothing, but he might just agree to keep me to stop the annoyance of a lawsuit. Or I could prove to him why I deserve to stay. Could I even go so far as to suggest who should go instead?

Most everyone has left the room now leaving just me and Jack and I find I don't know what to say. I decide to not say anything for the moment – it was Jack who asked me to stay, not the other way around; let him be the one to speak. I'm not in the mood to make this easy for him.

"Thank you for staying back Summer," Jack says as the last stragglers leave the room. He smiles and comes towards me. He sits on the table a few places down from me. "Tyler has a new project in the pipeline. It's for an up-and-coming tech company. They have had several projects in the works for a long time and they are ready to launch with a bang, but first, they want their own premises design."

I nod along, wondering why he's telling me this. Have I come across one of the owners before and somehow pissed them off to the point they are refusing to work with the company while I'm here?

"It's set to be a big project and Tyler has looked through all of the architect's portfolios and he's very impressed with yours and he wants you to work with him on it. That was him just now on my cell phone. He got caught up with a meeting running over so he couldn't make our meeting, but he's on his way in now and he asked for me to get you to wait here for him," Jack says.

The relief I'm feeling must show on my face because Jack frowns a little bit but then he laughs softly, his eyes crinkling slightly as he does.

"Oh my, I'm so sorry. You thought you were going to be let go, didn't you?" he says.

I debate denying it but what's the point? He knows it's not true and he doesn't seem offended or anything, so I nod my head.

"You don't have to worry about that here, Summer. I don't play games. And a bit of advice for you. If you ever find yourself working for someone who has to fire a member of staff for no reason just to get the other staff to do their jobs, that's probably someone you don't much want to be working for," Jack says.

I smile and nod my agreement.

"Good advice," I say.

He hops down from the table.

"I think you'll do well here, Summer," he says. "I look forward to getting to know you better."

"Likewise," I say as he heads for the door.

He smiles back at me before he pulls the door open and leaves me alone in the room. I'm a little bit lost as to what to do with myself. He didn't say how long Tyler was going to be and I hate just sitting with nothing to do. I don't think it will make a great impression if Tyler arrives and finds me messing around on my cell phone though so instead, I stand up and begin to tidy the chairs in the conference room. Why a group of adults have such trouble pushing their chairs back under the table after a meeting is beyond me, but there I have it.

I hear the door open, and I turn around. I'm expecting Tyler or one of the staff coming in to see if they've left something behind. Maybe even Suki or Gary coming to see if I've been let go. What I am most definitely not expecting is Len. Yes. That Len. Smoking hot one night stand Len.

"What the…" I start and then I stop. "Are you lost?"

I know as soon as I say it that it's a stupid thing to say but I just blurted it out in the moment. I'm distracted by being reminded of how damned hot Len is. If I thought he looked good in jeans and a t-shirt, it's nothing compared to how he looks in his expensive looking suit. The tailoring is perfect, the suit a perfect fit. If he was to turn around, I know his ass is going to look fine. I need to stop thinking like that though. I need to find out what the hell is going on.

"You're Summer Malone?" Len says after a moment of silence.

I nod my head.

"Yeah," I say. "What, are you stalking me or something?"

"Or something," Len says. He moves to the conference room table and sits down and gestures for me to do the same. I hesitate but then I go and take the seat beside him. I still have no idea what's going on but arguing about whether we sit down or stand up isn't going to help solve anything. "I'm Tyler Clark, part owner of Clark and Wilkinson."

That does it. I feel my jaw drop whether in surprise, horror, or both, I'm not quite sure. Len is my boss now? And his name obviously isn't Len. I don't feel so guilty about sneaking out on him now. He obviously didn't want me to be able to track him down or he wouldn't have given me a fake name. But it seems like he had a change of heart when he saw that I now work for him. I hope he doesn't think I'm one of those women who will sleep with the boss to get ahead.

"So, you bought the company," I say. "That explains why you're here, I guess. But really, out of everyone you chose me to work on this project. Am I meant to believe that's just coincidence?"

"You're not meant to believe anything," Tyler says with a sigh. "As I'm sure Jack explained, I've had a look through everyone's work portfolios, and I liked your style and I think we'd be a good fit for the project. But now that you mention it, it is a coincidence. How on earth could I have chosen you specifically? You never did tell me your name."

I realize that is true and I am a bit embarrassed now that I have accused him of stalking me. I need to get off the back foot here.

"Well at least I was honest about not telling you who I was unlike you who gave out a fake name," I counter.

"I didn't give you a fake name. I said my name was Tyler, but you obviously misheard. The first time you called me Len, I wasn't sure if I had heard you right or not and then when you said it again and I knew you had, it seemed too late to correct you, so I just went with it," he says.

For a second, we are quiet and then as one, we both burst into laughter.

"Oh my God, that's fantastic," I laugh. "So, I was calling you the wrong name all night?"

"Yeah," Tyler smiles. "And I have to say it was a little bit distracting hearing you scream some other guy's name."

I laugh again but I feel my cheeks go pink at his mention of what we did. I need to make it clear that it was a one-time thing, and it won't happen again. Even if I can already feel myself being drawn to him once again.

"About that," I say. "I'm not saying I didn't enjoy it because I did, but that's all it can ever be. Just that one night."

"Obviously," Tyler says. "You could have just told me you weren't looking for anything instead of running away though."

"I didn't run away as such, I just... we were done so I left. I find the whole morning after conversation about it icky and awkward," I admit.

"Like this one?" Tyler says with a smile.

"Exactly like this one," I agree.

"Ok, so let's draw a line under it. We had a night of fun and now it's over and we're nothing more than work colleagues who may or may not become friends," he says. "The sex meant nothing, and we have no intention of repeating it."

"Line drawn," I say. "Now tell me about this project."

Tyler begins to explain the project and I see that he is passionate about his work, and I like that. I think we will work really well together, but despite that and despite us drawing a line under what happened, I can't help but think of it as we chat.

As Tyler points to something on the blueprint he's currently showing me, I can't help but remember how good his hand felt on my body. I remember those spanks and I feel the heat in my face at the thought of them. If Tyler notices I'm blushing, he doesn't mention it which is a relief.

I shift slightly in my seat, trying to get my tingling clit to behave itself. It's no use. Now that I've started to think of that night, I can't stop, and the tingling only intensifies as I remember more and more details from that night.

I feel as though I can taste Tyler on my lips. I can almost feel his lips on mine, his tongue in my mouth. And his cock.

Oh my God I can almost feel his cock inside of me pounding into me, pushing me towards my limits and at the same time, pushing me towards my orgasm.

I wonder what he would say if I told him that actually, the line isn't drawn, that I have to have him one more time first. Would he be instantly agreeable, or would I have to seduce him?

I imagine myself slowly stripping for Tyler, dancing seductively as I peel off my clothes one item at a time, leaving myself in only a pair of black stockings and a red suspender belt and heels. And then I move to him, open his pants and push them down. I push his boxers down and tease him, running my fingernails lightly over his cock and then I push him backwards until his legs hit the conference room table and fold beneath him and he ends up on his back on the table.

I see myself climbing onto the table with him, not bothering to remove my stockings or my shoes. I straddle him and lower myself onto his cock and then I ride him. Oh, how I ride him. I give him no reprieve and when we come, we come hard, both of us screaming each other's name.

"Summer? Are you ok?" Tyler asks, pulling me back to reality.

I nod my head, but I'm blushing more deeply now as my eyes go to the spot on the conference room table where mere seconds ago, I was fucking Tyler in my head.

"Are you sure?" Tyler asks. "You look a little bit... flustered."

"I'm just a tad too warm," I say.

It's not exactly a lie. I am too warm but it's so much more than that. My pussy is so wet I'm afraid I will leave a puddle when I stand up and my clit is tingling so much it's maddening. God how am I ever going to be able to complete this project with Tyler when just being near him has this reaction in me.

I tell myself it will be fine. It's just because it's the first time seeing him since we had sex and because it was so unexpected.

I force myself to look at Tyler and I see that sexy little half smirk on his face, and I know that he knows. He knows exactly why I am flustered. Fuck. This is getting worse by the moment. Now I'm blushing so deeply I can feel it spreading down my neck and over my chest.

I am in so much trouble here. My God am I. The thing is though, despite everything, I still don't want to get tied down with a relationship that might interfere with my career. But surely Tyler won't want to interfere with my career. He's going to understand the long hours and all of that kind of thing, and he isn't going to want me to be slacking off when the company I work for is his.

I shake my head. No. I am not going down that route. Not now, not ever. I wonder though if Tyler would be open to a colleague with benefits kind of arrangement where we have no strings sex now and then. It would certainly liven work up a bit without being too distracting. I shake my head and shake off the thought. Thoughts like that might be nice, but they won't help me to stop thinking of Tyler as anything more than just a colleague.

"I'll send you copies of all of the blueprints and ideas we have played with so far and I'll send you the information about the client," Tyler said. "Have a look and see what you can come up with and we'll meet again in a few days' time."

"That sounds good," I say, pleased he is going to send me the things so I can take a look at them without his presence clouding my thoughts.

I have got to get myself together before our progress

meeting, but I think I will be able to. I think part of the reason I have found him so distracting today is because I wasn't expecting to see him. Now I am expecting it, it should hopefully get easier. It had better get easier. I can't be reduced to this cliché of a woman that goes all gooey just because a good-looking man happens to be in the same room as her.

3

TYLER

I'm sitting at my desk in my office waiting for Summer to come along. Our client has provisionally signed off on our designs but now we need to get them drawn out in detail and show them every little thing and see if they are happy. I think they will be. At worst there might be a few small tweaks, but I think overall, Summer and I both understand the vision the CEO of the tech firm has.

I still can't believe I'm working with Summer. It was so strange walking into the conference room on my first day here and finding out that Summer was a girl I had taken home a couple of months ago. Now I know it was just sex and I shouldn't have been so shaken at the sight of her, but for me, it wasn't just run of the mill sex. Let me explain.

A little over a year ago, I split up with my wife. I had been working late a lot of the time and working weekends too and don't get me wrong, I get why it was so frustrating for her, I really do. But as if cheating on me was the answer. But there we were.

She had been moaning about the hours, but noticeably not about the salary, and I decided that I was going to go home early one Friday afternoon and switch my cell phone off and spend the whole weekend with Chloe. I didn't tell her I was coming home early; I wanted it to be a surprise. And boy was it a surprise for the both of us although not in the way I had hoped.

I came home to what I thought was an empty house when I didn't find Chloe in the living room or the kitchen. I figured she must have gone out somewhere, so I decided to go and take a shower and change out of my work clothes and then start on a special dinner for her. I went up the stairs and I pushed open our bedroom door and that's when I found Chloe.

She was on her back, some guy between her thighs. She had her legs wrapped around him, her nails digging into his back, and he was thrusting into her. For a moment, I just stood there. I didn't know what to say or do to stop this spectacle that was still playing out in front of me. I made no sound, but my presence must have altered the atmosphere in the room or something because Chloe peeked over his shoulder and saw me.

We were both frozen in time for what felt like forever, but in reality, was merely twenty, maybe twenty-five seconds. In that time, we looked at each other, Chloe's face horror stricken, mine angry. And the whole time, the naked ass kept moving as that guy fucked my wife.

The spell broke finally, and Chloe pushed the man off her. He started to object but then he saw me standing in the doorway and he rushed to cover himself. I rolled my eyes. As if I wanted to look at him.

"It isn't what it looks like," Chloe said as I took a step into the room.

"Oh really?" I said quietly.

"Really," Chloe said.

"So, what is it then?" I ask. "Because it looks a lot like some scum bag is fucking my wife and I'm about to divorce her ass."

At that point, the aforementioned scum bag scurried past me, his jeans and shirt both still open and his sneakers in his hand.

"It... it didn't mean anything Tyler. I swear it didn't. Just you were never here and the odd time you were, you were always tired and stressed and well, a woman has needs," she said.

"Get out," I said.

Chloe frowned and then she nodded her head.

"Yes. I'll get out of bed and shower and then we'll talk," she said.

"No," I said, keeping my voice cold and neutral, not willing to let her see how much she had hurt me. "Get out of my house Chloe. We're done."

She got up from the bed and came towards me. She tried to put her hand on my cheek, but I pushed it away. I could smell him on her, and it was taking everything I had not to retch.

"Tyler please," she said, tears forming in her eyes. "I love you."

"Well, if this is your idea of love, I don't want it," I said. "Now get the fuck out of my house before I call the police and have them remove you."

She left, the divorce happened and that was it. Or at least it should have been it. But Chloe isn't one to accept feeling like she lost a battle, and she wasn't about to let me seemingly 'win' our divorce. She couldn't take me to the cleaners financially because we had an airtight prenuptial agreement that made it quite clear that if she cheated on me, she got nothing, and we both knew she wouldn't risk doing time for perjury by lying about that in court. So, she decided to hit me where it really hurt, and she went after me to my family and friends.

The first I heard of it was when I got a call from Angela, my sister. She was pissed off with me to say the least, shouting and screaming at me for hurting Chloe, telling me what a keeper she was and how I had been stupid enough to lose her. At first, I thought she meant the hours and stuff, the fact that I had likely neglected her needs somewhat and she had felt the need to fall into the arms of another man. But no. I eventually figured out that Angela was under the impression that I had been the one to cheat on Chloe.

Of course, I denied it and tried to explain to Angela what really happened, but she wasn't having any of it. Not a single thing I said convinced her that I was the one who had been cheated on, not the one doing the cheating. Chloe had always been one of those people that is just believed. I don't know why. Maybe it's because she's so damned good at playing the victim. Whatever it was, she had convinced my own sister that I was the bastard in our relationship.

Luckily, despite Angela thinking I had cheated on Chloe, she didn't want to actually fall out with me and in the end, we decided to make Chloe and all of that business a subject that was off limits. Chloe might have gotten Angela mad at me, but she couldn't actually take her away from me. The same can't be said about our mutual friends though.

Of course, some of the guys still come for a beer with me and we still hang out now and again, but it's not the same because all of their girlfriends and wives think that I am a cheat who broke their friend's heart, and it makes pursuing a friendship difficult to say the least.

So yeah. That's the story of Chloe and me. Fun, isn't it?

People say now that I'm not over Chloe, but I am. I know

why they say it. It's because I haven't made any effort to find another girlfriend since the divorce. Now don't get me wrong, I loved Chloe and it did take me a couple of months of feeling sorry for myself to get over her, but I did get over her. I just realized, in those months of singledom, that I preferred it that way.

If I stayed single, there was no chance of me getting hurt like that again which was a big thing for me. But it was more than just that. While I was single, I could pour all my time and energy into the business and make it work, something I hadn't been able to do when I was married. If Chloe thought the hours I was putting in when we were together was bad, she should have seen how many more hours I would have liked to have been able to put in. And once I was single, I could do it.

The last seven or eight months of constant hard work have been how we were able to afford to take over the company we have just bought out. Don't get me wrong, Jack is great at his job, and I wouldn't want anyone else as my partner because I trust him entirely, but he would have been happy to coast along at our small size forever, whereas I wanted more. Because he was happy, it seemed only fair that if we were going to expand it should be me who put the time in to make it happen.

Anyway, that's a little bit off topic. Where was I? Oh yes. Summer. Of course. It's always Summer on my mind these days.

So that night in the line for the cab. I started talking to Summer without even having seen her face. I was a bit tipsy and feeling social and well, I just thought why not strike up a conversation. It would make the time spent waiting for a cab go by faster. So, I spoke to her and then she turned around and for the first time in a long time, I felt something for a woman.

I felt my cock responding to the sight of her, the smell of her. But it was more than just that. I've had a physical response to women since Chloe – of course I have – but this was more than that. As we chatted, I felt an emotional connection with her. I felt like she was someone I would very much like to get to know.

And I told her she was coming home with me. Yes, told her. Not asked her. I'm no weirdo. If she would have said no, I would have left it at that, but it didn't feel weird telling her she was coming home with me. In fact, it felt like that was already a foregone conclusion and I was just confirming it out loud. And she just agreed like it was the most natural thing in the world.

We had the most amazing sex I have ever had. Chloe was very vanilla in the bedroom, even to the extent that she wouldn't let me go down on her. I love eating a woman out and it was the first thing I did with Summer and her reaction told me she loved it too. I found myself comparing Summer to Chloe. I didn't want to, but I found I couldn't help it, and Summer came out the winner in every category. I knew then she was going to be dangerous to be around. How was I meant to be around someone so amazing and not develop any sort of feelings for her?

After the sex I fell asleep thinking about the dangers of Summer. I knew if I wanted her to be around, there was a good chance I was going to fall for her. It would only really be a matter of time. And I knew there was a better than average chance I would end up in love with her. And if that happened, I was leaving myself wide open to getting hurt again. I knew it was a huge risk and I wasn't sure whether or not I was willing to take the risk.

I needn't have worried. The decision was taken out of my hands by Summer. I woke up the next morning to find her gone. For a moment, I had to question if she had ever really existed anywhere but, in my dreams, but I could smell her perfume on my bed and I could smell her juices on my skin. Oh, she was real alright. But she was gone, and I had no way to contact her. I didn't even know her name.

And for a while, that was ok. I kept finding her appearing in my thoughts, my dreams. And I liked fantasizing about her, both sexually and emotionally. She was the one that got away, the one who woke me back up to the possibility of love. And that was all she would ever be. And I would just have to be ok with that because what other choice did I have?

Of course, all of that was only until the day I walked into that damned conference room and found her arranging those chairs. At first, I thought it was a mistake, that I was seeing things, and this was just someone who looked a bit like her from behind. But then she turned around and I saw her face and it was her and I figured then it must have been a sign, that the gods themselves had sent her to me. But then she told me she hadn't wanted anything more than a one-night stand and she still didn't and I knew I would have to respect that and so I said I felt the same way about it too.

Yes, it was a little white lie but how awkward would it have been if she said that and I said, well, actually I think you might be the one so I'm just going to be over here wishing you would want me? Yeah, that was definitely not going to happen. The little white lie saved us both from a lot of embarrassment and it meant we could work together without any awkwardness. And it wasn't like it was malicious. The only person who stood to potentially get hurt from it was me.

And so far, it seems to have worked out ok. We have managed to work together on this project without any awkwardness. I know there's still a physical attraction there on both of our parts. Sometimes I look at Summer and I catch her staring at me. She always looks away quickly when that happens and that tells me more than the fact she happened to be looking in my direction when I glanced up. I like that she's still attracted to me. I like that when I feel my cock responding to her presence, making me want her, that her pussy is most likely doing the same thing to her, making her want me.

True to our words, we've never acted on our attraction again, but other than that first half hour or so in the conference room, we've never been alone together. There has always been either my personal assistant or Summer's secretary or another member of the team around. But tonight, we will be working alone, just the two of us in my office. And it's late enough that pretty much everyone else will have gone home for the day.

I am nervous, despite the fact that I've already told myself that nothing will happen between us. Nothing can happen between us. I'm not ready to get my heart broken again and the fact that Summer feels a physical attraction for me and no more means that would be the most likely outcome of anything that did happen. So then why am I hoping against hope that something happens then?

Because like I said earlier that girl is dangerous to me.

I look up when there's a light tap on my office door. The door is open, and I instantly see it's Summer at the door.

"Come in," I say.

She steps in and comes towards my desk. In her arms, she's carrying a load of files. They press her dark blue dress against her shapely breasts, and for a moment, I see her nipples straining at the fabric but then she puts the files down on my desk and her dress loosens again and I can no longer see them.

She sits down on the chair opposite me and flicks open one of her files. She's pointing to various features and talking me through them. I'm trying to listen, but I'm mesmerized by the sparkle in her brown eyes. One of her eyes is a solid brown but the other one seems to have flecks of gold through it that make it dance in the light. She is so beautiful.

"Are you listening?" she asks, looking up at me and smiling.

I nod my head but it's clear to us both that I wasn't, and I decide to just apologize and move on.

"Sorry," I say. "I was thinking about something else. Carry on."

She does and I force myself to listen to her words, not just the pretty cadence of her voice. And I force myself to look at her drawings, not at her shiny brown hair. And when she stands up so she can unfold one of the drawings and hold it up at full size, I'm sure to look only at the drawing, not at how her dress sits on the curves of her hips, curves my hand have been on, curves I want my hands to sit on once again.

By the time she's finished presenting everything to me, two hours have gone by. Two hours of delicious sexual tension and two hours of longing. I know this isn't one sided anymore. There have been more than a few stolen glances this evening. Summer is into me, and she is as aware as I am that this is the first time we've really been alone together since that first day in the conference room.

She has flicked her hair and ran her fingers down her neckline and over her breasts too many times for it to be innocent. She has made a point of fiddling with her hemline and drawing my eyes to her killer tanned legs. And when our hands accidentally touched, I heard the gasp of air she took in as she pulled back and I knew she had felt those sparks flying through her just the same as I had felt them flying through me.

Finally, we're finishing the discussion about the building's design, and we have settled on a lot of features that we are both happy with. We high five over my desk and then Summer stands up.

"You're not leaving, are you? We have pizza on the way, don't forget," I say.

"If you think I'm going home to cook dinner at this time, you're very wrong," Summer laughs. "I'm just going to the ladies' room."

I can't help but watch the way her ass moves underneath her dress as she leaves the office. Once she's gone, I get up and close the window that is left open. It's pretty warm out tonight but I don't want to forget to shut it before we leave. I feel the temperature go up a notch and so I loosen my tie and pull it off and put it on my desk. I open my top button too and untuck my shirt from in my pants.

Summer reappears and smiles at me.

"Looks like I'm just in time for the strip tease," she says.

She's laughing and so am I. It's obviously a joke, but then something changes, and the laughter fades and she takes a step towards me, and I feel as though I can smell her pussy from here and I want her, and I know she wants me. Before I can let my more cautious side talk myself out of it, I reach out and grab Summer's wrist and pull her towards me.

I mash my lips against hers, kissing her like I've never kissed anyone before. I feel as though I'm putting my very soul into my kiss, and Summer kisses me back, her own kiss feeling as desperate and passionate as mine. It's as though we both want this kiss to say everything we haven't been able to say to each other since we reconnected here. It's as though we've been unleashed, and every bit of pent-up desire is coming flooding out of us in that kiss.

I push Summer's dress up over her hips and around her waist and I push my fingers into her panties. I rub them through her slickness, stopping to massage her sweet clit. She moans into my mouth, and she brings her hands around to the front of my body and she begins to unbutton my shirt. When she gets the buttons open, she pushes it open and runs her palms over my chest and stomach. My skin tingles deliciously at her touch and my cock is going wild, craving being inside of her tight little pussy once more.

I move my lips from Summer's and I kiss her neck and keep massaging her clit. I can tell she is close to coming by the way she makes little 'ah' sounds and by the way her clit is thrumming against my fingers. I apply a bit more pressure and speed up the movement of my fingers and that does it. She hits her orgasm. She clings to me, her fingers digging into my shoulders, her face pressed tightly against my neck. I can feel her hot breath tickling my skin as she whispers my name.

Her body goes rigid for a moment and then a shudder goes through her, and she is gasping for air as her orgasm fades away. She lifts her head off my shoulder and kisses me again. Her hands go to my belt, and she opens it and then she starts to unbutton my pants. I'm more than ready for her and judging by how wet she was against my fingers only seconds ago, Summer is more than ready for me too.

"Hello? Anyone here? I have your pizza," a voice shouts from the hallway.

Summer and I jump apart like two teenagers who are

about to get caught together by a parent. We laugh as Summer pulls her dress down and I hastily fasten my belt.

"Coming," I shout as I start to fasten my shirt.

"Nearly," Summer says with a smile.

I laugh and shake my head and finally my shirt is buttoned up and it's just as well because the pizza guy has followed my voice and he's standing in my office doorway. I go to him and take the pizza and pay him. Once he leaves, Summer and I look at each other and start to laugh.

"Well, that was a close one," Summer says.

"Too close," I agree.

Summer nods her head and I think we've just made a silent agreement not to start up again or at least not here. Instead, we move to the more comfortable seats at the end of my office in the little alcove by the window. We eat our pizza, and our conversation goes back to the project we're working on. We finish eating and I know it's time to leave but I'm not ready to just give up on Summer tonight. Not after what just happened.

"Want to get a quick drink?" I ask her.

"Yeah, sounds good," she says.

We gather our things up and leave the building and head over to the bar across the street, a place I've been informed everyone from the company uses when they've had a rough day. It seems either no one has had a rough day today or it was so rough that they drank themselves into oblivion before ten o'clock because there's no one I recognize in there.

I go to the bar and grab our drinks and then I look around for Summer. I see her standing by the jukebox and I make my way over as she chooses a song. She nods to the table beside the jukebox, and I sit down and then she joins me.

"So, I think tonight has proved that we shouldn't be left alone together," Summer says with a grin.

"At least not somewhere public," I add, letting her know that I take her point, but I am more than open to being alone with her again. She knows exactly what I'm getting at because she bites her lower lip and looks down into her drink for a moment.

"Oh my God, imagine if that pizza guy hadn't shouted before he appeared," Summer says.

In my mind I see us again, her with her dress hiked up around her waist, me with my shirt open and my pants almost open. There would have been no disguising what we were doing and while it's not like we were doing anything wrong, it would have been pretty embarrassing.

"We'd probably still be there trying to apologize and him just trying to get away from us," I say with a laugh.

Summer laughs too and then we fall silent for a moment and we both drink some of our drinks before Summer breaks the silence again.

"So how are you finding the merge then? Are you settling in ok?" Summer asks me.

"Yeah," I say. "Everyone has been really nice and welcoming. I don't know if it's because I'm the boss or if it's because they're genuinely nice people, but it hasn't felt like I'm an outsider."

"Oh, it's definitely because you're the boss," Summer says. She laughs and shakes her head. "No, I'm joking of course. Everyone is really nice. I mean there's always a bit of gossip and shit going on, but that's just a part of the office life, isn't it?"

I nod my head. I know what she means. It was even worse before we bought out the new company. When it was just me and Jack and our few employees, I swear you couldn't even sneeze without someone knowing all about it. And the bits they didn't know? They made those up.

"I remember once one of the rumors got so out of hand that Maria was called to HR. Apparently, she had told everyone that Martin had gotten Diane pregnant, even though Diane was meant to be seeing Stuart," Summer says.

I frown. None of those names ring a bell with me except Maria.

"I guess they've all left now then?" I ask. "Was it because of the rumor?"

Summer laughs and shakes her head.

"That's the thing. They never worked there. There were no such people as Diane, Martin or Stuart. Maria was just showing people how a little bit of gossip can blow up. The HR rep wasn't too impressed when she learned that none of it was real and her time had been wasted protecting the rights of imaginary people I can tell you," Summer says.

"No, I don't suppose she was. HR people always seem to lack a sense of humor," I point out. "At least until you get them drunk."

We both laugh. I lift my glass to Summer, showing her it's almost empty.

"Another drink?" I ask.

She shakes her head.

"Not for me, thanks. I try not to have more than one on a work night. But you go ahead if you want another," she says.

I don't miss her implication. By not wanting another one but letting me know she will wait if I do, she's letting me know she's coming home with me tonight. I was going to have another drink, but I decide against it. I would much rather have her than a drink.

"No, it's cool," I say. "If I don't have another one, I don't need a cab home, I can take my car."

"Good point," she says.

We finish up the last bits of our current drinks and then we leave the bar and head back towards the office parking lot. Our two cars are the only ones left. We have to pass Summer's car to get to mine, but when we come adjacent to Summer's car, she stops and starts to fish her keys out.

"Oh," I said, trying and failing to hide my surprise.

"What?" Summer says, glancing up from her purse.

"No, nothing," I say.

"Come on, you were going to say something," she says.

She's finished digging through her purse and she's standing there with her car keys in her hand looking at me expectantly.

"It was just... I thought..." I sigh and start again. "I thought you would be coming back to my place, that's all."

"Oh, I see," Summer says. "You bought me a drink so I must be going to sleep with you, is that it?"

"What? No. That's not what I meant at all," I say. I can't believe she thinks that's what I mean. "Honestly I just..."

I stop talking when I see Summer laughing as quietly as she can.

"I'm sorry," she says, still laughing. "I couldn't resist that one. Of course, I'm coming back to your place, but I don't want to leave my car here. I'll follow you."

"I'll get you back for that," I say, laughing.

I'm still laughing as I head for my own car, but to be honest, I am more relieved that she doesn't really think so little of me as to think I'm someone that would expect sex after having a drink together. I get into my car and set off. I head towards home. I keep checking in my mirror making sure I haven't lost Summer along the way, although I'm sure she would find my place again if she wanted to. She managed to get home from there the other month.

I pull up on my driveway, leaving room behind me for Summer's car. She pulls up behind me and gets out of her car. She follows me to the house. I unlock the door and open it for her. She steps in and I follow her. I kick the door shut behind me and before I can even ask her if she wants a drink or anything, she smiles at me and takes my hand in hers and heads for my stairs. I don't resist her. I let her lead me upstairs and to my bedroom. She doesn't speak until we're in the room and then she smiles again.

"I think it's about time we finished what we started earlier," she says, and she drops to her knees on the floor in front of me and opens my belt and then my pants. She pushes my pants and my boxer shorts down and then she waits while I kick my shoes off. She peels my socks off and pulls my pants and boxer shorts off and then without warning, she grabs my cock and puts the tip of it in her mouth.

Within a second of her lips touching me, I'm hard. She sucks and pulls more of me into her mouth. The contrast of her smooth lips and her rough tongue is like heaven, and I can feel the pleasure moving through my body already.

I look down and Summer is quite a sight to see. She kneels before me, her head bobbing up and down, my cock going in and out of her mouth. I almost climax just watching her, but I hold myself back. I know I should stop her before I climax, but I don't want to stop her just yet. This feels too good for me to want it to stop. She keeps going, alternating between sucking and licking until she has me worked up into a frenzy and just when I'm about to reach the point of no return, she stops and releases my cock from her mouth.

She gets to her feet, and we stand looking at each for a moment and I need to have her now. I need the release; she is driving me crazy bringing me to the edge like that and then stopping.

She moves closer to me, and her lips rub gently across mine and then we're kissing hungrily once more. We make our way to the bed, still kissing, what's left of our clothes coming off as we go. When we reach the bed, Summer pulls back from our kiss and smiles at me and then she pushes me onto the bed and climbs on with me, straddling me.

She grips my cock in her fist and lowers herself down onto it and then she starts to move, lifting herself slowly up and down, teasing me. I try to resist the urge to buck my hips and let her set the pace. The teasing is torturous but it's delicious too and I am more than happy to lay back and enjoy it. The view is spectacular.

Summer's lithe body sits atop me, her breasts jiggling as she moves up and down on me. I'm surprised in the best possible way when she runs her hands over her body and starts to massage a breast with each hand. She closes her eyes and smiles slightly as she moves, her massage moving with the same slow pace as her up and down movement.

When she has worked herself up into a state, she leans forward and catches herself on one hand. Her other hand goes to her clit, and she begins to rub herself as she moves on me. I swallow hard. The sight of Summer touching herself is almost enough to send me flying over the edge, but I wait. I don't want to do anything that risks ending the show Summer is putting on.

As she plays with herself, her movements on me increase in speed as her rubbing gets faster and I know I'm not the only one who is close to losing it. Summer is rubbing herself almost angrily now and I can no longer stop myself from moving. My hips go in time with Summers and within seconds of me starting to move, I feel Summer's already tight pussy clench around me.

I can't do anything except explode at that point and I let myself go. Hot, urgent pleasure floods me as I empty myself into Summer's pussy. Her hand has moved away from her clit, and she's bent almost double, her hands clawing at the sheet on either side of me, her breasts hanging down, the nipples grazing my chest.

I call out her name as she tightens around me again and another burst of pleasure floods me. It's like fireworks exploding through my body, thrumming in time with my pulse. I have never felt pleasure like this, so pure, so unadulterated. It takes my breath away and makes spots of color dance in front of my eyes as a final wave cascades over me.

Finally, I come back down to earth, gasping and panting. Summer seems to be in a similar state to me. She has flopped onto my chest, and I can feel her heart racing, hear her panting. It's an effort to lift my arms up but I do it and wrap them around her.

She stays in place for a while and once we're both getting back to ourselves, she gently disentangles herself from my arms and lays down beside me. I turn onto my side so I'm facing her. She smiles lazily at me.

"Well, that was better than doing my taxes," she says.

"I should hope so," I say with a laugh.

Summer laughs too, a sound I love to hear, especially when I'm the one who made her laugh.

"No really, that was my plan for after work tonight. Go home and start sorting my taxes out," she says.

"Well, I'm definitely glad I could save you from that fate," I say.

"Oh, me too," she readily agrees. "Me too."

I WAKE up to sunlight streaming in through the window, the timer on the outside lights having turned them off. I yawn and stretch and sit up. I look to my right and the space beside me is empty but I'm not worried. Not this time.

I know exactly where I can find Summer today and I'm pretty sure she hasn't sneaked away because she didn't want to have a conversation with me today. I'm pretty sure it was more a case of her not wanting to be late for work. I'm guessing she knew if she woke me up, she would definitely have been late because I wouldn't have let her leave without making her come. There's nothing like a breakfast orgasm to start the day.

I pick up my cell phone from the ground where it must have fallen last night as our clothes came off. I check the time. It's after ten. I smile and shake my head. I can't remember the last time I slept in so late, especially not on a workday. Summer is going to be the death of me, but if that's the case, one thing is for sure; I will die a happy man.

4

SUMMER

I know to anyone passing by my office and dropping in
on me, I will look flustered. That's because I am
bloody flustered. I've just got here and it's nine
sixteen. That means I was fifteen minutes late to start work.
I've never been late for work in my life. Ok, that's a lie. But I
have never been late for work in my life because I slept in
from having hot sex half of the night before. The odd time
I've been late in the past it's been because I got a flat tire, or
because I was a witness to a traffic accident, and I wasn't
allowed to leave the scene until after I had given a state-
ment. This is just embarrassing. It's such a teenage thing to
do and it's the sort of thing my parents warned me about.

I can almost hear my mother's disapproving tone as she
tells me that it's not the nineteen fifties and being pretty isn't
a free meal ticket anymore, that I need to focus on my career
and then, when I am at the top of my field, then I can think
about maybe finding a partner. I always bite my tongue at
that point and refrain from pointing out that her and my
father were together and married by twenty-five. I know
what she will say. She'll tell me it was a different time back

then and all of that stuff and ultimately, I'll still be in the same position as I was, it just would have taken an hour for the lecture instead of ten minutes.

I shake my head. I'm letting my mother's voice into my head far too often these days. The fact that I'm never usually late isn't a bad thing; it means that me being late once probably isn't that big of a deal. And it was only fifteen minutes. It's not like I just didn't show up. I can make the time back easily enough.

I start replying to emails, my first task of the day. Most of the new emails in my inbox are just spam and I delete those as I go, leaving me three or four emails that actually need my attention. I try to focus on reading the first one of the four, but I can't stop thinking about Tyler. I find my mind drifting back to last night. I've never touched myself like that in front of anyone before. I always thought it would be cringey, but it didn't feel that way at all. It felt empowering, like I was in charge and taking control of my own pleasure, my own desire.

Of course, that's not to say that I didn't like it when Tyler took control the first time we had sex. I liked that very much but it's good to know I have it in me to take the lead sometimes. I wish now I had taken the lead again this morning and woke Tyler up before I left his place. If I had I would have been a lot more than fifteen minutes late for work. I probably still wouldn't be here now.

I wish I wasn't. I wish I had taken a vacation day and stayed with Tyler in his warm bed, in his warm arms. We could have spent the whole day in that bed just taking it in turns to make each other come. Why didn't I do that?

I'm getting myself seriously turned on now thinking about Tyler's tongue on my clit, his fingers inside of me. I imagine myself almost climaxing and Tyler taking his fingers out of my pussy and filling me with his cock instead. I know I would be climaxing right around now if this was really happening, and I don't feel like I'm far from it now.

I try to distract myself from Tyler and the way my clit is pulsing but it's too late. The only way I'm going to get any relief from this now is to finish what I have inadvertently started. I debate texting Tyler to come to my office, but I don't even know if he's gotten to work yet, and I don't think I can wait until he gets here. Instead, I go into my bathroom alone.

It's at times like this one that I'm particularly grateful that I've worked here so long that I have worked my way up to one of the largest offices and most importantly, one with a private bathroom attached. There's no way I would have even contemplated doing what I'm about to do in a public restroom.

I open my pants and pull them down followed by my panties and before I can change my mind, I slip two fingers into my slit and begin to rub my clit. I close my eyes and picture Tyler as I rub myself, imagining his hand working on me. I up the pace; now isn't the time to draw this out. I was already so turned on when I came in here that I orgasm within minutes of starting to touch myself.

I move my fingers away as my orgasm floods through me. It is intense and I reach out with my other hand and grip the edge of the sink as I experience the relief my orgasm has brought me. I wait until it has run its course leaving my skin tingling but my clit sated, at least for now. I quickly use the toilet while I'm here and then I go to the sink to wash my hands. I glance in the small mirror above the sink, and I'm pleased to see that I look normal.

My cheeks are perhaps a little bit flushed, but my hair is neat, my makeup isn't smudged, and my clothes are all in place. No one would look at me and know I have just had an orgasm. It's just as well that's the case because as I'm drying my hands on the plush red towel that hangs on the ring beside the sink, there's a knock on my office door.

I leave the bathroom quickly and go to my desk where I sit down.

"Come in," I call.

The door opens and a pretty redhead steps inside. It takes me a moment to place her, but I realize she's one of the new people. Jack's secretary, Ivy.

"What can I do for you, Ivy?" I ask, smiling at her.

She returns my smile.

"Jack would like to see you in his office," Ivy replies with a shy smile. "He said it's not urgent if you're in the middle of something for a client, but it's important enough that he wants to see you before lunch."

"Got it, thank you," I say.

Ivy nods to me and then she leaves my office. I wonder what Jack could want. Maybe he has a new project he'd like me to work on, but surely, he knows I'm swamped, what with all of my usual clients and then the project with Tyler too. Still though, if he needs me to work on something for him, I won't say no.

I decide that now is as good a time as any to go and see him and I lock my computer and get up. I drop my cell phone in my bottom drawer with my purse. I debate putting my jacket on but it's warm enough in the office and I'm already wearing a long-sleeved blouse which I think will be more than enough. It's not like I'm even going outside. Decision made, I leave my office and head towards Jack's office.

To get to Jack's office, I have to pass Tyler's office and of course that sets off all sorts of delicious memories from last night. It also brings back the funny moment where we were so close to being caught by the pizza guy. I wonder if Tyler is in yet. I decide to wait until I've seen Jack and am on my way back to my own office to knock on his door and see.

I reach Jack's office and knock on the door. He calls for me to come in and I open the door and step in. I smile at Jack as he nods to the chair opposite him at his desk. I notice he doesn't return my smile and as I sit down, I see that he actually looks really pissed off. Is this about me being late this morning? It's the only thing I know of that I've done that could piss him off like that.

"What the hell happened this morning, Summer?" Jack says once I am seated.

Wow. He really is pissed off about this.

"I was running a little bit late. I'm sorry and I promise it won't happen again. I know it doesn't make any difference, but for what it's worth, it was only fifteen minutes and I do plan to make the time back up," I say.

Before I'm finished talking, Jack is waving his hand, waving away my words. He shakes his head.

"I'm not worried about that. I didn't even know you were late this morning and I know you work late more days than not so I wouldn't be worrying about you making fifteen minutes up," he says.

Now I'm really confused. If he's not talking about me being late, then what is he talking about? I know I couldn't focus properly on my emails this morning, but I did look over them enough to know none of them were pressing matters.

Jack is watching me and after a few seconds, when it's become clear to him that I have absolutely no idea what he's talking about, he sighs.

"You missed your ten am meeting with Scarlet Bond about the redesign of her holiday home," he prompts me.

Oh fuck. I didn't just miss that meeting, I forgot it existed altogether. How could I have been so careless? Scarlet Bond is by far my richest client – hell she is by far the whole company's richest client - a multi millionaire, she likes the finer things in life and that includes bespoke designs on any property she invests in. Scarlet is no trust fund brat – she's earned every cent she has and as such, for her, time is money, and I have just wasted a chunk of her time. I can see now why Jack is pissed off. I'm pissed off too and I'm sure Scarlet is pissed off enough to put both of us to shame.

"I... I don't know what to say," I stammer as Jack sits waiting for an explanation. "I wish I could give you an explanation that could excuse this, but I can't. I don't know what happened. I just genuinely forgot about the meeting."

What can I do but be honest? There's nothing I could invent on the spot that would be big enough to excuse my behavior without it coming back to bite me in the ass down the line. I might as well take the ass kicking now.

"You realize I have fired people for less?" Jack says.

Ok, I wasn't expecting that. An ass kicking is one thing, but to be fired from the company I have worked for since I graduated from college is a step too far in my opinion. I don't think pointing that out is a wise move right now though.

"All I can do is apologize and promise you that I will make it up to Ms. Bond," I say.

Jack nods curtly once. I think that means I'm not getting fired today. At least I hope it does.

"Ok," Jack says. "And I trust that this won't happen again?"

"Definitely not," I say, and I mean it. I am more than embarrassed this has happened once. If it happened again, I think I would quit on the spot out of the sheer mortification of it all.

"Summer, let me ask you something," Jack says. The anger seems to have gone out of him and he's looking at me with a look that feels more like a concern for me. "Is there something going on in your personal life that's affecting your work? A bereavement, or some other form of stress?"

I shake my head, hoping the fact that I'm blushing is not something Jack will pursue. How can I tell him the thing affecting my work is Tyler?

"Are you sure? Just from what I've seen of you, this is extremely out of character for you, and I know your old bosses thought very highly of you too so I'm assuming your performance to date hasn't been some sort of act to make Tyler and me think you're a good employee," he says.

"I value my career and I enjoy what I do. I'm also damned good at it which is why my old bosses thought highly of me. I've made a huge mistake today but let me assure you that is the anomaly, not me performing well. There's nothing specific going on, but I think I was just flustered with running late today and that's caused me to forget in my panic to get caught up," I say.

"Ok," Jack says. "If you make this right with the client, I see no reason for this to go on your permanent record."

I nod my head, grateful to him. Reading between the lines, he was debating giving me a written warning, but he has decided against it if I can appease Scarlet. And I really think I can.

"Thank you," I say. "I won't let you down again."

"Please see that you don't," Jack says. "And if there is something bothering you, my door is always open, Summer."

I understand that I'm being dismissed from Jack's office, and I stand up and nod to him.

"Thank you," I say again. Although the thought of coming here and pouring my heart out isn't exactly a comforting one, I know that Jack means well.

I leave Jack's office and head back towards my own, still mortified that I have let this happen. I would have been upset about any client getting forgotten about like this, but it's even worse when it's my biggest and least forgettable client. I need to seriously sort myself out and make sure nothing like this ever happens again.

Unfortunately, I know what that means for me. It means I can't see Tyler anymore. We have to go back to being just colleagues and nothing more. Sure, his presence will still affect me, but I won't be late because I've been up half of the night having sex and if I'm not thinking constantly of when I can next have sex with Tyler, I might be able to keep my head on my job long enough to remember when I have meetings.

I'm almost at Tyler's office now and I remember that I was going to knock on his door on the way back to see if he was in yet. I should and let him know last night was a one off, but I decide against it. I want to try and sort this mess out with Scarlet first. Or at least that's the reason I give myself.

I'm past Tyler's office and doing my best not to think of him at all when I hear him calling my name from behind me. If I pretend I haven't heard him, he's only going to call after me again. I turn around and smile.

"Hi," he says. I smile wider, not trusting myself to speak at this moment. I'm afraid I will just blurt out that I can't have sex with him again and the last thing I want to do is blurt it out at work. "Want to grab some lunch in about an hour?"

I should ask him if we can go into his office and say no to the lunch and explain why, but instead, I nod my agreement. Maybe it will be easier to talk to him over lunch, away from the office altogether and hopefully the Scarlet mess is sorted too.

"Sounds good," I say. "Just swing by my office when you're ready to go."

"Will do," he says.

"See you then," I say, and I hurry away before he can instigate anymore of a conversation.

I'm soon back in the relative sanctuary of my own office and I sit down at my desk and sigh. I know what I need to do to appease Scarlet. It's something I told her couldn't be done. Of course, by that I meant it can be done but it is an absolute shit ton of work for no reason other than to fulfill her whim.

Basically, Scarlet's need to be different has reached another level. She wants a standard pool at this new holiday home, but she also wants another pool, which is a perfect sphere. As I said, I can design it and I know I can find people who can do it, but they'll absolutely hate me because the work it will take just isn't worth it. But if calling in a favor with someone appeases Scarlet then so be it. I'll do what I have to do.

I type out a quick email to Rick, one of my most trusted contractors and basically beg him to do this. He emails me back quickly saying thank you but no thank you and so begins the negotiation. He ends up with twice the original offered price, which I know Scarlet won't care about and he also gets a promise of a favor owed from me. I can't say that went too badly. Now it's time to get my ass chewed off by Scarlet and then hopefully bring her around.

I pick up the receiver of my desk phone and find Scarlet on the contact list stuck on the phone. I type her number in and wait. It's her cell phone number. We've worked together long enough that I no longer have to go through any of her PAs because she knows I will only call if I need to speak to her about something important.

"Hello," Scarlet says after a few rings, her voice rich and throaty.

"Hi Ms. Bond," I say. "It's Summer Malone."

"Ah I see. You've remembered I exist now, have you?" she says.

Her tone is matter of fact, but her voice is as cold as hell, and I know she's still pissed off about me missing the meeting.

"I'm so sorry about missing our meeting," I say. "And I'm not going to insult your intelligence by lying to you about why I missed it. The truth is, it slipped my mind and all I can do at this point is apologize and promise you that it won't happen again."

"I'm going to let it go this once because we've worked together for a long time, and I love your designs. But don't think that my time isn't important. If it happens again, we're done," Scarlet says.

I have to swallow hard to stop myself from telling her to kiss my ass. I know I can't do that, and I can't even really be annoyed that she's speaking to me like this. It is my mistake that's brought us here after all. I do feel like I've apologized enough now though and to keep doing so would just be kissing her ass and so I move the conversation on to what I hope will nip this whole thing in the bud.

"While I have you on the line, I have some good news," I say.

"Oh?" Scarlet says, her attention clearly piqued.

"I've found a contractor skilled enough and willing to do your spherical pool," I say.

"Shut up!" Scarlet says, but her tone tells me she doesn't mean it literally. She is happy again. "For real?"

"For real," I say. "If you have your PA call through to mine, we can set up another meeting and then once you sign off on the design, we're good to go."

"That sounds good, thank you Summer," Scarlet says. "And please forgive me if I was a little brusque earlier. I realize mistakes happen. Take care."

With that she hangs up and I smile to myself. I'm vindicated and if anything, this will make our working relationship stronger because I've managed to deliver something Scarlet believed to be impossible. Her hanging up without a goodbye used to worry me, make me think I had upset her somehow, but I soon realized that was just her way and now it doesn't bother me at all. As little quirks go, I wish all of my clients had such easy to deal with ones.

I quickly email Jack explaining that the situation with Ms. Bond is sorted and she understands that mistakes happen, and she has accepted my apology and we are going to reschedule the meeting. His reply pings back in quickly. It's a simple three words – good, I'm glad – but they say more than just their face value. They tell me that Jack is cool with me now too.

With everything right in the world of work once more, I go back to my emails. Once I have dealt with those, I get to thinking again. Yes, I made a mistake. Well, two mistakes. Yes, I allowed myself to lose my focus for a moment. But is that really a good enough reason to give Tyler up? Is it at least possible that I could keep seeing him and not be distracted like this?

I don't get a chance to decide the answer to that question for myself because my father's voice in my head decides it for me; don't throw away everything you have worked for in exchange for a brief fling that might not even go anywhere.

I know that voice is probably right. I could give it a chance I think, if Tyler and I didn't work at the same company but being so ditzy and distracted because of him when he works here too is just too embarrassing. And people would surely put the pieces together at some point and everyone would know that deep down I'm as mushy and romantic as those women I have laughed at over the years for giving up their careers for relationships.

5

TYLER

I was a little bit nervous asking Summer if she wanted to get lunch with me, although I never would have shown it. I know she's into me – anyone with eyes could see it – but she did say she wasn't looking for anything more than a one-night thing before. But then again, I wasn't looking for anything. I'm not looking for anything. But then I think of Summer and how could I not be looking for her? Or at the very least, how can I not be pleased that I have accidentally found her?

I suppose deep down, I always knew this moment would come. That I could say I wasn't looking for anything and mean it, but that a special someone would still come along and make me not care if I was looking or not.

Realistically, I know that Summer isn't my ex. She is absolutely nothing like her. Just because Chloe turned out to be a fraud and cheated on me, it doesn't mean Summer will do the same. It doesn't mean that anyone I get with will hurt me. But until Summer landed in my life, I had never met anyone who I liked enough to risk it for. Now I have Summer in my life, I guess it's fair to say that for once, I'm not looking to the past, but to the future, and I very much want that girl in my future.

So yes. What I'm trying to say is that I am pretty happy about the prospect of a little lunch date with Summer. It doesn't matter how much I try to remind myself to be cautious, or how much I claim to myself that I'm still not ready for a relationship, I can still feel myself falling for Summer.

My office door opens and for a moment, I think it's going to be her, that she's here to fuck me into oblivion. I can't think who else would come into my office without knocking. My heart sinks when I see Jack. He's my partner, of course he comes into my office without knocking when he knows I'm not with a client. He smiles at me and comes and sits down opposite me without waiting for an invite. I feel a bit annoyed about it and I tell myself to let it go. I'm only annoyed because I thought Jack was going to be Summer and he isn't.

"What's up?" I ask.

"Hopefully nothing," Jack says. "You've been working closely with Summer Malone these last few weeks, right?"

I make a noncommittal grunt. Where the hell is this going? Has Jack somehow found out about us sleeping together? I don't see how he could have, and even if he has, there's no rule to say we can't be in a relationship together.

"How does she seem to you?" Jack asks. "I mean is she ok?"

"As far as I know she is. Why?" I say, relieved that he's not here to lecture me, but confused as to what he's getting at.

"Well, she was late this morning, but I'm not so worried about that. It was only a few minutes and that can happen to anyone. I wouldn't have been concerned if that was the only issue, but she forgot she had a meeting with a multi-millionaire client too. I'm just wondering if she maybe needs some support?" Jack says.

It takes everything I have not to grin. I know why Summer was distracted this morning and it's definitely not something she needs support with. I believe the phrase I'm looking for would be guilty as charged, your honor. Still though, I have to give Jack an answer that doesn't involve my cock distracting Summer from her job.

"She hasn't given me the impression she's struggling, and she hasn't forgotten anything important on our project. Maybe she was just flustered with already being late. Or maybe she was sick or something and just didn't want to say," I add, knowing that both of those explanations are a bit lame but not able to come up with anything better on the spot.

"I'm probably reading too much into it," Jack says after a moment. "It's a one-time thing and as long as it stays that way I'm not going to make a fuss about it. I've told her she can come and talk to me if she needs to and that's really all I can do without pressuring her."

"I'll keep an eye out too," I say. "But I really don't think I'll find anything for us to be concerned about."

I'm about ready to go and collect Summer and go for lunch, but I wait for a moment to let Jack get back to his office. I don't want it to look like I've gone running to talk to her the second after he left my office, not after what that conversation entailed. Having said that, in some ways, what Jack has just told me could work in our favor. If we are spotted and Jack asks me about it, I can just say I was thinking about what he had said, and I took her out to lunch to make sure she was definitely ok.

When I figure enough time has passed by that I would

have had time to contemplate our conversation further and then decide to take Summer to lunch, I stand up. I grab my wallet and put it in my pants' pocket. I don't bother with my jacket. It's a warm day and I'll only be too hot. I go to Summer's office. Her door is closed. I almost just push it open but then it occurs to me that she might be with a client, so I tap lightly on it.

"Come in," she calls.

I open the door and poke my head around it.

"Are you ready to go for lunch?" I ask.

"I just have a quick call to make and then I will be," she says.

"Ok, how about I go on ahead and grab us some food and meet you in the park on the next block and we'll have a little picnic?" I ask.

"Yes, that sounds good," she says smiling at me. "Can you grab me a roast beef sandwich and a Coke please?"

I nod my head and go to the elevator. I go down, cross the lobby and step outside into the warmth of the sun. I go to my favorite little place just down from the office. I decide Summer's choice sounds good so I order two roast beef sandwiches and two Cokes and then I make my way to the park.

I find an empty picnic bench beside what, in the winter, becomes the outdoors ice rink, but what, at the minute, is just a circle of concrete. It's perhaps not the best view but I sit facing it so Summer can sit opposite me and have the view of the trees and the pretty flower beds that grow between them, their soil alive with reds and oranges and yellows that seem to dance in the sun their fiery colors making them look almost like they are a part of it.

I look up as a shadow falls across me and Summer is slipping onto the seat opposite me. I hand her sandwich and

Coke to her and then I open my own sandwich and take a bite. The beef is juicy and tender, and I definitely made the right decision copying Summer's choice. Summer opens her can of Coke and sips it and then she begins on her sandwich. She's about halfway through it when she drops a bombshell on me.

"This is nice Tyler, really it is, but it can't happen again," she says.

"Huh? We can't have lunch together anymore?" I ask when I've swallowed my mouthful.

"Not just lunch," Summer says. "Any of it. I'm sorry Tyler, I thought it would be ok, us fooling around, maybe even dating, but I was wrong."

I feel like I've been punched in the stomach, but I keep eating, trying not to show Summer how much of an effect her words have had on me.

"I'm sorry," she says again after a moment of silence.

I shrug my shoulders like it's no big deal and finish my lunch. Summer finishes her sandwich just after me and she sits and plays with the bag it came in, looking down at her hands and not at me.

I could just let this go, just put it down to Summer telling me before she wasn't looking for anything serious, but I feel like it's more than that. I feel like there has to be a better reason than her just not being actively looking for a relationship.

"Can I ask why?" I ask.

"Why what?" Summer asks me.

"Why us dating isn't ok," I say.

She sighs and keeps fiddling with the bag, but eventually, when I don't rush to fill the silence, she looks up at me.

"I fucked up big time at work today. I forgot I had a meeting with one of my top clients. I've appeased her now, but I could have lost her. I've worked too hard to throw my career away," she says.

"There's no rule to say we can't date Summer. You're not throwing your career away," I say.

"No, it's not that," she says. "It's... look I can't stop thinking about you, ok? About us together. And I'm so distracted I can't concentrate on my work or on anything. So, I'm sorry, but I have to put my career first."

I burst out laughing at that. I know I shouldn't, but I can't help it. Summer frowns at me.

"What's funny?" she says.

"You are," I reply.

"What, you think me risking my career that I have worked so hard for is funny?" she says.

I shake my head.

"No of course not," I say. "What I think is funny is your logic."

She frowns again and I just smile at her. I can see she is dying to know what I mean but I don't make it easy for her. I wait for her to either ask or drop the subject, knowing that she won't be able to resist knowing and that she will ask. She doesn't disappoint me.

"What's wrong with my logic?" she demands after a few seconds.

"Well," I say. "If you think it's distracting now when you can touch me whenever you want to, kiss me whenever you want to, fuck me whenever you want to..."

I pause, watching with amusement as Summer's eyes glaze over the way they always do when she's turned on. She swallows hard and I go on.

"Imagine how much more distracting it's going to be knowing I'm just down the hallway from you and that you can't do any of those things," I finish.

I laugh softly again when I see Summer's expression change. It's clear she hadn't considered that, and I must admit I'm enjoying watching her squirm. It will be hard for me too, knowing she's so close but not being able to touch her, but it will be harder for her because she'll know that it's her own dumb fault.

"I..." Summer starts and then she stops and shakes her head.

"I'll make you a deal," I say. "When you change your mind – and yes, that's when, not if – and you come to me wanting me, I won't say I told you so."

"How do you know I'll change my mind?" Summer asks, frowning again.

"Because I can see it in your eyes," I say. "So, I'll be waiting. But this time, it has to come from you."

"You think I'm just going to give in, don't you? That I want you so badly I won't be able to resist you," she says.

I nod my head and smirk at her, watching her squirm in her seat. I know what that smirk does to her and I'm not afraid to use it.

"Well then you're in for a long wait," Summer says. "I can control myself quite easily, thank you very much."

I'm laughing again as I stand up and gather up the trash from our lunch and take it to the nearest trash can.

"Whatever you say," I say with a grin when she joins me, and we head back towards the office.

We reach the office building and get into the elevator. I can feel the sparks flying between us as we stand there, alone in the tiny box. I can almost taste the sexual tension in the air. I bite the inside of my lip to keep from smiling. I give Summer three months tops before she breaks and comes for me.

6

SUMMER

I put down my fork after finishing the last bite of my cheese and ham pasta salad. Rebecca is still eating her chicken and bacon sandwich. She watches me as she chews.

"Ok, out with it," she says after she swallows.

"Out with what?" I ask.

"Oh, come on Summer, it's obvious something is bothering you," she says.

"What do you mean, something other than the presentation I have to give after lunch?" I ask. "You know I hate doing presentations."

"Yeah, I do know that. But you're not usually so quiet. You normally babble on when you're nervous," she says.

"I don't babble on," I interrupt her. "I share my thoughts and ideas."

"Whatever," Rebecca says. "This is different. It's him, isn't it?"

It's been almost a month since I told Tyler that nothing can happen between us. I'm pleasantly shocked with myself that I've lasted this long without crossing a line. It's been hard. Damned hard. Especially with us working so closely together. Every day it's been a struggle to bury my attraction to him, but I have managed it. Or at least I have managed to not let it influence me. A couple of days in, I was having a particularly hard time resisting Tyler and I called Rebecca and asked her to go out for a drink. She obliged and I ended up telling her everything.

I nod my head sheepishly.

"The presentation is the last part of us working together. If the client likes the design, and I see no reason why they won't as it's been approved every step of the way, then that will be it. I mean obviously we'll still work in the same building, and we might see each other around, but it won't be the same," I admit.

Rebecca puts the last piece of her sandwich into her mouth and chews it slowly then she takes a long drink of her Sprite.

"I still don't get it," she says.

"You would if you saw him," I say.

"No, I don't mean that. I get that you're attracted to him, and I get that sometimes you just click with someone and it's magical and all of that. What I still don't get is why you can't just be with him," she says.

"I told you why already," I say with a sigh. "Being with Tyler is all consuming and I find myself too distracted. I don't want to fuck up at work again and risk losing my job."

"Ok. Let's just pretend for a moment it's you talking and not your mom," Rebecca says. I roll my eyes, but she ignores me and goes on. "You just have to learn to separate your emotions."

"Right," I say. "I'll just go see a witch doctor or something huh?"

"You're being ridiculous," Rebecca says. "Let me

explain." She's quiet for a second and then she smiles. "Ok, I've got it. You like a few cocktails when we go out right?"

I nod my head, wondering where she's going with this.

"But at work, you wouldn't sit and drink cocktails, because being drunk would be distracting. Right? So, work Summer doesn't drink cocktails, but real Summer does. And I'm sure there's been times sitting at your desk, too hot, bored or restless, that you have liked a nice cocktail. But you don't because you're work Summer and work Summer doesn't pull that kind of a stunt," Rebecca says. "Are you with me so far?"

"Well yes, but what does this have to do — " I start, but Rebecca cuts me off before I can finish. — "

"It has everything to do with Tyler," she finishes for me. "Imagine Tyler is that cocktail. Work Summer knows she can't have him because he would distract her. Even if she really wants him, work Summer knows better and ignores her desire. But real Summer, the Summer that you are outside of work, the Summer that drinks cocktails, that Summer, she could date Tyler."

I finally see where she's going with this. It makes sense on a logical scale, but when Tyler and I allow ourselves to touch each other, to kiss each other, every bit of logic goes out of the window.

"It won't work," I say. "God Rebecca it's hard enough not to jump on him every time I go into his office now and we aren't together. Imagine how much harder it would be not jumping on him knowing that I can because we're together."

"I genuinely think that will make it easier. Every time you resist that urge right now you deny yourself something that you want forever. If you and Tyler were together but still professional at work, you would only be denying yourself what you want until the evening comes. You could even make a sexy little game out of it," Rebecca says.

"Ok, yeah, I could do that," I say. "I'm not really some sex mad maniac. I would be able to control myself at work. I would hate to be one of those workplace couples that make everyone else uncomfortable. That's not what I'm worried about. I don't know how to explain without sounding pathetic, but when we're together, as in having sex, it's great but when we are physically apart, I can't stop thinking about him."

"It doesn't sound like you can stop thinking about him now," Rebecca says. "At least my way you get to stop thinking and start having fun for at least some of the time."

"I wish it was that simple," I say.

"But that's the thing, Summer. It is entirely that simple but you're making a big thing out of it. Look, just promise me you'll at least think about what I've said ok, because I hate to see you like this," Rebecca says.

"Like what?" I ask.

"Unhappy," Rebecca says as though it should have been obvious.

Maybe it should have been obvious. I mean I suppose I am unhappy because I know how good I could feel if I was with Tyler and I'm not. But I thought I was doing a much better job at hiding it. Rebecca laughs softly and when she speaks again it's as though she's read my mind.

"Don't worry, no one else would notice, but none of them at work know you like I do," Rebecca says. She glances at her watch. "And knowing you like I do; I know you'll want to be back a bit early for your presentation, so I reckon it's time to go."

I smile and nod, grateful Rebecca isn't going to insist we still have time before I have to be back at work even though it likely means she'll be going back to work earlier than she really has to as well.

We leave the café and go our separate ways. It's less than a two-minute walk for me and I'm back in my office in no time. I go back through each slide of my powerpoint presentation. I know this stuff back to front and inside out, but it never hurts to check everything over – it's better to check too many times than not enough.

When I'm as confident as I'm ever going to be, I take my laptop and go through to the conference room. It's the conference room where I first saw Tyler and realized I would be working with him and I smile a little bit at the memory, but I push it away. I have more than enough on my plate right now without letting myself think about that.

I set my laptop up so my screen is displayed on the wall of the room. I pull the screen down and the display sits perfectly on it, and I close the blinds so there's no glare on it and all is good. Now I just have to wait for Tyler and the client to arrive. My stomach is fluttery, and my heart is racing with a strange mix of nerves at the thought of the presentation and excitement because I genuinely think the client will love the design. I'm not nervous because I anticipate a bad reaction; I'm always like this when I have to deliver a presentation or a pitch. Once I get going, I know I'll be fine.

Tyler comes in a few minutes before the clients are due. We greet each other and as always when I first see him, my stomach gives a little roll, and my breathing quickens a little bit.

"I see you're all prepared," he says, nodding to the screen.

"Yeah. I hate doing the set up in front of people. I always find if I do it that way, something goes wrong and I end up fighting with everything and looking stupid," I say with a laugh.

"I wish I'd known. I would have come along earlier and had a good laugh," Tyler says.

"Oh, you don't count," I say, and we both laugh. "It's only clients seeing me square off with technology that worries me."

The conference room door opens then and Janine, one of the main receptionists stands in the doorway.

"Alex Carrol and Jonathon Maynard for you," she says.

"Thanks Janine, please show them in," Tyler says. Janine nods and scurries away and Tyler flashes me a smile. "Show time."

My nerves are shot at this point. My palms are sweating, and my throat is dry. The conference room door opens again and this time, Janine stands back and allows the clients to enter. Tyler and I both stand, and I quickly wipe my hands down my skirt and then I shake their hands in turn as does Tyler.

I offer the two men refreshments. They both decline a hot drink and ask for water. I go to the fridge at the back of the conference room and take four cold bottles of water. I tuck them under my arm and get four glasses from the cupboard above the fridge. I return to the table and hand out the drinks.

Once the pleasantries are out of the way, we are ready to get started. I grab my bottle of water, open it, and pour some into my glass. I take a few sips then I move to the front of the room and begin my presentation. I haven't gotten through the first slide when all of my nerves fall away, and I begin to enjoy showcasing our design.

The presentation flies by and when I finish, both Alex and Jonathon are smiling. They look impressed and I know then we have done good. Even if they request anything to be changed, it's going to be minimal. I beam at them.

"Do either of you have any questions?" I ask them.

It's Tyler's turn to talk now. That was what we agreed. I would do the initial presentation and Tyler would handle any questions the client had. They ask a few questions, nothing that Tyler can't handle and nothing that makes me change my mind about us having nailed this.

After a few questions, Alex and Jonathon look at each other and nod. They turn their attention back to us and Jonathon speaks up.

"Thank you, guys, this is great," he says. "You've done a fine job and you've answered all our questions. We're going to go back to our office and have a chat to discuss it all, but I have to say that your work is good, and I'm impressed."

"Me too," Alex agrees. "We'll get back to you by close of business today."

"That's perfect, thank you," Tyler smiles.

I smile and nod my agreement and Alex and Jonathon stand up. We all shake each other's hands and then Alex and Jonathon leave the conference room and Tyler and I beam at each other.

"That went exceptionally well," Tyler says.

I nod my head.

"Yes, it did," I agree. "Way better than I expected it to if I'm being totally honest."

I get up and roll the screen back up and disconnect my laptop from the projector. Tyler is up too and we both head for the door.

"Let me know as soon as you hear from them," I say.

"I will," Tyler says.

We reach the door and we both reach out for the handle at the same time. My hand comes down on the handle with

Tyler's hand over mine. My hand tingles and I have to catch my breath. Tyler doesn't move his hand immediately and for a second, I debate turning to him and kissing him. I know it would be a bad idea, but it doesn't stop me from wanting to do it. Tyler moves his hand.

"Sorry," he says, and the moment is gone.

I shake my head and open the door.

"It's ok," I say.

We leave the conference room and hurry away, both of us, I think, knowing how close we came to crossing that line once more. I don't relax again until I'm tucked back away in my office, sitting in my chair with my laptop back on my desk.

I don't really know how I feel about this project being as good as completed. From a professional point of view, I'm more than happy about it. We did a great job, providing a design the client loves and we did it within the promised time frame. On a personal level though, it's a little bit more complicated than that.

On the one hand, I have to admit it will be easier not having to work so closely with Tyler. Not seeing him up close and personal at least once every few days will make moving on from him a hell of a lot easier. But on the other hand, the truth is, I don't want to move on from him, and it's hurting me to know that after today, we won't be working so closely together.

To say the day has dragged by would be an understatement. Fridays always seem to drag because of the promise of two days off work, but this one is even worse than usual waiting to hear back from Alex and Jonathon. Two or three times

I've almost gone to Tyler's office just to check in and make sure that he hasn't heard from them and just forgotten to come and tell me. I've resisted the urge though. I'm sure he won't forget to tell me considering how much work I've put into this project.

I check my watch again. It's half past four and they said we would hear by the close of business today. Many times, I'm in the office until nine, ten o'clock, and I have no doubt that as a fairly new start up, Alex and Jonathon could say the same thing, but it's a universal thing that when you say close of business, you mean five pm not the time you leave the office for the day. Which means we will be hearing something any time now. Oh God what if they forget to get in touch and go home and we have to wait until Monday to hear from them? I tell myself they won't do that. They are professionals and they want to get this moving every bit as much as we do.

I am a little bit nervous about what they'll have to say, but I'm mostly excited. There might be some minor tweaks, but I really think that overall, they are happy and are going to approve our design.

It is five to five when the light tap finally comes on my door. This is it I think to myself.

"Come in," I call.

The door opens as I stand up. Tyler comes in and steps towards me and I step around my desk. He looks at me and I feel the familiar buzzing in my body but this time I ignore it completely, focused only on the project for the minute. Tyler is wearing a total poker face and he's giving nothing away. We meet in the center of my office, out of the line of sight of the ajar door.

"Oh my God, tell me," I blurt out. "Did they like it?"

"No," Tyler says and my heart sinks. How could I have

gotten this so wrong? His face melts into a smile and he goes on. "They didn't just like it Summer, they absolutely loved it."

Relief floods me followed by that pure euphoria I always feel when my designs are loved. Tyler grins at me and holds both hands in the air, palms outwards. I give him the double high five he's looking for and then we stand and grin stupidly at each other for a moment.

Slowly, our grins fade but we don't move away from each other. We stay in position, facing each other, our eyes locked on each other's eyes, and I feel the atmosphere in the room shifting from one of celebration to one of sexual tension. I look into Tyler's eyes, watching them flicker slightly from side to side as he looks into mine. He leans a tiny bit closer, and I know we're going to kiss if I don't move away. I stay in place. I'm hungry for the kiss that's coming, but it never does reach me.

"Ah there you are," Jack says from the doorway of my office.

Tyler and I jump apart. He quickly sits down on the visitor's side of my desk, and I practically run back behind it and take my seat there. If Jack notices our behavior is pretty strange, he doesn't ask any questions about it.

"What can I do for you Jack?" I ask.

He has crossed the floor and now sits beside Tyler at my desk.

"I was looking for Tyler to find out how we are on your big project. When he wasn't in his office, I figured I'd find out in the morning brief, but then I saw your office door was open and so I thought I'd ask you Summer," he says. "But it seems like I found my man. Come and update me when you have a moment, Tyler."

Jack stands up, the last part of his sentence directed at Tyler who stands up too.

"I can come now," he says. He glances at me. "You're not rushing off, are you? There was something I wanted to ask you."

"No, it's fine, I can wait," I say.

I feel like I'm holding my breath until Jack and Tyler leave the office and then I let my breath out in a long sigh. Would we have kissed if we hadn't been interrupted? I really think we would have. I shudder at the thought of how embarrassed I would have been if Jack had appeared a moment later and caught Tyler and me mid kiss.

I think of what Rebecca said, about resisting Tyler at work because to do anything else is just unprofessional, but then to have a relationship with him outside of work. While I'm still not convinced her theory is fool proof or even really a good idea, I do know that it would have prevented what almost happened there. If I knew I could kiss Tyler the second we were out of the office, I wouldn't have even let it get to the point where we almost kissed.

Could it work? Could we make it work?

I shake my head. It's not so much a no as it is a don't even think about it because it's all too complicated right now.

To distract myself, I gather up my things. I decide to leave my laptop here; I have another for personal use at home and if I take this one home with me, I'll only be tempted to do work over the weekend and I think, after the intensity of the project we've just finished, I deserve a weekend off.

I put my cell phone in my purse and grab my jacket, which I hang over my purse and then I put it down on my desk and sit down to wait for Tyler. If I was waiting for anyone but Tyler at five twenty on the one Friday I had promised myself I wasn't staying late, I would be cursing both myself for agreeing to wait and them for not being quicker, but it's Tyler. I don't mind waiting for him. I kind of like the idea of getting one last look at him before we will be apart for two whole days.

I don't have much longer to wait before Tyler reappears in my office door. He smiles at me as he comes back in.

"Right then. That's Jack all up to speed," he says. "That will save me a job Monday morning."

"Is he happy?" I ask.

"He's way beyond happy," Tyler says. "He's very impressed with your input on this one."

I feel myself blush and look down at my knees.

"It was a team effort," I say.

"And you were a big part of the team," Tyler insists. "Don't sell yourself short Summer. You did really well on that."

I force myself to look up and smile at him even though I'm still blushing.

"Thank you," I say. "Now what did you want to ask me?"

"Oh, yeah," he says. "I wanted to ask you to come for a drink with me."

I start to open my mouth to tell Tyler I don't think that would be a good idea, despite my body screaming at me to say yes. My answer must show on my face because Tyler hurries on before I get further than the word I.

"Come on Summer. One drink. No funny business. It's not a date, it's a celebratory drink between colleagues," he says.

"I don't know," I say.

It's less of a no than it was and Tyler smiles.

"If you'd worked on this project with Jack and he asked

you for a celebratory drink when you smashed it, would you assume he was coming on to you?" Tyler says.

"What? No of course not," I say, shocked he would even ask.

His grin becomes a laugh.

"So do me the same courtesy then," he says.

I realize I have backed myself into a corner now. The only way I can continue to refuse a drink with Tyler is to send the message that I don't believe he can go for a drink with a colleague without being some sort of creep.

"One drink," I say, standing up.

We leave the building and I automatically head for the bar across the street, but Tyler shakes his head and turns left. I shrug and follow him thinking he must need something from his car first, but he passes the parking lot and keeps walking.

"Where are we going?" I ask.

"There's a nice little bar around the corner. I thought we could go there," he says.

"Ok," I say, dragging the word out a bit.

"Is something wrong?" he asks.

"Well, no, I just assumed we'd be going to Jazz like we always do," I say.

"We can if you want to but ask yourself this. Do you really want to spend more time than you have to with everyone from the office?" he says. I frown and he laughs. "I don't mean any offense to them. They are all great people, but whenever we are all together like that, all we do is talk about work. And I don't know about you, but I am more than ready to forget about work for the weekend."

"Fair point," I say.

We reach the bar Tyler is taking me to. It looks a lot more upscale than Jazz and I look down at my white blouse and black pencil skirt. Am I dressed ok for a place like this on a Friday night? I tell myself to stop overthinking everything. It's still only afternoon really and probably half the people in here will have come from an office somewhere nearby and will be dressed in a similar manner.

Tyler pulls the door open and gestures for me to go inside. I do and I'm pleasantly surprised when I step inside. The bar is reasonably busy but not crowded and the people are all dressed in office wear or casual clothes like jeans and shirts, and I don't feel so underdressed anymore.

It looks like a nice place though, the tables spread out enough to give people a bit of privacy. The seats are all plush leather couches and low coffee tables, and the floor is a beautiful oak. I could definitely get used to coming here instead of Jazz.

I follow Tyler towards the bar, and he waves towards an empty table.

"Why don't you go grab us that table and I'll get the drinks. What would you like?" he asks.

"A glass of Prosecco please," I say.

He nods and keeps going and I go and sit down. Tyler soon joins me, and he raises his glass.

"To you," he says.

I lift mine and clink it.

"And to you," I say.

We drink and then put our glasses down.

"That's it, no more work talk," Tyler said with a grin. "Tell me about your childhood."

I'm kind of thrown by the abrupt shift from professional to personal, but I don't really want to spend the time here talking about work, so I go with it.

"There's not really a lot to tell," I say. "My parents are both doctors, so we were fairly well off when I was growing up. We weren't rich but we weren't poor. My parents focused on my education a lot and while I suppose in one sense, I should be grateful, in another sense, it was a bit selfish on their part because they were so focused on me becoming a doctor like them."

"Did you never want to do that?" Tyler asks.

I shake my head.

"No. When I was little, I wanted to be a teacher, then I decided I wanted to be a flight attendant. And then finally I settled on architecture. My parents weren't happy to say the least, but I suppose it was better than a flight attendant in their eyes," I say with a smile.

"Do you have any siblings?" Tyler asks me.

"Nope. So of course, that made everything worse because all of my parents' focus was on me. Do you have siblings?" I ask.

"One. A sister. She's thirty-six, a year older than me. We're not really close. It's not that we don't get along, we do, it's just, well we used to be closer, but you grow apart from people sometimes, don't you?" he says.

I nod my head. I want to ask him more questions about how he and his sister drifted apart because I feel like there's something big that he's not telling me, but I decide against it. If he wanted me to know he would have told me more. It's not for me to go poking around in his private life.

"What do your parents do?" I ask instead.

"My dad is an electrician," Tyler says. "He runs his own firm. I mean technically he's retired now, and the firm has a manager in place. And my mom left her job as a librarian when Angela was born. She brought us up and by the time we were old enough to be left alone, my dad's business was doing so well they didn't need the extra income, so she never bothered going back to work."

Tyler's mom is exactly who my parents fear I will become.

"Is your mom happy?" I ask. "Doesn't she miss having her career?"

"No," Tyler says. "I mean no she doesn't miss her career, not no she isn't happy. She's by far the happiest out of all mine and my friends' parents. As she says, working is to finance your actual life and her life is financed without work. It gives her plenty of time to spend spoiling Angela's little one and painting and gardening and doing all the things that she wants to do."

"That sounds amazing," I say.

"It does, doesn't it," Tyler laughs.

Would it really be so bad to give up work and be a wife and a mother and, if Tyler's mom is anything to judge by, all sorts of other things? I think I would miss work too much and I would feel like all of that time and money getting my degree had just been a waste, but it doesn't sound as bad as I have been led to believe it would be.

Our glasses are empty and Tyler nods towards mine and I shake my head.

"No, it's my round," I say.

"Your round? Really?" Tyler laughs.

"Yup," I say. "It's not a date, remember. If you were here with Jack, would you buy his drinks all night?"

I laugh to myself for using his own argument against him and he shakes his head but he's laughing too.

"No, but I did bring you here to celebrate the project," he says.

"Well, I would very much like to celebrate your part in it too," I say. I stand up before he can argue. "What are you having?"

"I'm not going to win this one, am I?" Tyler laughs. I

shake my head and smile. "Fine. I'll have a rum and Coke please."

I go to the bar and get our drinks and head back to the table. I'm well aware that I said I was only having one, but the conversation is flowing and I'm enjoying Tyler's company and it's not like I have to be up early for work in the morning.

"Did your dad ever want you to follow in his footsteps and work for the family business?" I ask when I am back seated, and we have started our fresh drinks.

"He didn't try to pressure me into that route, but he did make it known that there would be a place for me if I wanted it. And one for Angela too," he says. "When I said I was going to college and I was going to be an architect, he was supportive and never tried to guilt me into the business."

"That's amazing," I say, meaning it. I wish my own parents had been more supportive like that. "What about Angela? Did she take up your dad's offer?"

"Yes, she did. She's one of his electricians. She was one of those kids who is always taking something apart just to see how it works, you know the type?" Tyler looks at me and I smile and nod. "My dad started to teach her about fixing electrical items from an early age and she never really looked back. It's funny though because I bet now you are picturing her as a tomboy, right?" I nod my head again. "Everyone always does when they hear what she does, but she's actually a really girly girl. She will think nothing of going out to rewire a building with a full face of makeup on and her nails done."

We both laugh at that.

"I think I would like her," I say.

"Yeah, I think you would too," Tyler says. "And she would adore you."

We keep chatting about our families for a bit then we move onto old friends, new friends, our dreams for the future and everything in between. We discuss hobbies, movies, books, and music. I feel like I know Tyler as well as I know my best friend by the time twelve o'clock rolls around. For a time, the bar became really busy, all of the tables full and people standing around too. Then it quietened back down again as it started to get later, and people moved on to other bars or clubs.

"Are we outstaying our welcome here?" I ask Tyler when I realize the time.

He shakes his head.

"No, they're open until one," he says. "Sometimes later. They..."

He trails off and I follow his gaze. A blonde-haired woman in a form fitting cream dress printed with red roses has just walked in. I feel a surge of jealousy flood me, hot bile rising in my throat at Tyler's reaction to her. I force down a swallow of my drink and raise an eyebrow to Tyler.

"Sorry," he says, and he genuinely looks it. "I thought that was my ex-wife for a minute there."

I suppose that is marginally better than him just staring at strangers like that, but it doesn't change his reaction to the sight of her. I hate that I hate it, but I do.

"How long ago did you get divorced?" I asked.

"Just over a year ago," Tyler says.

"And you're still in love with her?" I press him.

"What? No. God no," he says.

He sounds like he really means that. In fact, he sounds almost like he hates her. But his reaction to the woman he thought was her can't be ignored.

"Are you sure? You caught sight of someone you thought was her and you just stopped talking mid-sentence," I say.

"I can promise you I am not in love with Chloe. I was just shocked when I thought I saw her, that's all. She's honestly the last person I want to see," he says.

"Bad break up?" I ask.

"Something like that," Tyler says. "Now, I'm going to ask you something very important." He pauses and I find that I'm quite nervous all of a sudden. "Harry Potter. The books or the movies?"

I relax and laugh. I don't know what I was expecting but it wasn't that. It's obvious that Tyler just wants to move the conversation away from his ex and that's fine with me. I can understand if he had a messy divorce he doesn't want to dwell on it.

"I love the books," I say. "But I haven't seen the movies yet."

"What do you mean you haven't seen the movies?" Tyler demands, his face showing his shock. "One Sunday you are coming to my house, and we are having a Harry Potter movie marathon."

"Ok," I laugh. "I guess it is about time I watched them."

"It's past time you watched them," Tyler corrects me.

The bartender shouts for last orders. We both have almost full drinks, so we don't bother ordering another. Tyler goes off to order a cab and I debate ordering us some shots, but I decide it's better if Tyler thinks I at least have a little bit of class and somehow doing shots feels like the opposite to that.

Tyler comes back to the table.

"Five minutes," he says.

I nod and we start to finish up our drinks. I swallow

down the last mouthful of mine and put my empty glass down on the table with a laugh.

"Not bad for someone who was only having one drink huh?" I ask.

"Not bad at all," Tyler agrees.

He has finished his drink now too and we start to get ready to leave. I pick my purse up off the floor and take my jacket from it and put it on. Tyler's jacket is on the back of his chair, and he too puts his jacket on.

"I'm just going to pop to the ladies' room before we go," I say.

I hurry through to the ladies' room and quickly do my business. I wash my hands and pull my fingers through my hair, tidying it up a little bit, and then I go back out to see Tyler still at our table. He sees me, stands up and we meet in the middle of the bar. Then we head to the door and leave.

Our cab is there waiting for us, and Tyler opens the door for me. I get in and slide across the seat and he follows me and closes the door.

"Where to Mister?" the driver asks.

"We'll drop you off first," Tyler says to me. "Where to?"

Tyler looks at me as he asks me where I am going, and I know this is it. The moment I make a decision that might change the rest of my life. But I'm done missing out. I'm done depriving myself of things. I can hear Rebecca's voice in my head telling me to live a little bit, that I truly can have it all if I just trust myself to make it work.

Something shifts in that moment, and for perhaps the first time, I put my emotional needs before anything else. I don't take my eyes off Tyler's as I answer his question.

"Miller Square," I say. "I don't remember the number."

Tyler swallows hard.

"Ten ninety-three Miller Square please," he says.

He's talking to the cab driver but he's looking at me and the air is alive between us. I can almost see the sparks dancing between us. On some unspoken cue, Tyler and I both lean in and before I know it, his lips are on mine and we're kissing.

His kiss awakens a desire in me that's so strong it should be scary but it's not, because when I'm with Tyler, nothing scares me.

One of Tyler's hands rests on my cheek and the other one is on my hip. My hands are flat against his chest. I can feel his pecs through his shirt, and it drives me crazy that I can't yet touch his skin. It's taking a lot of willpower to not rip his clothes off and straddle him and I have to keep reminding myself that we are in a cab.

Tyler pulls back from our kiss, and he kisses gently across my cheek and then his lips are on my ear.

"You are so beautiful," he whispers.

His breath tickles my ear, and a delicious shiver goes through me. I don't know if it's the tickling sensation or his words that cause it. He kisses down towards my neck and then back up and his lips find mine once more. I push my tongue into his mouth but then I remember myself once again and dart it back out again. We kiss gently now, a tender, almost loving kiss and it should slow my racing heart, but it doesn't. It just makes me want Tyler more.

Finally, when I can take no more, I have to break the kiss and I pull back from Tyler. He smiles at me as I look at him, my chest heaving as I pant for air. Tyler is smiling, I can see he is in a similar state of longing, and I have to bite my tongue to not yell at the cab driver to hurry up.

Tyler and I move apart slightly, although I can still feel the heat of his thigh against mine. He reaches out and takes my hand in his and that has to be all for now, until we are at his place. I look out of the window, urging the landscape to pass by faster.

The journey can't have taken more than twenty minutes when we finally arrive at Tyler's place, but it feels as though we've been trapped in the cab for hours. I'm relieved to get out and know I can kiss Tyler as passionately as I like now.

I get out of the cab and wait for Tyler. He pays the fare and gets out of the cab. We head for his gate as the cab pulls away. Tyler takes my hand in his and smiles at me as we walk down his front path to his door.

"You know, this is the third time you've been here," he says. "I think it's time you saw that I do indeed have other rooms."

"You don't want me in your bedroom?" I say with a raised eyebrow.

"Oh no, I do. I most definitely do. I just thought we should have a drink first, make it last," Tyler says.

I smile and nod my agreement, although I'm not sure either of us will be able to hold out long enough to drink anything before we are on each other.

7

TYLER

We get inside of the house, and I point the living room out to Summer and then I keep going until I'm in the kitchen. I find a nice bottle of Grey Goose and a bottle of lemonade. I make us each a vodka and lemonade and I go through to the living room.

I take it in with one long glance, looking for anything that's too messy. Luckily the place is pretty tidy, and I don't think there's anything to gross Summer out. The room is undoubtedly masculine but it's clean and tidy. I try to look at it through an outsider's point of view.

The room consists of three white walls with a dark blue feature wall that contains a brick fireplace. The furniture is all glass and chrome aside from the couch and the armchairs which are leather in the same shade of dark blue as the feature wall. Above the fireplace, a huge TV is mounted on the wall.

"Welcome to my humble abode," I smile as I go and sit down on the couch beside Summer. I put our drinks down on the coffee table in front of us.

"I'm not sure humble is the word," Summer laughs. "It's nice though. I like it."

"Really?" I say, a little bit surprised. "My mom, my sister, every female really tells me this space is too full of masculine energy that I need accent pillows or some shit to feminize it a bit."

"Oh, what bullshit," Summer says. "They're just intimidated by the clean lines and the minimalist feel. Sure, it's not for everyone, but the last thing you want is accent pillows. Or cozy little throws. Or any of the other shit they suggest."

We both laugh and then Summer picks up her drink and takes a mouthful. She winces.

"Sorry, is it too strong?" I ask.

She shakes her head.

"No, it's ok. I just wasn't expecting it to be that strong," she laughs. "I've gotten too used to bar measures."

She takes another drink and this time, she doesn't wince. I take a sip of mine and I see she's right; it is a bit strong but in reality, she's right; it's probably just strong compared to pub measures.

"Should I put some music on?" I ask.

Summer nods her head and I get up. I put my cell phone in my docking station, so the music comes through the main sound system and then I find my chill-out playlist and start it. By the time I sit back down, Summer is humming along to the music.

"I love this song," she says with a smile.

She puts her drink down and stands up and reaches for my hand to pull me up with her.

"Oh no, no way," I laugh.

Summer shrugs one shoulder.

"Your loss," she says.

She goes to the other side of the coffee table and stands in the center of the room. She sways her hips and raises her hands up in the air and dances. She looks so good, and I'm already starting to wish I had gotten up with her, but at the same time, I'm more than happy to sit here and enjoy the show. And what a show it is turning out to be.

Summer is still swaying her hips and moving her body from side to side, but her hands are down now. Her head is back slightly, and her eyes are closed. Her fingers are working their way down the front of her blouse opening the buttons as she goes. She reaches the waistband of her skirt, and she takes her blouse in both hands and pulls it loose. She opens the last few buttons and then she shrugs the blouse off her shoulders and down her arms and lets it fall to the floor.

The song changes, but Summer doesn't stop her little strip tease. She's onto her skirt now. She runs her hands over her hips where the material sticks to her body and makes her curves look insanely good. She reaches behind herself, and she must open her skirt because the next moment, it drops to the floor. She side steps then lifts the skirt on one foot and flicks it away.

She continues to dance. Her arms are up in the air again as she stands before me, swaying, in nothing but her white lacy panties and matching bra and her high black heels. My cock is already rock hard and watching Summer's show is doing nothing to make me feel any more comfortable down there. The only way I will be able to be comfortable down there is by taking Summer and my god I have to have her right now.

I stand up and go to her. I start to reach out to wrap my arms around her, but she catches my hands and holds them out to our sides, involving me in her dance. I let her move me around a bit and I even sway my hips a bit with her, but I am not here to dance, I'm here to have Summer. I drop her hands and reach for her again, but she ducks out of my reach and shakes her head. She smiles at me, her eyes sparkling.

"Not until you've stripped for me," she says.

I'm more than open to taking my clothes off, but I hope Summer doesn't expect me to put on a show like she did. Where she looked sexy and set the mood, I would look stupid and kill it.

I'm taking my jacket off even as I think that, and I throw it down on the armchair near me. I pull my shirt out of my pants and then I loosen my tie and pull it over my head, dropping it on the ground. I undo the top couple of shirt buttons and then I pull that over my head and throw it to the ground. I pause for a moment and Summer and I stand watching each other. I can feel the desire pumping through my body and I know I have to have this girl soon or I will explode.

I move my hands to my pants opening the button and fly then push them down. I lift one foot up and pull off my shoe and sock then the pants leg. I repeat the same with the other foot. I stand before Summer in just my boxer shorts. Her eyes roam over my body and she makes a low moaning sound in the back of her throat. The noise is so fucking sexy, and I reach for her, but she jumps back. She shakes her head, that teasing smile back on her face.

"All of it," she says, looking pointedly at my boxer shorts where they are still in place on my body.

"You're still in your underwear," I point out.

"Oh. So, I am. Let me fix that," Summer says.

She reaches behind her back and unclasps her bra. It slips down her arms and she lets it fall and then she pushes her panties down, kicks them off her legs and stands there naked and smiling. I rush to follow suit, kicking my boxer shorts off to who knows where.

Summer looks at my hard cock and licks her lips and it's my turn to moan. I reach for her and this time, she doesn't dance away. I pull her into my arms and kiss her. Our hands roam all over each other's bodies, our lips locked together.

I push one hand between Summer's legs and put two fingers inside of her slit, finding her clit and massaging it as we kiss. My other hand holds Summer tightly against me. Her hands are up and down my back and sides and then they are in my hair and then they are back on my back again.

I massage Summer's clit until she is dripping wet and I know she's ready to come and then I stop. Her mouth leaves mine but before she can object, I push my same two fingers inside of her pussy and use my thumb on her clit. I work my fingers and thumb together and I push Summer backwards towards the couch. She moves easily with me and when we reach the couch, I support her with one arm around her and lay her on her back with my other hand still keeping her right there on the edge of her orgasm.

I push one of her legs off the couch, so she is wide open and then I kneel between her knees. I up the pace of my probing fingers and I feel Summer's pussy clenching as she starts to orgasm. I reach up and wrap my spare hand around her throat and squeeze gently. Her eyes flicker open in alarm for a second but then the alarm is gone, and her eyes glaze over as her orgasm takes her away.

She arches her back and I squeeze her throat a bit harder. She goes rigid, her back still arched and her mouth opens and closes as she tries to breath but finds her airway restricted. I keep working her clit and her pussy and she floods my hand over and over again.

She clenches around me again and her hands come up and grab my upper arms, her nails digging in hard enough to hurt. The stinging pain wakes my nerve endings right up and as it moves through my body, it becomes pleasure rather than pain.

I take my hand from Summer's throat as she begins to come down from her second orgasm. She gasps in a big breath, and she's panting as I lean forward and gently kiss where my hand has been on her throat. I pull my fingers out of her pussy and then I move so that I'm lying on top of her, and I push my cock into her pussy instead.

She cries out as I fill her and then I start to thrust inside of her, and she moves her hips in time with mine. Her hands reach for my ass cheeks, and she wraps her legs around me, trying to force me in deeper, deeper.

We are well into our rhythm when Summer thrusts extra hard, sending me lurching to the side. I tumble from the couch, and she comes with me, straddling me where I land on my back. She smiles down at me and moves up and down on my length, clenching and unclenching her muscles, making her already tight pussy even tighter around me.

I'm so close to coming when she slows down completely. She moves slowly, deliberately up into the air until I'm almost out of her and then she takes me back in, her downward movement just as slow. I feel her slippery warmth on every inch of my cock as I slip inside of her, and it's delicious and it's amazing, but it's not enough. I'm on the edge and I need to climax. The need is almost a physical pain and I want to hold off and make this last, but I can't.

My primal drive takes over and I can't stop myself any

longer. I grab Summer's hips in my hands and push her towards the couch. I keep a hold on her as I slip out of her and get to my knees. She turns so she's on her knees, bent at the waist, her upper body laid on the couch.

I kneel behind her and penetrate her once more and I pound into her, our bodies slamming together with each thrust. I try to make it last as long as I can, but my body takes over in the end and before I can stop it, I'm coming, hard. I feel Summer clench around me and I realize she is coming with me. I hold her in place as we both moan and gasp.

Pleasure floods me, my whole body is alive and tingling and delicious. I feel pleasure through every part of me from the top of my head all the way down to my toes. I'm so overwhelmed by the feeling that I can't think for a moment. I can only feel. I cling to Summer, sure that if I don't, I might just float away.

She screams my name, and her scream brings me back to myself in the best possible way and I spurt into her over and over again as I hold her in place, the tip of my cock pressed against her cervix.

Finally, it's over and it is at once a relief and a disappointment. I have never felt anything that intense before and it scared me a little bit, but I'm already ready to feel it again. I slip out of Summer, and she turns towards me. I move off my knees and sit on my ass with my legs folded in front of me and then I hold out my arms to her.

She moves into my lap and puts her head on my shoulder, and we wrap our arms around each other as we take a moment to recover. I only have to look at Summer, her dazed eyes, her slightly swollen lips, her flushed cheeks to know that she felt that like I did, and I love that I can make her come as undone as she can me.

When I feel like I am pretty much back to my normal self, I lean down and kiss Summer on the top of the head. I feel her cheek move against my chest as she smiles and then she tilts her face up and I kiss her lips. There is passion there - I don't think there will ever be a time when Summer and I come together and there isn't passion there – but this kiss feels like it's about more than just passion and attraction. It feels like the difference between fucking and making love.

It's scary for me because it can only mean one thing – I am falling for Summer and if I let myself fall for her, I'm leaving myself wide open to getting hurt. But who am I kidding when I say if I let myself fall for her? As if I could somehow stop myself. I need to stop over thinking about this and just go with it and see where we end up.

As we kiss, Summer moves so she's sitting astride me, and I can feel the heat of her pussy on my cock. I'm hard again already. This is what she does to me. I shuffle back slightly so that my back is against the couch and then I deepen our kiss. Summer moans into my mouth and then she moves her hips slightly so that her slit rubs over my cock leaving behind a warm, wet trail.

I need to be inside of her again. I put my hands underneath Summer's ass and then I move back onto my knees and stand up, holding her to me. She wraps her arms around my shoulders, her legs around my waist and I carry her towards the stairs.

She moves her head to one side and kisses my neck and then along my shoulder and back to my neck. Her kisses send goosebumps scurrying over my skin, her light, teasing touch makes me want to throw her down right here and fuck her, but I'm afraid the stairs will hurt her back and the last thing I want to do is hurt Summer so I force myself to wait.

I reach the top of the stairs and head for the bedroom. I don't even have the bedroom door open yet when Summer reaches behind herself. She grabs my cock in her fist and starts to move it up and down my length. I moan and almost tumble as pleasure assaults me. I take a moment to experience the ecstasy her touch awakens in me. I stand outside of my bedroom, the door still closed, my forehead pressed against it beside Summer.

She works me and her other hand curls around my neck and peels my head from the door and we're kissing again, the deep, passionate kisses that I can't resist. I get myself together and open the bedroom door and as I kick it closed behind me, Summer stops moving her fist on my cock and instead, she pushes me inside of her.

I moan her name as I turn around and slam her against the wall. I take her arms and lift them above her head, running my hands up them to her wrists. I take both of her wrists in one hand and pin them above her head and then I lean in and run my tongue lightly up and down her neck.

I stop thrusting, just holding myself still inside of Summer as I tease her with my light licks and kisses. She moans and writhes and tries to move her hips, to make me start thrusting again. I press myself against her, jamming her pelvis against the door, rendering her motionless and then I use my one spare hand and my tongue and lips to bring her into a frenzied state where she is begging me to fuck her.

I ignore her begging for a moment and keep pushing her. She is so wet, so ready, and I know she can't take much more. I release her wrists and her hands come down into my hair. I kiss her deeply as she tries once more to move her hips and make me fuck her. I tease her for a few more seconds until it becomes more than either of us can bear, and then I whisk her away from the wall, carry her to the bed, we get on the bed and then I'm fucking her.

I'm slamming into her, filling her up physically while fulfilling the need in us emotionally. Our bodies come together in a series of intense thrusts that are so hard, so passionate, it almost hurts.

I know Summer is close to orgasming and I reach down with one hand and work her clit. She comes within seconds of me touching her, a bomb waiting to go off. She whimpers as her face twists and then her mouth drops open in a silent O of pleasure.

Her pussy tightens around my cock but this time, it stays tight, locking me inside of her, making each thrust feel even more amazing than the last one. Her fingers cling to me and her legs tighten around me. It's as though she wants to consume me, and I'm more than ready to be consumed by her.

With an animalistic sound that is half a scream, half a moan, a gush of liquid rushes out of Summer and coats my balls and my thighs. It's too much for me to bear and I can no longer hold back my own orgasm and once more, I spurt into Summer over and over again, holding her against me, whispering her name against her neck as I push the side of my face into her shoulder.

As we come down, I pull out of Summer and roll off her and we lay side by side, spent, panting, our skin glistening in the silvery moon light that streams in through the window.

When I've got my breath back, I realize just how good I feel. I feel sated, my muscles heavy but relaxed. I feel my eyes closing and I reach out to Summer, not wanting to fall asleep without her being in my arms. She shuffles closer to me and lays her head on my shoulder, and I wrap my arm around her. She cocks one of her legs over mine and wraps an arm around my waist. I make a contented "mmm" sound and when I feel my eyes closing again, I don't try to stop them.

I'm not sure how long we lay like that, but I'm almost asleep when I feel Summer stirring beside me. I want to ask her where she's going but I don't have the energy to even open my eyes, let alone speak. That is until I feel her lips running gently over mine and my eyes spring open then. She kisses me then pulls back a bit and smiles.

"You look tired," she says. She makes a point of turning her head to look down at my cock which is hard once more. She has that effect on me. She only has to kiss me, and I'm rock hard and ready for her. "I hope little Tyler isn't too tired for me."

"There's nothing little about Tyler Junior," I retort. "And as for him being too tired, why don't you go down there and find out for yourself."

Summer grins at me and she cocks her leg over me and sits astride me. She leans down and kisses me again and then she starts to shuffle backwards, and I can feel her warm, wet trail moving down my legs and I love that she's leaving her juices on me.

She kisses her way down my neck, my chest and over my belly. She kisses my pubic bone and then my cock and then she moves onto one of my thighs. She kisses down to my knee then moves to the other thigh and kisses back up it. She lays down between my legs and smiles up at me. I smile back and then she starts to lick my cock and I lay back, my arms folded behind my head, my eyes closed.

She sucks me into her warm mouth and begins to move her head up and down, running her lips over every inch of me as she sucks. I want to fuck her once more, but the truth is, I really am tired and the rhythm of her sucking me feels so good and I don't want to move. I just want to lay here forever and enjoy the feeling of her lips on my cock.

As she sucks on me, she runs her nails lightly up and down my inner thighs, adding to my pleasure. I can feel myself getting close to coming now and I move my hands from behind my head and I grab a handful of the comforter in each hand, twisting it between my fingers as I lift my ass, thrusting into Summer's mouth.

She keeps sucking me, sucking me, and I'm ready to explode when she takes her mouth away. Before I really know what's happening, she's straddling me again and she holds my cock in her fist, and then she lowers herself, impaling herself on me and I'm inside of her again and the tiredness is gone and I find that I want this as much as she does.

She isn't messing around teasing me this time. She is moving up and down fast, her breasts hopping wildly around as she moves. I match her pace, thrusting away inside of her. She throws her head back and pinches her nipples and the visual is too much and I come hard. I can't stop myself, the pleasure is racing through me, my cock emptying once more.

I moan Summer's name as my whole body contracts and releases, sending thrumming pleasure through me. It seems to move in time with my pulse and the way my heart is racing means my body is practically buzzing with electricity. It fades and I relax and slip out of Summer.

She is still in place on top of me and I realize she hasn't come. I can't have that. I won't leave her disappointed. I sit up and wrap an arm around Summer. Her eyes flutter open at my touch, and she smiles lazily at me.

"See he was up for it," she laughs.

I kiss her as she stops laughing and she kisses me back, her hands gripping my hair. I hold her with one arm around her waist and the other hand I push between us and use it to bring her clit back to life. I begin to move my fingers side to side, slowly at first. I can feel how engorged Summer's clit is already, how ready she is for this.

I keep moving my fingers. I move them faster and faster and Summer pulls her mouth away from me, gasping and panting but she can't seem to get enough air. I don't give her a break. I keep working, working her, and she goes rigid, and I feel that now familiar rush of warm juices coat my hand and then she's moaning my name on the last bit of air she has and her mouth is opening and closing, opening and closing, and she manages to gasp again and then she flops forward, sagging against my chest, her face on my shoulder. I can feel her hot breath as she pants and gasps there and I hold her letting her come down at her own speed.

Finally, she pushes herself back up and smiles down at me. She flicks her leg over and lays back down beside me. I pull her against me, and she snuggles into me and within seconds, she's asleep. I don't think I'm far behind her.

I WAKE up and smile to myself when I see that Summer is still beside me. She's laying on her front, her face turned away from me, her hair all fanned out. I prop myself up on one elbow and move her hair back away from her neck and then I kiss the exposed skin. Summer moans and her eyes flutter open. She smiles.

"Good morning," I whisper.

"Good morning," she replies.

"So, you're still here then," I say.

"It looks like it," Summer agrees. She sits up and smiles down at me. "I need to shower. I feel stickier than a pulled pork sandwich."

I can't help but laugh at her choice of words but I kind of know what she's getting at. I will be right behind her once she's finished in the shower. I watch her walk naked across the room to the door. Her ass is so perfect and the curve of her hips and the shape of her legs. Alright. All of her is so perfect. She looks back at me and I smile at her, and she raises an eyebrow.

"What?" I ask.

"Nothing. I just wondered what you were doing. Are you waiting for a written invitation or something?" she says.

She turns away and leaves the room before I can reply but I'm out of the bed and moving. I didn't even realize she meant she wanted us to shower together but now that I do there's no stopping me. Summer looks over her shoulder and smiles when she sees I'm now behind her.

"Next one," I say as she reaches a door and glances back at me again.

She keeps going and opens the bathroom door and steps in. She smiles when she sees my big, double shower. She slides the door open and steps in. I follow her and slide the door closed and she starts to mess around with the water until the temperature suits her. She picks up a sponge and my shower gel and squirts some of it onto the sponge. She starts to wash herself and I take the sponge from her and gently sponge her down.

As soon as I start to rub the sponge over her body, my cock starts to crave her. It hardens and I make no effort to hide it. Summer must know the effect she has on me by now. I'm pretty sure it's the same effect I have on her too.

I pay particular attention to Summer's breasts and then between her legs, neither of which she objects to, although she does gasp and grit her teeth when I rub the sponge over her clit. I'm guessing she's still tender from last night. Her clit took a good few hot and heavy sessions.

When I finish washing Summer's body, I reach for my shampoo. I squirt a little bit into my hand and begin to lather up her hair. I wash her hair, bringing the length up onto her head and then I run my nails lightly over her scalp. When I've finished, I gently rinse the shampoo out of her hair and then I take a moment to admire her. She really is perfection personified.

When I've drunk her in for as long as I can without fucking her, I grab the shampoo bottle again and I wash my own hair. I put my head back into the thick of the spray, close my eyes and rinse the soap away. I grab my shower gel, but Summer takes it from me. I open my eyes and grin at her. She grins back.

She doesn't bother with the sponge. She spreads the shower gel over her palms and then she slowly, deliciously, rubs her hands all over my arms, my neck, my chest, my sides, my back. She reloads her hands with shower gel and rubs her hands over my ass cheeks and then down my thighs, missing my cock altogether.

She kneels down on the shower floor and washes my calves and then she puts more shower gel on her hands, and she grabs my cock when I'm least expecting it. She moves her hands up and down and all around on it, washing it but also turning me on so much.

When she tires of washing my cock, she rinses her hands off and then she pulls me forward so that I'm standing right in the spray and all of the shower gel slowly washes away. Throughout all of this, she stays on the ground, and I'm about to lean down and help her up but then she grabs my ass cheeks in her hands and I'm glad I didn't.

She takes my now washed and rinsed cock in her mouth and begins to suck it. The sensation of her sucking me with the warm water massaging my chest and cascading down my body is such an amazing sensation. And what a sight Summer is. Her head bobs back and forth, up and down. I can see my cock going right into her mouth and then coming most of the way back out. The water runs down her hair, down her face, leaving her skin glistening and making me throb with need.

I hold off for as long as I can, enjoying Summer's mouth on me and then when I know I don't have long left, I reach down to her and pull her to her feet. We stand for a moment, drinking in the sight of each other as the shower water runs over us both. After a moment, I reach out and turn Summer around. She faces the wall, and she bends down at the waist, pressing her palms against the shower wall.

The spray hits her back and runs down her sides and through the crack of her ass. I move forward, take a hold of her hips and slam into her. I can feel her warm tightness, and as I pull out to fill her again, I feel the tickling sensation of the shower water drumming against my cock. It is both strange and amazing.

Summer cries out as I slam into her and I slow down, moving slowly through her warm, tight pussy. I don't want to hurt her when I know she is sore from last night. She stops crying out when I move slowly and as an added bonus, the water on my cock brings a whole new sensation to us.

After moving slowly for a few minutes, Summer begins to move faster and when I match her pace she doesn't cry out. I think she must be getting used to the friction, maybe even learning to like the red raw feeling.

"Faster," she pants. "I'm ok. Don't hold back."

"Summer if I don't hold back, then I won't be able to stop myself once I start," I say.

"Good," she says.

I take her at her word and tighten my hold on her hips, I slam back into her, and I begin to move in and out of her harder and faster, harder and faster. When she cries out again, it's accompanied by a clench of her muscles, a squirt of warm juices and I know this time, it isn't pain making her cry out. I let go myself and let my own climax hit me.

I hold Summer in place as I pump into her and then I cry out her name as I spurt. I release her when we're both done, and she turns to me and we kiss beneath the shower. Finally, when the water starts to run cold, I reach out and turn off the spray. I slide the door open and step out of the shower and I pick up a clean towel and hold it open. Summer smiles and steps out of the shower. She turns away from me and I wrap the towel around her. I grab another one and wrap it around my waist and then I go to the sink and get my toothbrush and the toothpaste.

I put some toothpaste on my brush and then I realize Summer needs a toothbrush. I open the small cabinet above the sink and find a new toothbrush still in the packet. I hand it to Summer. She smiles and opens it up and holds it out for toothpaste. We brush our teeth and then move back to the bedroom.

"Would you like a robe?" I ask.

"Please," Summer says.

I hand her a dark blue robe which she instantly puts on and ties. It's far too big for her but she looks so cute. She takes the towel I wrapped around her and starts to rub her hair with it.

While she dries her hair, I pull on a pair of jogging pants and a t-shirt. When I'm dressed, I smile at Summer.

"Do you want to go out for breakfast?" I ask.

"Actually, if you don't mind, I would rather stay here so that we can talk," she says.

"Ok," I agree. "But I only have toast or cereal."

"As long as you have coffee, I'm happy," Summer grins.

I go to the kitchen and put a pot of coffee on, and I put two slices of bread in the toaster. By the time Summer comes out of the bedroom, the coffee is made and poured into two mugs with cream added to both and the toast is cooked, and I have added jam. Summer is dressed and she's brushed her hair although it's still wet. All of her makeup is long gone, but she looks just as beautiful without it.

She sits down and takes a drink of her coffee. She makes an appreciative sigh and drinks again. I stay propped up against the counter and I nibble on my toast. Summer starts on hers. When we finish the toast, I take our cups and refill both of our coffees and then I smile at her.

"I'm guessing when you said you wanted to talk, you're going to say this was a mistake, but I don't believe that Summer. You see, I don't make the same mistake twice. And certainly not three times," I say. "I know you're worried about your career, but I promise you I'm not going to stand in the way of your career. It's not the fifties. I'm not about to try and lock you in the kitchen all day. And besides, you work for me. I'm hardly going to choose to distract you, am I?"

"Ok," she says.

It wasn't the response I was expecting after my soliloquy, and I frown.

"Ok what?" I ask.

"Ok, let's say fuck it and give us a go," she says. "But I really want us to take this slow Tyler. I know right now the thought of us falling out seems ridiculous, but it can happen and if it does, I want to get ahead of it and leave us in a place where we can still work together."

"I get that," I reply. "We can take things as slowly as you want to. I don't want to rush into anything myself. I think if it's meant to be, we have forever so there's no rush. And if it isn't meant to be, we can enjoy the ride for as long as it lasts."

Summer smiles and sips her coffee.

"One more thing," I say. "I'd prefer it if we didn't make it public knowledge at work just yet. Not until we're sure we're in it for the long haul. I don't think there's any need for us to be hot office gossip until we know for sure it's going to work."

"I agree," Summer says.

I go over to her and kiss the top of her head.

"You realize us getting dressed was just a waste of time right," I say.

Summer laughs and nods her head. I bend down and pick her up. She squeals playfully as I carry her back to the bedroom and kick the door closed behind me.

8

SUMMER

THREE WEEKS LATER

"**R**emind me again why I let you talk me into this," I say as I lace up my ice skates.

"You'll love it," Tyler says, smiling at me.

I don't think I will love it. In fact, I think I'm about to make a massive fool of myself, but when Tyler suggested coming ice skating, I couldn't resist agreeing. At the time, I saw us in my mind, hand in hand, bundled up in gloves and scarves and mitts, sipping hot cocoa and gliding gracefully around the outdoor ice rink in the park, our breath forming white clouds before us. What I didn't realize was that Tyler didn't just mean it for some point in the future when the winter rolled around. He meant it for today, a normal Sunday morning at an indoor rink where there are no cute hats, gloves and scarves and no graceful gliding. I'm guessing the concession stand might sell hot chocolate but I'm only going to spill it if I even attempt to skate with it in my hand.

"I honestly can't believe you've never been ice skating before," Tyler says.

"Even as a teenager I valued my pride enough not to

attempt something that meant balancing on something so slippery with something so thin," I say.

Tyler laughs and stands up from the bench we're sitting on. He holds his hand out to help me up. I take it and he gently pulls me to my feet. Walking in the skates is a bit strange but I have walked in stiletto heels all my life so I can cope with that. It's the ice I'm dreading. Tyler leads me to a gap in the barriers that circle the ice rink. He steps onto the ice and turns back to me. He takes my other hand in his other hand.

"Ready?" he says.

I want to say no I'm not ready, I will never be ready. But I don't want him to think I'm boring and I know if I say I'll just watch, he won't bother skating himself and I will feel like I've ruined what was going to be a good day. I nod my head and tighten my hold on his hands as I step onto the ice. Tyler laughs and looks down at our hands, I have him in so much of a death grip that my knuckles have gone white.

"I'm not going to let go of you," he says, still laughing. "You can relax your grip a bit."

I try, I really do, and I think I do release him a little bit.

"Ready to try and skate?" he asks.

I shake my head and he laughs again.

"Come on Summer. What's the worst thing that can happen?" he asks.

"Oh, I don't know," I say. "I could fall over and show myself up in front of everyone."

"So what?" Tyler says. "So could I but it's not going to stop me from having a good time. It's not like you're going to see these people again, is it?"

When he puts it like that, I can hardly argue with him, and I try again to relax a bit. Tyler smiles at me.

"Right," he says. "You hold onto the side and watch me, and I'll show you how to skate."

I do as he says, leaning against the barrier and watching him. He points at his feet.

"See. One then the other in like a V shape," he says.

He shows me another couple of times and then he comes over to me. He stands beside me and takes my left hand in his left hand, pulling my arm across the front of his body. He puts his other arm around my waist and holds my other hand at my side. I have to admit that as far as being on ice feels, this feels safer than I imagined it would.

"Right leg first," Tyler says. "On three. One... two... three."

I move my right leg the way he showed me and then my left leg. It's kind of awkward and shaky but I am doing it and I am still on my feet which is far more than I expected to be honest. By the time we've done a lap, I'm confident enough that my knuckles are no longer white from clinging to Tyler so hard and by the end of the second lap, I'm confident enough to try only holding hands between us.

After a few more laps, if I'm honest, I feel as though I could probably do it myself now but I like the feeling of Tyler's hand in mine and so I keep quiet and keep holding his hand. He makes no effort to make me release him and I think he probably knows as well as I do that at this point, we are just holding hands because we want to.

"Where did you learn to ice skate?" I ask as we skate around the rink again.

"My mom used to take me and Angela to a rink not far from home when we were kids. I think I was skating practically before I could walk," he says. "I haven't done it in a long time now, but it's not something you forget how to do."

I smile imagining a tiny Tyler staggering around on the ice giggling.

"I bet you two were so cute then," I say.

"You say that as if I'm not cute now," Tyler laughs, and I join him.

"You know what I mean," I say.

"I do," he agrees. "I just want to be sure you don't underestimate my current level of cuteness."

"Never," I laugh.

When the bell rings and the announcement comes to say that the hour is up for everyone wearing a yellow band, I'm shocked. It doesn't feel like we've been skating for an hour. After my initial fear dissipated, I have done nothing but smile the whole time we've been on the ice. I've smiled and laughed so much my cheeks ache. My legs ache a bit too and I think I'm going to be awfully stiff in the morning.

Tyler leads me off the ice and we sit down again and take our skates off. He picks them up and takes my yellow wrist band then goes to join the line at the counter leaving me sitting watching the people still skating around. Even though the line is fairly long, it goes down quickly, and Tyler is soon back by my side with both of our shoes. He sits down and hands me mine and we both put them on.

"Where do you want to get lunch?" he asks me when we have our shoes back on.

"I don't know," I say. "I don't want anything massively heavy though."

Tyler nods to the food stand and the tables at one end of the ice rink.

"Do you want to just go there? They make a surprisingly nice burger," he says.

"Yeah sure, why not?" I ask.

We walk over to the area and Tyler asks me what I want.

"I want you to sit down. This is my treat," I say. He opens his mouth, but I laugh and shake my head. "I wasn't asking you; I was telling you. Now either tell me what you want, or I will just get you something."

"A cheeseburger and an orange soda please," Tyler says finally.

I go up to the counter and order the food – Tyler's cheeseburger and orange soda and my cheeseburger and banana milkshake. The woman shouts my order back to the workers in the kitchen area. She pulls a tray up and puts it on the counter. She goes off and gets the drinks and straws by which point, someone else has my food ready. They all end up on the tray at roughly the same time and I pay the server and then go to sit with Tyler.

I put his cheeseburger on the table in front of him and put mine in front of me and then I do the same with the drinks then I put the tray on the ground under the table for now so it's out of the way. I unwrap my cheeseburger and take a bite and I have to admit that Tyler was right. The cheeseburger is surprisingly good. I was expecting a fast-food type of burger, but it doesn't seem like it is. It seems like a decent quality of meat and if it's seen the inside of a microwave, I'd be shocked.

"It's nice, isn't it?" Tyler says and I nod my head.

"Yeah," I say. "I was just thinking that. I'm surprised at the quality of it."

We eat and Tyler tells me a story about him and Angela ice skating when they were little and how he came to break his wrist. Angela wanted to join the end of a line, they were all holding hands and skating in a big circle. She grabbed Tyler's hand and took him with her. He said it was fun at first – being at the end of the line made it really fast. But then he started to feel a bit sick, so he decided to let go of

Angela's hand. Instead of coming to a stop like he had thought he would, he went flying, hitting the barrier and going straight over the top of it and landing awkwardly on the other side.

"Ouch," I say when he is finished. "I'm surprised you dared go back on the ice after that."

"It wasn't so bad," Tyler shrugs. "And for a whole week I got away with murder and Angela got in trouble for every little thing. That was enough for me."

We both laugh at that and then we go back to eating our cheeseburger. I put the last bite in my mouth and then I pick up my milkshake and sit and sip it. I turn slightly to watch the ice skaters.

"They all look so graceful," I say.

"You did too once you got the hang of it," Tyler tells me.

"Even once I got going, I didn't feel graceful, just slightly less clumsy than before," I say with a soft laugh.

I feel my purse vibrating at my side where my cell phone is getting a text message, but I ignore it. It seems rude replying to it while we're sitting, having our lunch. We talk a bit more and then Tyler excuses himself to go to the bathroom and I'm able to get my cell phone out. I frown when I see it's a text from my mom. She never texts me; she always calls. I open the text and read it.

"I thought it best to text you as it seems you're too busy for phone calls these days," the message starts. I roll my eyes. There's the first guilt trip because I forgot to call the other day. I did apologize but it obviously hasn't been forgiven quite yet. I read on and the message goes from bad to worse. "Why don't you make it up to me by coming for dinner on Tuesday evening. And bring that boyfriend of yours. Your father and I want to meet him."

I immediately click out of the text thread and open the one with Rebecca instead. I type angrily.

"You told my mom about Tyler?" I say in the message.

The answer comes back fast as it always does with Rebecca.

"I'm sorry. I ran into her in the mall, and she was asking me all of these questions and it just slipped out. I was going to tell you but I knew you'd be angry so I just waited, hoping your mom would forget about it. X," Rebecca's response reads.

"Fat chance of that. She wants me to invite him to have dinner at their place," I type.

"So do it," she texts back. "What's the worst thing that could happen?"

I roll my eyes at that one. She knows my parents well enough to know the answer to that one.

"How long have you got?" I reply.

My cell phone pings almost instantly, with a laughing emoji. Yeah, it's ok for her to sit there and laugh after causing this. I put my cell phone down on the table. I don't put it away yet because I haven't replied to my mom's text. I wait for Tyler to come back from the bathroom. He frowns as he approaches the table.

"What's wrong?" he asks, retaking his seat.

"Nothing," I say.

"Ah ok, my mistake," he says. "I didn't realize you always looked shell shocked and sat shredding straw wrappers."

I can't help but laugh at that and Tyler laughs too but he soon turns serious again.

"Come on, out with it," he says.

"My mom texted me. She wants you to have dinner with me and my parents at their place on Tuesday. I get it if you don't want to, please don't think there's any pressure or..."

I know I'm babbling but I can't seem to stop myself. Tyler interrupts me and that stops me in my tracks.

"I'd love to have dinner with you and your parents," he says.

"Really?" I say, waiting for him to laugh and say no of course not, but he doesn't. Instead, he nods his head.

"Really," he says.

"Ok, I'll text her back and tell her to expect us about seven thirty?" I ask.

Tyler nods.

"Yeah, that should be enough time for us to get home from work and get showered and changed," he says.

I quickly type out a reply to my mom letting her know we would love to come to dinner. She replies quickly, saying it's great and she's looking forward to seeing us. I can imagine her shocked expression. She would have been expecting me to say no chance. Normally, I would have. Does this mean Tyler and I have just gone to the next level now that he's meeting my parents? I don't know and I refuse to let myself dwell on it. After meeting my overbearing parents, he'll probably run as far away and as fast as he can from me anyway.

We finish the last bits of our drinks and then I pick the tray back up from underneath our table and load it up with our trash. I take it to the trash can and empty it off and then put it on the return stack, then I head back to the table. Tyler smiles and holds his hand out to me as I reach him. I slip my hand into his and we head towards the exit of the building.

I love that even after three weeks together, none of the spark has faded between us even a tiny bit. We still always want to be touching each other, whether that's holding hands or having our arms around each other snuggled up on Tyler's couch or mine. And the sex. Oh my God, the sex. If anything, it's only gotten better, something I would have said was impossible after the first few times. I swear I have never felt anything like the way I feel with Tyler. I don't know if it's because we have a deeper connection than anything I've had with past boyfriends or if he's just so much better in bed than anyone else I've ever slept with but whatever it is, I'm certainly not complaining.

I've even managed to do what Rebecca advised and compartmentalize everything. So, at work, Tyler is just my employer, not my boyfriend. Out of work I can touch him when I want to, kiss him, caress him and ride him. But in work, I can't do any of those things and sometimes it's hard not to, like when we're working late and nearly everyone has gone and we could just lean up against one of our office doors and get on with it and no one would ever know. In a way though, holding back when all I want is to be with Tyler makes it even better when I can be with him and touch him. And now I've gotten used to keeping my work and my personal life separate, I don't find being with Tyler distracts me from my work, and it certainly doesn't mean I'm neglecting work and finishing early or anything like that. If anything, I've probably worked later more often than usual while I'm waiting for Tyler to finish.

We reach the exit and leave the building, crossing the parking lot and head for Tyler's car.

"What do you feel like doing now?" he asks me.

"I don't mind," I say. "I'd be happy not to do anything, just go back to your place and chill."

We both know what that's code for and Tyler grins at me and starts the engine of his car and pulls away. He leaves the parking lot, joining the slew of traffic. I know we're not going to get anywhere fast, and I lean forward and turn the radio on. I'm humming along to a song until it ends and the DJ starts talking. I'm not really listening to him, but one word catches my attention: magic.

"We could start that Harry Potter marathon you promised me," I say.

"Sounds good to me," Tyler says. "If you're a good girl, I might even make you some popcorn."

"Is that so," I say. "If you're a good boy, I might let you slither-in side of me."

I burst out laughing at the look of disgust Tyler gives me. He starts laughing when I do.

"Do you have to?" he says.

"What? Don't you want me to see your wand?" I ask.

"Oh my God Summer, stop it. You're ruining Harry Potter for me," Tyler laughs.

I burst out laughing again. I can't help it. Even though Tyler is laughing, he looks so serious at the same time.

"Right," he says after we stop laughing. "Have you got that out of your system?" I nod my head. "Anymore?"

"No, I'm done," I say. "Oh. Wait. I have another one. If you make me popcorn, I might just let you see my chamber of secrets. I swear that's it now."

We are both laughing again, and it feels nice to just laugh and have fun together.

"Definitely done?" Tyler asks with a raised eyebrow.

"I think so. There's definitely something I could say about a basilisk, but I can't quite decide what yet," I say.

"Oh God help me," Tyler says.

We're pulling up outside of Tyler's house when it comes to me. We get out of the car, and I blurt it out.

"I've got it. If you show me your basilisk, I will be your dumble-whore," I say.

Too late, I see the couple walking past. They turn and

look at me in surprise and I feel myself blushing but then they are past us. Tyler and I grab each other's hand, both laughing like crazy, and we make our way to his front door. We are still laughing when we get there, tears streaming down our faces. Tyler gets his keys out and unlocks the door and we step inside. He leads me to the living room, and I sit down.

"I'll go and grab the DVDs," he says.

He isn't gone long, and he reappears with a boxset in his hand and goes about switching on the TV and the DVD player and loading the first disc. As we wait for the movie to start, he laughs, and I look at him.

"What's funny?" I ask.

"The fact you used the word dumble-whore and more so, the fact that two complete strangers heard you using it," he says.

"That wasn't part of the plan," I admit. "I was just happy to have thought of it and I blurted it out without looking around."

"Ah well, it sure must have brightened up their Sunday afternoon. I bet they laughed as soon as they were out of sight," Tyler says.

"Or they've never watched or read Harry Potter and they think I'm a complete loony," I say.

"Yeah, or that," Tyler says with a grin.

The film starts and we fall silent and start to watch. At some point, Tyler goes off to make us the promised popcorn and grabs us some sodas. I think we're onto the third movie before Tyler's basilisk comes out to play.

Ok, so here's the deal. I have never in my life been shy and I have never been someone who gets nervous about meeting people. I can talk to pretty much anyone regardless of their background and I usually make a decent impression on people, or at least I think I do.

But today, I am nervous. I'm going to meet Summer's parents for the first time and I really want them to like me. I think back to the first time I met Chloe's parents. I don't remember feeling nervous about it. I remember thinking along the lines of either they like me, or they don't, it's Chloe I'm with, not them. The fact that I don't feel like that about Summer's parents liking or disliking me tells me that I am falling fast for Summer. Not that I really need anything to tell me; I know it.

Up until I met Summer, I genuinely believed I loved Chloe. And I think in a way I did. I just had nothing to compare that feeling to. Now I know what falling in love really feels like and what I felt for Chloe was nothing compared to this. It's all consuming, like Summer is my whole world. Her laugh, her smile, the scent of her, the taste of her, everything about her is perfect and amazing and I can't get her out of my head.

I kind of want to tell her all these things but we agreed to take things slowly and I hardly think telling her she is my whole world after three and a half weeks of dating is taking things slowly. I can keep up the pretense of taking things slowly though until Summer is ready to take things to the next level. God, I hope she does want that at some point.

I swallow all of that down. I'm not going to make a good impression on Summer's parents if I'm thinking about that kind of thing and making myself more nervous. I just have to be myself and hope to God, they like me. Or at the very least are willing to tolerate me because Summer likes me.

"Are you almost ready? We're going to be late," I call out to Summer.

She is still in her bedroom getting ready. I arrived to collect her fifteen minutes early so we could make a good impression. I've now been here for twenty minutes.

"Calm down," Summer shouts back. "We're going to my parents' house. It's not like they're going to give our table to someone else if we're late."

"But it's rude," I shout.

I hear her laughing as she comes down the hallway.

"Oh, my parents are going to love you," she says. "They usually give me a time half an hour earlier than they actually want me to arrive so if I'm earlier than that you're in their good books."

I turn around to answer her, but I stop in my tracks when I see her. She's wearing a silver-colored thin jumper that hangs off one shoulder leaving it bare. The jumper hangs to her mid thigh and she's wearing black leggings with it. Her hair is in some sort of clip, tendrils hanging loose around her face.

It's a simple outfit, but on her it looks exquisite, the bit of bare skin on her shoulder making me want to tear her clothes off and see all her skin.

"You look amazing," I say.

"Don't let my dad see you looking at me like that," she giggles. "You look like you want to eat me."

"I do want to eat you," I say. "The only thing stopping me right now is knowing it will make us even later. Now let's go before I change my mind."

Summer laughs again and shakes her head but she picks her purse up and drops her cell phone into it.

"Keys, keys, keys," she says to herself as she looks around. She spots them on the countertop in the kitchen area of her open plan living space. She snatches them up and holds them up triumphantly.

"Keys," she says again. "Ok, let's go."

We leave her apartment and go down to the lobby and step outside. Summer has already told me to leave my car at her place so I can have a drink tonight as her parents' place is within walking distance of her place. While her parents could easily afford a huge place out in the middle of nowhere, they instead have opted for an apartment in the city so that they are closer to the hospital and don't have much of a commute. We arrive at their place in under five minutes.

"It looks very similar to your block," I comment.

"Yeah, from here maybe. Wait until you see inside," Summer laughs. "I mean some of the smaller apartments are probably similar to mine, but Mom and Dad are in the penthouse. It's honestly ridiculous that two people think they need that much space."

We get into the elevator and Summer hits the button for the second to top floor. I frown at her questioningly. Didn't she just say her parents lived in the penthouse apartment? That's surely the top floor. Summer sees me looking and rolls her eyes.

"We'll have to walk up the stairs to the last floor. The elevator can only go to the penthouse for people who have a card," she says. "I have one somewhere at home but honestly, it's easier to walk up a flight of stairs to the penthouse than it is to find the damned thing."

We step out of the elevator when it stops. I'm pleased that we are finally free of it, because it was getting harder and harder to look at Summer's bare shoulder and not kiss her.

I follow her up the last flight of stairs and along a thickly carpeted hallway to the only door on the floor. She pushes it open and pokes her head around the door then steps inside.

"We're here," she calls.

I step in behind her and gently close the door. I find myself in another long hallway, the black carpet here even thicker and more luxurious. The walls and ceiling are both perfect white as are all the doors. The door handles are chrome, and they all shine like they have been polished to perfection.

A door opens and I hear Summer's mom before I see her.

"Well don't stand out there, come on in," she says.

"I didn't know if you were in the living room or the dining room," Summer says, stepping into the room.

I follow again in time to see Summer taking the hands of her mom and the pair of them kiss a cheek. Summer then moves to one side, and I get my first proper look at her mom.

She doesn't look a day over forty, but Summer is twenty-nine so realistically, she has to be closer to fifty. Her hair is blonde, but it doesn't look bleached blonde. She's a little bit on the plump side but she suits it, her curves accentuated by the dress she's wearing.

"And you must be Tyler," Summer's mom says.

She steps forward and shakes my hand.

"It's a pleasure to meet you Doctor Malone," I say.

"Oh, now unless you're wanting stitches or something, let's stick to Melanie, ok?" she laughs.

"Melanie it is," I reply.

"Sit down, both of you. I'll get you some drinks and let your dad know you're here. He's making chicken curry and he's made enough for half of the block, so I hope you're both hungry," she says.

"Actually Mom, Tyler is a vegan. Didn't I tell you?" Summer says.

Melanie's face falls but she quickly covers it with a smile.

"That's ok, I'll get him to find something," she says.

"I'm not a vegan," I say at the same time.

I give Summer a what the fuck look and she laughs.

"Sorry I couldn't resist," she says.

"Oh, you bugger, you had me there," Melanie laughs. She's still laughing as she leaves the room. "A vegan. As if."

"What the hell was that?" I hiss at Summer when I'm sure Melanie is out of ear shot.

"I don't know. It just came to me that it might be funny," she says. "Seriously though, lighten up."

"I promise I'll lighten up if you promise not to do that again," I say.

"Deal," Summer says.

Melanie comes back with two glasses of white wine in her hands and a man behind her.

"Jason, this is Tyler," she says. I stand up and we shake hands. "Tyler, this is Jason, Summer's father. And it's just Jason. None of that doctor shit, ok?"

"Ok," I say.

"I don't mean to be rude, but I really don't want dinner to burn. We can have a proper chat later," Jason says.

"I look forward to it," I say with a smile and then I sit back down as Jason hurries away.

Melanie hands me and Summer our drinks and raises her glass.

"To a good night," she says.

Summer and I raise our glasses and repeat her words and we all drink. Melanie smiles and sits down in the chair opposite the couch Summer and I are sharing.

"So how did you two meet?" Melanie asks.

I cringe inside and I hope it doesn't show on the outside. Summer starts to tell her about the takeover and how we met at work, and I'm so relieved she didn't say it was in a line for a taxi home from a nightclub.

Melanie and Summer are chatting away, and I'm quite content to listen and just add in the odd comment and laugh along with them. Melanie is very different to how I imagined her to be. For starters, I expected her to be a lot older and I expected both her and Jason to be quite cold and unwelcoming with what Summer has told me about them being determined she should focus only on her career and how they were so disappointed when she didn't want to be a doctor. I expected Summer's parents to be quite traditional, maybe even old fashioned, but that is definitely not the impression I'm getting from Melanie.

After around half an hour, the door opens, and Jason pokes his head around it.

"Dinner is ready," he says.

We get up and I follow the women through to a dining room where the table is laid elegantly with shiny silverware and glassware and a beautiful floral centerpiece. The dark mahogany wood of the table and the frames of the chairs with the red velvet of the seats should have made this room feel a little bit dark and dingy, but the real fire crackling away in the fireplace compensates for it and makes a lovely, cozy feeling room.

I like the taste of the couple. Their apartment and its décor and furnishings scream good taste and class rather than gaudy look at me, I have money. It's not always easy to stay on the right side of that line, but so far, the Malones have absolutely nailed it.

I pull a chair out for Summer and then hurry around to the other side of the table to get Melanie's chair. She smiles and thanks me and I go back to my side of the table and sit down beside Summer. Jason comes in through a different door pushing a hostess trolley. I can smell the tantalizing smell of the spices and the meat, and it makes my mouth water.

Jason begins to unload the trolley. He places large silver dishes on the table then takes the lid off of them one by one. One is a huge container of chicken curry. The other ones are a big pile of white rice and a big pile of chips plus a stack of naan bread. I see what Melanie means now about there being enough food for half of the block and when it's my turn to help myself to food, I don't hesitate to help myself to a nice big portion.

I try the curry and it tastes every bit as good as it smells.

"Wow," I say. "This is amazing. You'll have to give me the recipe."

"I will," Jason says. "It's literally the only thing I can cook but I do cook it well, even if I do say so myself."

We all dig into our food and for a while, everything is quiet as we eat. After a while, I turn my attention to Jason and Melanie.

"What sort of a doctor are you both?" I ask.

"I'm a surgeon," Melanie says.

"And I work in the ER," Jason says. "And the answer is one Lego block, two mini micro machines and a small remote control"

"Huh?" I say, confused.

Jason laughs.

"Usually, the first question I get when I say I work in the ER is what's the weirdest thing you've had to remove from someone's butt. And that is the answer. And yes, they were all in one person's butt and it was the same occasion."

"And let me guess. They fell on them?" I say which gets an approving laugh from Jason.

"Every damned time," he says.

"And the weirdest thing I ever removed from someone was a small doll's head," Melanie adds on. "Now if that was a child, I'd say not that weird. Kids swallow some random stuff. But no. This was a woman in her thirties. She said she did it for a dare and she believed it would just pass through her, but the hair got tangled around her lower intestine and caused a blockage."

"Mom, we're eating," Summer says but she's laughing.

"You're not squeamish are you, Tyler? Because we talk about anything and everything here," her mom laughs.

"No, I'm not squeamish," I say. I'm quite enjoying their stories and I genuinely don't mind talking about this kind of thing. In fact, I want to hear more. "What's your most crazy 'how are they even alive' story?"

"I had one once, a young man who tried to take his own life. He jumped from the top of a five-story building. The fall should have killed him outright, but he landed on a fence post. It impaled him, but it stopped him from smashing his head open. He got rushed to surgery with the fence post still in position through him, but that post had missed every damned one of his vital organs. I pulled out a few splinters and put in a lot of stitches and he was fine," Melanie says. "And when he recovered physically, he was referred for counseling and he very much wants to live now."

"You kept in touch with him?" I ask.

"Not as such," Melanie says. "Last year he started working at the hospital as a volunteer."

"Oh wow," I say. "Someone definitely wanted him to live."

"Didn't they though," Melanie says.

"Mine would be the guy who was shot point blank in the head," Jason says. I turn to him, my eyes opening wide in shock. "The guy was in a bank, and it got robbed. Wrong place, wrong time. One of the robbers grabbed him to use him as a human shield and a hostage. He had a gun to the guys' temple and was using that fact to get the bank tellers to do what he wanted them to do. Things got out of hand, and he ended up pulling the trigger, whether by accident or with intent isn't for me to work out.

"I don't know what the hell his victim's skull is made of, but that bullet went in, ricocheted off his skull, went up over and burst back out of the top of his head. He had two nasty holes that needed stitching, especially the exit wound, and he lost a lot of blood, so he was touch and go for a while, but the bullet itself did absolutely no damage at all except to his flesh and skin. From his skull, you would never have known what happened to him."

"Wow," I said. "His bones must be made of titanium or something."

The conversation takes a small lull and I turn to Summer.

"Are you ok?" I ask.

"Yeah why?" she says with a smile.

"You're being really quiet," I reply.

"Oh, I've heard all of these stories before that's all. But it's nice seeing the shock on people's faces when they hear my parents' stories for the first time," she tells me with a laugh.

I'm loving these stories and if Summer is loving watching me hearing them, then what's the harm in asking for some more.

"What's been your weirdest case?" I ask.

"Mine would have been really early in my career. I had just finished my internship and I was working in a hospital that required each of its surgeons to volunteer once a week at a clinic for people with no insurance. I was at the clinic, and I had just taken out the appendix of a man who would have died if he'd waited another hour to come for treatment. I just wanted to grab a coffee and chill for a few minutes, but as I made my way to the break-room, I heard a woman screaming in reception. She was shouting that her baby needed help, that he was going to die just because she had no insurance. Naturally I rushed out into the waiting area shouting that I could help and for her to come straight through.

"She was clutching this tiny bundle to her chest and I'm running her down the hall to the examination room wondering what sort of an absolute bastard of a doctor could turn away a baby this tiny for lack of insurance."

Melanie pauses and takes a drink of her wine. She grins.

"And that's how I ended up performing heart surgery on a Jack Russell," she finishes. "It wasn't a baby in the blanket, it was a damned dog. And her vet wouldn't do the surgery the dog needed without her having insurance or an up-front payment, neither of which she had. I suppose I could have turned her away when I saw it was a dog. The rules would say I should have.

"But the way she had lit up when I said I would help her, I didn't have the heart to turn her away. Plus, I could see the love she had for that dog, and I would like to think that by saving her dog's life that day, I might also have saved her mental health.

"My boss wasn't too happy when he found out, but I was pretty pleased with myself."

"I would have been too," I say, and I mean it.

The dog deserved a chance and I instantly hate the vet that wouldn't save his life without getting the money up front.

"My weirdest one was a woman that came to the ER originally because she felt ill at work," Jason began when it was his turn. "Her boss brought her to the ER because she lived alone, and he didn't want to risk her being alone without being seen as she was saying she felt sick and dizzy and like she might pass out.

"To be honest, when I read over the chart before calling her in, I expected to find she was dehydrated. I went to the waiting room to call her name. I called her and she stood up and then she collapsed onto the ground. I rushed over, still sure she was dehydrated, and it had caused her to faint.

"That woman had no pulse, and she wasn't breathing. She had literally just dropped down dead on the ER waiting room floor. I called for a crash cart, and we managed to resuscitate her. Within half an hour, all of her vitals were fine and you wouldn't know anything had been wrong with her. She wasn't dehydrated, she wasn't anything. Every test we did came back normal. To this day I can't explain what happened."

"Wow. She was lucky that she was in the ER when it happened. Imagine if her boss had just told her to go home and get some rest or whatever," I say.

"Yes, she definitely had a guardian angel looking down on her that day," Jason agrees.

"Tell us some of your stories," Melanie says.

"Oh, mine are all boring compared to these," I say. "Like my weirdest client would be someone who wanted a glass walled bathroom, that kind of thing."

We all laugh but Melanie insists so Summer and I spend some time regaling them with stories about our work, none of which match up to their stories, but to give them their dues, they listen intently, and they seem genuinely interested.

Somewhere along the way, a dessert of toffee and strawberry flavored cheesecake comes out and more wine is poured. Then the cocktails come out and we go back through to the living room and chat and laugh and drink the cocktails. Somewhere during the course of the night, my nerves have well and truly gone. I really like Summer's parents and either they like me, or they should have gone into acting rather than medicine.

Another round of laughter makes me realize how badly I need to pee. I stand up.

"Excuse me a moment," I say. "I just need to visit the bathroom."

I leave the living room and realize I don't know where the bathroom is. I look down the hallway and I decide that it's going to be the door right at the end, the furthest from the main living area. I walk along to it but when I get there, I see that what I thought was the end of the hallway actually isn't. It's the back wall of another hallway that runs at a right angle to the one I'm in. The other hallway goes off to the left and to the right and there are so many doors. I don't think it would be a good idea to get caught opening doors at random looking for the bathroom, so I head back to the living room to ask for directions.

I reach the living room door and put my hand on the handle ready to open it, but right at the last second, I hear Melanie say my name and as much as I don't want to eavesdrop, I can't help but stand and listen for a moment.

"I didn't say I didn't like him, Summer," Melanie says. "I do like him for the record, but you have worked so hard to get to where you are in your career. I just don't think you should be throwing all of that away to be in a relationship."

"How am I throwing it all away?" I hear Summer ask. "You know it's possible to have a boyfriend and a job, right?"

"Don't take that tone with me Summer, you know what I mean," Melanie says.

"Actually, no, I don't," Summer says. "I've spent so long single because I keep thinking of you saying I can't have both. But I can and I am, and I don't know why you are so sure it won't work."

"A job is one thing," Jason puts in. "Of course, you can have a job and a boyfriend. But a job is the sort of thing where you clock in and clock out on time and outside of those hours, you don't care about the place. A career is entirely different, and you know it. You stay until everything is done. And you take work calls on your day off and you don't resent it."

"I get all of that," I say. "And I have no intention of not focusing on my career."

"You say that now," Jason says. "And I'm sure you mean it. And if you've talked to Tyler about it and he's in agreement, I'm sure he means it too. But there will come a time when he gets sick of you being late or not being there at all, sick of the calls and the emails you have to deal with outside of work time. And at some point, you will have to choose between him and your career. I just think it would be easier to choose your career now rather than let yourself get too attached to this man and have it be a more difficult decision down the line is all I am saying."

"It's not like that with us though is it. Not only is Tyler an architect himself so he gets the hours and everything, but he bought the company I work for. Like literally if I blow work off, he loses out. He's hardly going to encourage that is he?" Summer says.

It goes quiet for a moment, and I think the conversation is done but then Jason speaks up again.

"I guess that is slightly different," he admits.

"Yeah," Melanie says. I can imagine her smiling over at Jason. "I mean us both working shitty hours and understanding that the end of a shift doesn't necessarily mean the shift will end worked for us."

"See," Summer says.

"Just keep your head in the game Summer, that's all we're asking," Melanie says. "And if you can find a way to make this work, then good because Tyler seems like a good one."

"He is," Summer says, and I beam. "In fact, I might as well say it now. We're going to have to find a way to make it work because I don't want to give him up. I think I'm falling in love with him."

I do walk away from the doorway then, my face aching because I'm smiling so widely. I still don't know where the bathroom is and it's far too late to go back and ask now so I start opening doors as I walk along the hallway. I find the bathroom and go inside and lock the door. Once the door is locked, I fist pump into the air.

Summer is falling in love with me. Summer is falling in love with me. Summer is fucking falling in love with me.

It's all I can think about. When I heard her say it, I wanted to open the living room door and just go in there and grab her and kiss her, but of course I knew I couldn't. It wasn't just that she would know I'd been listening in at the door, and it wasn't even the fact that her parents were there. It was more a case of me not wanting to embarrass Summer or push her into saying something she's not ready to say to me yet. When she's ready to tell me herself that she's falling for me, then I am more than ready to hear it, and then I will kiss her like she's never been kissed before, but until then, I will hold onto that memory like it is a precious stone and never mention it to Summer.

I finish in the toilet and wash my hands then I flush the toilet and leave the room and head back for the living room. I can hardly keep the smile off my face. What I have just heard has literally made me the happiest man alive. I go back into the living room and sit back down beside Summer. She looks at me in concern.

"Are you ok?" she asks me quietly.

"Never better," I say. "Why?"

"You were gone ages," she says.

"Oh," I say. "That." I decide to tell a half truth. It's better than Summer and her parents thinking I had some sort of stomach issue which they clearly are. "So, I left the room and started along the hallway and then I realized I didn't know where the bathroom was. I was a bit embarrassed to come back in and ask and I kind of just stood there, indecisive for a bit. By the time I decided I was being silly being too embarrassed to ask where it was, too long had gone by and I ended up just opening doors until I found it."

"Oh Tyler, you don't have to be embarrassed around us. Especially not about toilets or bodily functions. Doctors remember," Melanie says with a laugh.

We all laugh, and the potentially awkward moment passes, and we go back to the easy chatter and laughter of before. I hold Summer's hand in mine as we chat and I feel like I'm floating. I can't believe this gorgeous, amazing, talented, funny woman is falling in love with me. I do know though that it's past time that I stopped letting Chloe's indiscretion ruin my life. I refuse to let the insecurities she gave me ruin my relationship with Summer.

10

TYLER

I put my book down and sigh. I'm worried about Summer. She said she's fine, but she's been really quiet all night since we finished work and came back to my place and then an hour ago, she asked if I would be ok if she had a bath and an early night. That was at like eight thirty. It's definitely not like her.

I decide to go up and see if she's still awake and see if she wants a cup of tea or anything and see if I can get out of her what's wrong. I think if she felt physically ill like a headache or some sort of flu coming on, she would just say that, so I think it's more that she's upset about something. I hate not knowing what it is. How can I help her if I don't know what the problem is?

I head up the stairs and I decide to go and use the bathroom before I go in to see Summer. The door is open so she must be finished with her bath. I push it further open and step in and then I see Summer sitting on the side of the bath. She's wrapped in a towel, and she has another towel on her head. She's holding something in her hand, something she tries to hide behind her back when I come in.

"Sorry," I say. "I thought you were in the bedroom."

"It's ok, I'm almost done," she says, smiling at me like I haven't just found her sitting on the side of the bath looking all forlorn and hiding something from me.

"Summer," I say as she stands up. "Is that what I think it is?"

"I don't know what you mean," she says.

I reach out and cup her cheek in my hand and gently stroke it with my thumb.

"Summer, I saw the pregnancy test. Are you pregnant?" I ask gently.

She sighs and sort of sags against my hand.

"I don't know," she says with a sheepish smile. "I haven't had the courage to do the test yet."

"Do it now," I say. "And we'll find out together."

She nods her head and I step out of the bathroom so she can pee on the stick in peace.

"Let me know when you're done," I say, pulling the door closed behind me.

I'm not sure how I feel about this. I guess I had kind of given up on the idea of having kids once Chloe and I got divorced, but that's not to say I wouldn't want to be a dad. In fact, I would love that. I'd love a mini version of me and Summer running about the place. Barely thirty seconds has gone by, and she calls me back into the bathroom. I go back in and sit down beside her on the side of the bath again.

"We just have to wait for three minutes now," she says. "It's going to feel like three hours while we just sit here waiting."

"Is this why you've been quiet tonight and why you wanted to go to bed so early?" I ask.

Summer nods.

"Yeah. I was going to wait until tomorrow at work to do

the test, but I kept thinking about it in my purse and soon it was all I could think about, and I knew I had to do it. I'm sorry, I should have told you, but I figured I might as well find out if there was anything to tell you first," she says. "I guess I thought it seemed pointless to us both stressing out about the possibility of me being pregnant and I decided it made sense for only one of us to have to do that."

She pauses. "I'm sorry," she says again.

"You don't have to apologize," I tell her. "But you didn't have to do this alone either."

She smiles at me, a slightly wavering smile, but a smile nonetheless and I feel a bit better for knowing that I've made her feel a bit better. I put my arm around her shoulders and give her a quick squeeze. I release her but I keep my arm around her.

"So, what makes you think you're pregnant?" I ask. "I mean you're on birth control, right?"

"Yes," Summer says. "But I forgot to take one and my period is like a week late, so I thought it best to check. It's probably nothing – I've never really been regular with my periods even when I'm on birth control."

"It's definitely best to check," I agree. "It's easier to deal with when you know one way or the other."

"By deal with, do you mean..." she trails off and I realize what she thinks I meant.

"God no," I say quickly. "I meant emotionally deal with it. Like..."

I stop talking when a beeping sound comes from Summer's cell phone where it sits on the closed toilet lid.

"That's my alarm to say three minutes have gone by since I peed on the stick," she says.

For a second she makes no move to pick the test up from

the side of the sink, but after a while, she takes a deep breath and leans forward and grabs the test. She looks at it and the relief on her face is unmissable. She smiles and then she's laughing.

"Oh, thank God. It's negative," she says.

I find myself smiling back at her but it's not because I'm excited to know that she isn't pregnant. I'm smiling just because I'm caught up in her happy mood. The truth is, I'm not sure I am as happy about it as she is. I had kind of wanted to be a dad for a moment there, but judging by Summer's reaction to the negative result, that isn't something that is going to happen for me if I want to be with her. Her reaction seems like someone who definitely has decided she doesn't want children.

"Come on," I say, standing up and taking her hand in mine. "Let's go through to the bedroom instead of perching on the side of the bathtub."

She opens the trash can with her foot and drops the negative pregnancy test into it and then she lets me lead her out of the bathroom, down the hallway and into the bedroom. I walk her over to the bed and we sit down on the soft mattress side by side. Our backs are against the headboard and our legs are stretched out in front of us, although we aren't underneath the covers.

"So, you seem pretty relieved," I say.

That's an understatement really but I don't want to say she seemed ecstatic in case I have gotten the wrong idea. I haven't though. I know I haven't, and Summer confirms it when she nods her head and laughs softly before speaking.

"Damned right I'm relieved," she says. She peers at me with a frown. "Wait. Aren't you relieved too?"

This is it. This is the moment when I either admit I want

children and risk losing her, or the moment when I tell her I too am relieved and give up any notion of being a dad but having this beautiful woman in my life. It's a no brainer really.

"Yeah, I guess I am relieved as well," I say. "I didn't really have time to process it enough to be so outwardly relieved that's all. Don't get me wrong Summer, I would have stood by you whatever the test result was, but to be honest, I've never really pictured myself as having kids."

That's it. That's the decision made. It was never really like I had a choice. I love Summer far too much to lose her and if being with her means I can't have children of my own, then that's a price I am willing to pay. Of course, I could have told Summer that, but I'm afraid that she will think I will resent her or whatever down the line if she thinks I do want kids and I'm only holding off on having them because of her. She might decide that she is better off ending things because of it.

I will never resent Summer. This is one hundred percent my choice but it's definitely going to be easier not having to try and convince Summer of that. Plus, I never want her to see men with their children playing in the park or walking down the street or whatever and have her feel guilty because I don't have that. I'm the one who has decided my choice, not her. She has no reason to feel guilty, but I still think there's a fair chance that she would, and I would hate that for her.

She smiles at me and shuffles closer to me on the bed. I put my arm around her shoulders and gently pull her against me. She seems happy that I don't want to have children and I think I made the right decision by taking away any possibility of her feeling guilty about me not getting to be a father.

I know we're meant to be taking things slowly and I have never wanted to jeopardize that but right now, I feel like I need to tell Summer how I feel about her. It's not like we're actively taking things slowly as such anyway. We're together pretty much every evening and all weekend. And she did tell her parents that she thought she was falling for me. I have to do it before I lose my nerve, and if it scares her, well then, I will have to deal with that when it happens.

"Summer?" I ask.

She makes a "hmm" sound and I wait for her to look at me. After a few seconds, she lifts her head up from where she has rested it on my shoulder and looks up at me.

"I know this is crazy and far too soon, but I need you to know, I love you," I say.

For a second, she just looks at me, her face expressionless, not speaking, and I panic. I have done the wrong thing. She's trying to find the words to let me down gently. Oh God, what have I done? Why did I have to ruin things? Am I going to lose her?

All of those thoughts tumble through my mind in the split second after the words leave my mouth and not even a second later, Summer smiles at me. She looks down for a second and then she looks back up, looking me in the eye.

"You're right. It is far too soon, but that doesn't change the facts, does it? I love you too," she says.

I lean in and kiss her, and I pull the towel off her head, releasing her still damp hair. I push my fingers into it, close my eyes and deepen the kiss. Summer pushes herself up onto her knees without breaking her mouth from mine and she cocks her leg over me and sits down on my thighs.

Then she moves her mouth from mine, kissing down my neck and then running her tongue up it. I open my eyes and my cock springs to life when I see that Summer has removed the other towel and she is now sitting on me completely naked.

She straightens up and smiles at me. I reach out and cup Summer's breasts, one in each hand. I massage them, feeling her nipples harden beneath my palms. I run my fingers gently over them, teasing her, and then I take a nipple between my thumb and forefinger of each hand and pinch them. She moans and I pinch them harder. She gets that look in her eye, the one that says she is about to fuck the life out of me. She leans forward and grabs the bottom of my t-shirt, pulling it up and forcing me to release her breasts. She pulls the t-shirt off of me and throws it off the bed onto the carpet.

She grins at me and then she lifts herself up and tugs at my pants. I lift my ass and let her pull them down, my boxer shorts with them. They come off and get thrown onto the floor as well and we're both naked. Summer grins at me again and then she puts her forefinger into her mouth and sucks on it. Making a tight O with her lips, she pulls her finger out of her mouth. It is glistening with her saliva, and I hear myself moan when Summer lifts herself again and slips her finger between her lips and starts to rub herself.

I watch the show for as long as I can bear it. Summer has almost brought herself to orgasm. Her eyes are closed, her lips parted. Her head is slightly back, and she has a half smile on her face. She's panting and her hand is working so fast it's almost a blur. Watching her like this is making me want her so bad and she's not the only one who is on the verge of climaxing.

When I can't stand the torment any longer, I reach out and pull her hand away and replace it with my own. I slip two fingers inside of her and I push my thumb against her clit. As I massage her clit, I move my fingers inside of her, running them over her g-spot. Within moments, she's coming, screaming my name, warm liquid running down my hand and coating my thighs beneath it.

I pull my hand away from her pussy and her clit and then I push my cock inside of her before her orgasm has even finished. Her eyes fly open as I fill her, and she bites her lip in a way that makes me moan. I pull her towards me and kiss her as I buck my hips and she moves up and down on my cock.

She runs her hands over my head and down to my shoulders and she clenches her pussy around me. She pulls her mouth from mine and moves her head beside mine. She nibbles on my ear lobe and then runs her tongue down my neck. As she teases me with the feather light touch of her tongue, she slows down on my cock, lifting herself slowly until I'm almost out of her and then coming back down even more slowly, taking me into her in tiny stages.

It's delicious but it's also like torture and I can't stand it much longer. I run my hands down her bare back and caress her ass cheeks and then I move my hands to her hips, moving her up and down faster. She fights me and I can't take it anymore and I push her to the side, and we roll. I'm on top of her now and I fuck her hard and fast. She grips me with her knees, moving with me, no longer teasing.

My orgasm floods me and I slam into Summer one more time, hard. It hits the spot for her, and she orgasms with me. We are a mix of gasps and moans and tingling pleasure and liquid – so much liquid – as we both come.

Finally, it's over and I roll off her and we hold each other as we lay beside each other getting our breath back. Summer smiles over at me when she has herself back under control.

"If I'd known you were going to do that to me, I would have told you ages ago I loved you," she says.

I laugh softly and kiss her again. Her saying she loves me is something I will never get sick of hearing, even if we both were to somehow live forever.

11

SUMMER

I feel like I'm floating on air. I have felt like this since Tyler and I said I love you to each other. I knew I had fallen for him long before we actually said the words, but I also knew that we had both said we wanted to take things slowly, so I kept it quiet, but then when he said it to me first, I realized that we were kidding ourselves. It was one thing to say we were taking it slow, but that didn't mean it was actually going to happen. You can't stop yourself from falling in love once you start, no matter how much you try to slow it down.

I have to keep pinching myself to make sure that it's real. It sort of feels too good to be real, and I keep thinking that I'll wake up one day and it will all have been a dream. Either that or something will go wrong, and I'll lose Tyler for good. I tell myself it's stupid, that I'm just being paranoid, and each time the feeling comes over me, I manage to push it away and go back to my walking on air feeling, but it's annoying. I have never felt like this before, and I guess it's because Tyler is the first person I've been afraid of losing. I don't want to spend all of my time with him afraid though. I want to have fun with him, enjoy our time together. I have to find a way to stop myself from overthinking everything.

Tyler and I sat down the other day and had a good talk about our relationship and everything. We decided that now we are officially together and in love, it seems pointless keeping it a secret at work. Having said that, we both agreed that we're not going to start with the whole PDA thing. I want to be taken seriously at work and that's not going to happen if I get seen kissing the boss or holding his hand. We also agreed that some sort of announcement would be pretty tacky, so we came to the conclusion that we weren't actually going to go off into work and spread the word, but it was just no longer a secret. There is a difference. We worked it out.

Like if someone asks me what I did over the weekend, I'll tell the truth and say I did whatever with Tyler and if he wants to make plans with me for after work, it will no longer have to be whispered behind closed doors. So yeah. We're not going to be cheesy and do a big ridiculous announcement, but we're not going to be doing anything to keep our relationship a secret either.

Tyler did say he wanted to tell Jack. As his business partner, he felt like it should come from him rather than it being brought to Jack's attention through the office grapevine, and I completely understood that and told him it was fine. So far, he's the only person who knows at work, or at least I think he is. I'm sure plenty of others suspect something is going on when we leave together and arrive together, often in the same car, but no one has actually come and asked me or Tyler about it.

As is our new normal, we arrive in the office parking lot together in Tyler's car. We get out and walk across the parking lot together and enter the building. At this point in our journey, anyone seeing us together could assume we had just crossed paths in the building, and I relax a little bit. It's not that I don't want people here to know about Tyler and me; it's just that I don't particularly want to become the next piece of juicy office gossip. I know it will happen once the truth gets out. But, I kind of like having him all to myself, the stolen kisses, the long, lingering glances when no one else is looking.

Oh well, I tell myself, at least they're talking about me for something I'm happy about and not criticizing me for a mistake I've made or something. And it's not like people knowing about us will make me want to stop looking at Tyler or stop kissing him.

We get into the elevator and stand at the back as more and more people crowd in. When the doors close and the elevator car starts moving, Tyler reaches out and rubs his hand over my ass. I give him a stop it look but he just grins at me and runs his fingers up my spine sending goosebumps rushing over my skin.

He brings his hand to the front of my body and runs it over my stomach and down between my legs. He presses his fingers against me, rubbing me through my dress. I have to fight not to moan and draw attention to myself. I love this, the fact that we could get caught at any second makes me so wet. But at the same time, I'm worried that the combination of how turned on I am, and Tyler's probing fingers will leave a wet patch on the front of my dress. That would not be a good look for me.

We reach our floor without anyone noticing Tyler's probing fingers or my flustered state and Tyler steps off the elevator without looking back as I follow him, now feeling even more flustered and frustrated, my clit screaming for more. When the elevator doors ping closed behind us, Tyler looks over his shoulder at me and grins.

"What the fuck was that?" I hiss.

"Just a little something for you to remember me by when you're in your office alone," he says.

I feel a pulse of desire go through me and I shake my head.

"Like I could forget you," I say. "How about a keyring next time?"

Tyler throws his head back and laughs and I can't help but join him, my pretense of being mad at him slipping away. We reach the point where we have to go our separate ways.

"See you later," Tyler says. He drops his voice to barely above a whisper. "Don't even think about finishing yourself off in there. I'll be doing that for you after work tonight."

Another pulse of desire goes through me, and I can't find my voice, so I just nod my head. God Tyler is so fucking sexy when he gives me commands like that. We part and I head for my office, knowing that not touching myself and bringing forth the release I need is going to be torture, but also knowing that I won't do it. I will wait until tonight knowing that every excruciating second will be worth it.

I reach my office, hang my purse up and go into my bathroom. I stand up on my tip toes so I can see my crotch area in the mirror. There's no wet patch and I breathe a sigh of relief.

I head back out of the bathroom and into my main office where I sit down. I wiggle on the seat, trying to find a way to sit that doesn't tease my clit. I barely manage it, but I know I have to find a way to get on with my work and ignore the delicious throbbing feeling between my legs. Somehow, I manage to get through my emails and when my secretary comes to my office with a few telephone messages and some papers for me to look over and sign, she doesn't look at me like there is anything amiss.

By the time my lunch time meeting with Scarlet rolls around, I've found a way to live with the buzzing feeling inside of myself and still work properly, which is good, because I can't let her down again and I don't want to go against Tyler's sexy command.

The meeting with Scarlet goes really well and she approves ninety percent of my drawings which is more than I was expecting for a first draft mock up. Even the changes she's requested aren't anything major and I leave the restaurant feeling full and happy and ready to tackle the next stage of the design.

I'm concentrating so hard that I don't immediately notice Tyler approaching my open office door, but after a moment, it registers with me that I can feel eyes on me, and I look up. I smile when I see Tyler leaning against the door frame.

"Don't stop on my account," he says. "You look like you were well engrossed there."

"I was," I say. "But I can take five minutes off." I beckon him over. "Come on in and I'll show you what I'm working on."

Tyler comes over and stands behind me. I talk him through my design, including the spherical swimming pool I promised Scarlet.

"Wow," he says when I finish. "This is really good. That pool is spectacular."

"You don't have to sound so surprised," I say.

I'm joking but deep down, I am pleased that he likes my work. I'm pleased because he is my boss, but more than that, I'm pleased because I want him to love everything about me like I love everything about him, and my designs are a big part of who I am.

"I'm not surprised at all," Tyler says. "Not after working with you on our last big project."

I flash him a smile and turn back to my drawing for a moment, stroking a few pencil marks onto it, before turning back to Tyler with a questioning frown.

"Sorry, you obviously came here for a reason. What's up?" I ask.

"Oh Angela, my sister, she's having a barbecue on Saturday. My parents will be there too. I wondered if you would like to go and meet them," he says.

I nod my head slowly and then I smile.

"Yes, I'd love to go, thank you," I say. My smile widens. "I want to see all the baby pictures your mom wants to show and hear all the embarrassing stories Angela has about you."

"That's not fair. Your mom didn't get baby pictures out when I met your parents," Tyler says.

"Ah that's true, but that's because you didn't think to ask her to," I say laughing.

"Well damn," Tyler says, also laughing. "I can't even uninvite you now because if Angela finds out, she'll kill me."

We laugh for a moment longer and then I look at Tyler, serious now.

"Seriously though, it will be good to meet your parents and your sister," I say.

"I think you'll like them, especially Angela and Mia," he says.

"Mia?" I prompt.

"Oh. My niece, Angela's little one," he says. "I'm her favorite uncle. And it's not just because I'm her only uncle."

I laugh at that. I feel a bit nervous at the thought of

meeting Tyler's family but if they're all as laid back as him, I'm sure we'll all get along. I just hope they like me.

"We'll sort out the details later," Tyler says. "I just wanted to let Angela know one way or the other because she wants to start getting some of the stuff today. So, I can tell her we're definite yeses?"

"Yeah," I say.

"Cool, see you later," Tyler says.

He leaves my office and I look back down at my work. He has barely been gone for twenty seconds and he's back again. I look up and smile, wondering what he's forgotten but it's not Tyler that's standing in my office door, it's Camille, one of the architects who came over with Tyler and Jack. I have spoken to her a few times, and she seems nice enough, but I wouldn't say I know her well.

"Everything ok?" I say, because she is just standing there and not coming in or speaking.

She nods and then she does come in and she pushes the door closed behind her. Ok, that's a bit weird, I think to myself, but I let it go. She might want to talk about something private, although I can't imagine what that might be considering how little we know each other.

"So, you and Tyler huh?" she says. I am genuinely confused for a second and she rolls her eyes. "You can drop the act. I just heard you two making plans for a lovely barbecue with his sister and his niece and his parents."

"Oh. That," I say.

"Yes, that," Camille says.

"Tyler and I are in a relationship. It doesn't affect work, so we generally don't feel the need to announce it around the office," I say.

"Fair enough," Camille says. By now, she's moved to sit down opposite me. "I wouldn't want to announce something like that either. I couldn't be bothered with everyone talking about me. Especially the ones laughing at me. Or worse, the ones pitying me."

"And why would they be laughing at me or pitying me?" I ask with a raised eyebrow.

"Oh, you know, with Tyler being such a player. But I can see a difference in him. I think he's really into you so if anyone can tame him, I reckon it's you," Camille says.

"Well, umm, thanks," I say, not really sure what else to say.

Of course, I want to ask her what she means about him being a player and me taming him, but that feels way too close to being office gossip and the last thing I want to do is get involved with gossip about Tyler, especially with a virtual stranger and especially about stuff that sounds like it's supposed to be putting me off him or something.

"So, are you like the jealous ex or something?" I ask.

Camille laughs and shakes her head.

"Good God no. I have some self respect," she says. I glare at her, and she reddens slightly. "Sorry, that just slipped out. What I mean is... right. Let me start over. I'm not Tyler's ex and I am not in love with him or anything like that. I am just warning you, woman to woman, that he has a bit of a reputation. Just take it slow and don't get hurt, ok?"

I can't quite decide if Camille is genuinely warning me from a place of her not wanting me to get hurt or not. Her words feel genuine, and she doesn't seem like the type to be just causing trouble for fun. She doesn't know Tyler like I do though. She doesn't know that he has told me he loves me and that he wants us to be together forever. And I have no intention of telling her that. Instead, I just smile.

"Well thanks for the warning," I say.

Camille stands up and smiles down at me.

"Which you are going to completely ignore and that's fine," she says. "I've done my bit. I've told you what he's like and to be careful and if you choose to ignore me, well that's on you. I don't have to feel guilty for not warning you what he's really like when he breaks your heart."

She leaves my office before I can think of a response to her parting shot that is more sophisticated than fuck off. I don't really know what to make of her warning. Is Tyler really going to break my heart? I don't know but I'm not about to let an almost stranger ruin our relationship. That would be me breaking my own heart. And that would just be crazy.

Assuming Camille was telling the truth when she said she's not a jealous ex or someone who is in love with Tyler and wants me out of the picture – and I do believe that much; there was no passion in her voice when she spoke of him, no spark in her eye when she said his name - then what reasons does that leave for her to come and say those things to me? To be honest, there's another reason why I believe her when she says she's not either an ex or someone who is in love with Tyler. While I didn't like her proclamation that she has too much self respect to date Tyler, it felt real, like it slipped out before she thought to sugar coat it. And if she feels like that about him, she certainly doesn't want him for herself.

That leaves two options. Either she's lying to cause trouble, which seems unlikely, or she's telling the truth as she sees it. I think that is probably the most likely option. And if she's only ever known Tyler when he was single, then maybe she has a point about him being a bit of a player. I mean he took me home with no intentions of anything other than sex when he was single. I highly doubt I was the only girl he took home during that period. That's probably all she means. Maybe he liked to come in and gossip about his conquests over early morning coffee before work started. I'm suddenly glad I didn't tell him my name all of those months ago now, just in case that is the truth.

I go back to work, putting Camille and her warnings out of my mind, but when it's time for a quick break that afternoon, I find that despite myself I'm still thinking about it. I sip my coffee and try to push my thoughts away, thoughts that involve Tyler having at least one side chick, but it's hard.

"Summer? Are you even listening to me?" Suki says.

I could bluff it, pretend that I was indeed listening to her, but what if she asks me something about what she's just said. I'll look stupid and it will be obvious I lied.

"Sorry," I say. "I was thinking about something I heard earlier. What were you saying?"

"Nothing important," Suki says. "What did you hear?"

Do I tell her? Why not, I think to myself. She's a good friend, one who won't repeat what I say. And now that Camille knows about Tyler and me it's only a matter of time before the whole office knows about it. I would rather Suki hear it from me.

"So, Tyler and I have been seeing each other," I start.

"Oh, lucky you, he's gorgeous," Suki says with a dreamy looking smile on her face.

I return her smile whilst picturing Tyler's gorgeous face and I nod my head.

"I know," I say. "Anyway, Camille overheard us arranging to go to a barbecue this weekend and she made a point of coming to my office and warning me not to get too attached to Tyler because he is apparently a bit of a player and I'll get hurt."

Suki snorts down her nose.

"I wouldn't pay too much attention to that one," she says. "At least not when it comes to Tyler."

"Why not?" I ask.

"Because she's friends with his ex-wife," Suki says.

"That explains a lot," I say.

And it really does. After our break, I go back to my office a lot happier than I was when I left it and I'm no longer thinking about Camille's warning. Or should I say Camille's attempted sabotage.

12

SUMMER

I look down at myself. I'm wearing a pair of denim short shorts and a black tank top with a pair of denim wedges. A large, silver heart shaped pendant sits on my tank top between my breasts.

"Are you sure I look ok?" I ask Tyler for the hundredth time.

"You look great," he says. He gives a soft laugh. "At this point, I feel like you're just fishing for compliments."

I roll my eyes.

"I don't mean it like that. I mean are you sure I look ok for the barbecue? Are you sure everyone will be dressed casually?" I ask.

"I'm sure. Summer it's a barbecue not a royal gala or something. Just relax ok," he says.

I nod my head, but I don't know if I can actually do it or not. I suppose it's pointless to keep asking if I'm dressed ok or not now that we're in the car on the way to Angela's place anyway. Even if Tyler changes his mind and decides actually that I don't look ok, I don't think he'd say so at this point. And even if he did, it's not like I have a spare outfit with me to change into and if we were to go back for me to change my outfit, we'd be late and then I'd worry about being seen as rude instead of worrying about being under dressed.

Ah fuck it, I think to myself. This is me. They will either accept me as I am, or they won't. I can't be one of those women who totter around in skyscraper heels and wear beautiful dresses all day every day. It's just not who I am.

"Well, here we are," Tyler says as he pulls up at the curb.

I get out of the car and look at the house. It's a nice house, well looked after, but it's nothing as grand as Tyler's house and I start to feel better. This seems more like the sort of place I will be able to relax in.

Tyler walks around the car and joins me, and we head for the house. He leads me away from the front door and instead to a green-colored gate in the middle of a tall wooden fence at the side of the house. He puts his hand over the gate and releases the bolt and then he pushes the gate open and gestures for me to go through it. I step through and wait while Tyler follows me and then locks the gate behind us. He takes my hand in his and leads me around the edge of the house and into a large back yard.

The bottom half of the yard is mostly grass with a swing set and a small trampoline that is currently being bounced on by a cute looking toddler. A small building is nestled in the bottom corner. The top half of the yard is all decked out and covered with patio furniture. I figure Angela must entertain out here a lot to have this many outdoor tables and chairs.

Just across from the seating area, a large trestle table loaded with salad, buns, condiments, plates and napkins sits, waiting to be filled with meat from the smoky barbecue that sits beside it. An older man is flipping chicken breasts and steaks with tongs on the barbecue. Everyone else is congregated around the tables on the various seats.

The back door to the house is open and I can see the array of drinks laid out on the countertop of the kitchen. Music drifts out through the open door. Angela sure knows how to throw a party it seems.

People have started to notice our arrival and a woman stands up and comes over to us. Tyler releases my hand and takes both of hers in his. They air kiss a cheek and then Tyler releases her hands and puts one hand on the bottom of my back, pushing me gently forward.

"Angela, this is Summer. Summer, my sister, Angela," he says.

"Hi," I say, holding my hand out to shake hers.

"Nice to meet you," Angela says.

She takes my outstretched hand, but she doesn't shake it. She uses it to pull me in and gives me a hug which I return awkwardly. She releases me and then takes my hand and starts leading me away from Tyler into the main part of the yard.

"Come meet everyone," she says.

I glance back at Tyler as Angela pulls me along. He just smiles and I laugh softly and give in, allowing Angela to take over.

"Mom, this is Summer. Tyler's girlfriend," Angela says, leading me over to a woman with short gray hair. She's wearing dark blue pants and a pretty blouse, and she smiles at me.

"Hi Summer, I'm Sally," the woman says with a warm smile. "I've heard a ton about you."

"All good I hope," I say with a laugh and then cringe at how much of a cliché it is to say that.

"Of course," Sally says. She winks at me. "And don't worry. I have a ton of embarrassing baby photos for you."

We both laugh and I feel myself relaxing slightly. Angela gently takes my elbow and steers me away towards the barbecue where Tyler now stands with the man cooking. He's holding the little girl from the trampoline on his hip.

"Dad, this is Summer. Summer this is our dad," Angela says. "And head chef for the day apparently."

"Don't act all innocent Angela," her dad says with a laugh. "We both know you knew I would take over the barbecue."

Angela laughs and nods her head.

"It's a pleasure to meet you Mr. Clark," I say when the laughter fades.

"Call me Keith. And the pleasure is all mine," he says.

"And this little monkey," Angela says, bopping the nose of the toddler as she says the word monkey and getting a sweet little giggle in return, "is Mia."

Mia regards me with huge brown eyes, and I smile at her.

"Hi Mia," I say.

"Hi," she replies.

She says something else, but I don't catch it and I look to Angela to explain. Angela smiles and does so.

"She said, will you push me on the swing?" Angela says.

"Sure, I will," I say to Mia.

She untangles her arm from around Tyler's neck and holds her arms out to me. I'm a little bit taken aback that she is so happy to come to a complete stranger but I take the little girl and hold her.

"You've got a friend for life if you're willing to push the swing," Keith laughs.

"Swing," Mia agrees.

I carry her over to the swing, put her on the seat and start pushing her gently.

"Higher," Mia shouts.

"Ok, hold on tight then," I say.

I push her a little bit harder, and she squeals with delight, and I smile to myself. Oh, to be this young again.

Over the next few hours, I spend time chatting to Sally and Keith and getting to know them a little bit and I also chat to several of Angela's friends. Most of my time is spent either talking to Angela or pushing Mia on the swing. I barely see anything of Tyler, but I don't mind. He has friends and relatives here to catch up with and I'm enjoying getting to know his family, Angela in particular. I can definitely see us being friends.

Mia is taking a nap on her trampoline, and I'm sitting chatting to Angela and her friend Penny. I'm absolutely stuffed full from the burgers, sausages, steaks and chicken breasts I have been constantly presented with, not to mention the huge chunk of garlic bread I was given. It's a pleasant feeling. I'm that kind of full that makes you drowsy. I'm surrounded by nice people and the sun is shining. What more could I want?

"Summer, you have to try this," Sally says from behind me.

I can't eat another thing, but I know I will feel rude saying no when she sounds so enthusiastic and I turn around, trying my best to smile. My fake smile becomes real when I see she's holding a silver tray full of large glasses of red juice. She holds it out to me, and I take one of the glasses.

"Thank you," I say. "What is it?"

"It's Keith's famous punch," she says.

I sniff it and the smell of rum almost takes my breath

away. I sip it and I have to admit it tastes delicious. The taste of rum is there, but it's nowhere near as strong tasting as it smells. On top of the rum, there is a hint of apple and cinnamon, a citrusy orange tang and a definite taste of cherry.

"Oh, wow that's delicious," I say while taking another drink.

Sally smiles and goes around the group handing the drinks out. Angela takes one but Penny declines. Is Penny the sensible one? Maybe she is but I suddenly don't want to be the sensible one. I am enjoying myself and I don't want to stop.

"Where's Mia?" I ask, noticing she is no longer on the trampoline.

"Oh, I was worried she might catch too much sun sleeping there so I asked Tyler to take her up to bed," she says.

"Ah ok," I say.

That answered my next question too which was going to be where Tyler had gotten to. By the time Tyler reappears, I've finished my glass of punch. He notices my glass is empty and brings me another glass of the punch when he gets himself one. I'm more than aware of how potent this stuff is, and I tell myself no more after this one.

"Is she still asleep?" Angela asks.

"Yeah," Tyler says. He reaches into his pocket and pulls out a baby monitor and sets it on the table we're sitting around. "And no doubt she'll make it known when she's awake again."

"It probably won't be long. She barely naps through the day now, but the heat and the excitement has gotten to her a bit today," Angela says.

"Mine is the same," Penny says. She pauses and then laughs. "And she's sixteen."

We all laugh and then Penny and Angela get into a conversation about whether the terrible twos are worse or the hormonal teen years are worse. Tyler touches my arm and I turn my head and smile at him.

"Are you having a good time?" he asks me.

"Yeah," I say. "Everyone is being so lovely and welcoming."

"I told you you'd have a new little bestie with Mia, didn't I?" he says with a laugh.

"Aww she's adorable," I say.

Tyler's cell phone starts to ring, and he pulls it from his pocket and looks at the screen.

"Shit. I have to take this, sorry," he says.

He gets up and goes into the house and I tune back into the conversation. They have moved on now to talking about someone named Jean who apparently lives on Penny's street and is a neighbor from hell. I can't help but giggle at some of the stories and Angela and Penny join in with the giggles and before long, we are all howling with laughter, tears pouring down our faces. Every time the laughter starts to die down a bit, one of us adds on another funny comment and we start up again. The laughter is finally stopping when Tyler comes back over to the table.

"What's funny?" he asks.

"Everything after two glasses of this stuff," Angela says, holding up her nearly empty glass of punch.

I realize my own second drink is also nearly empty, and I think maybe Angela has a point. Tyler puts his hand on my shoulder.

"Listen, I have to go, I'm sorry. There's a problem with one of my clients and he isn't going to rest until I've been out there and spoken to him in person," he says.

"Oh," I say, quite disappointed that we have to cut the

day short but understanding that it has to be done. "Give me a minute to go to the bathroom."

Tyler is shaking his head before I've finished speaking.

"Don't be silly, you stay here," he says. "I shouldn't be too long, and I'll come back for you."

"Oh no, I couldn't impose on Angela like that," I say.

"You're not imposing, you're an invited guest," Angela puts in. "And besides, do you know what kind of temper fit Mia is going to have when she wakes up and Tyler is gone? If you're both gone, I'll never hear the end of it. Stay. Please."

"Well, if you're sure," I say, not really sure whether I'm checking with Angela or Tyler.

It doesn't matter which of them it was because both of them answer me and both of them tell me they are sure. Tyler bends down and kisses the top of my head.

"See you soon," he says.

I watch him walk away and then I'm pulled back into conversation. I was a little bit worried that things might be awkward once Tyler has gone but they aren't. We are chatting and laughing, and I feel like I've known these women for ages.

At some point, we hear Mia crying over the baby monitor and Angela excuses herself to go and see her, leaving me and Penny, still chatting.

"Do you have kids Summer?" Penny asks me.

"No," I say.

I don't elaborate. What am I supposed to say? I've never had a real relationship where it might have happened and now, I am in one, Tyler doesn't want kids? I suppose there is a part of me that would have liked to have had kids one day, but at the same time, I had kind of resigned myself to the fact that it wasn't going to happen for me, and I had made my peace with that so Tyler not wanting kids isn't that big of a deal for me.

"Do you want to borrow mine some time? She comes with a huge chip on her shoulder and an attitude to match," Penny laughs.

"Hmm you're not the saleswoman you think you are," I say, and we both laugh.

Angela comes back with Mia in her arms. She looks around the garden and then at Angela.

"Where Unkie Tyler?" she asks.

She really is adorable with her little curls tumbling over her forehead and her cute little voice.

"He had to go sweetie," Angela says.

"Go night nights?" Mia says.

"Yup," Angela tells her.

She wrinkles up her small nose, but she doesn't cry which is a relief. I realize Angela only said what she said to give me an easy reason to stay, and I feel a flood of warmth for the woman. She really is a nice person.

She puts Mia down and Mia goes toddling off to see her nana and Angela rejoins us at the table.

"Anyone for more punch?" she says.

Penny nods her head. "What the hell, yeah I'll have one," she says.

I open my mouth to say no thank you, but I surprise myself instead.

"Yes please," I say.

Angela goes back into the house again and returns a couple of minutes later with three more glasses of punch. She hands them out and sits down. We chat some more and as people start to leave, Sally and Keith come over to join us and we all chat. They ask me about my job and my family and where I grew up and I feel like we're all starting to really get to know one another. I'm a little bit disappointed when they say it's time for them to leave.

We're down to just the three of us – myself, Angela and Penny – and little Mia of course. Angela is keeping the drinks flowing, although the punch is all gone and we're back to more sensible drinks. She keeps trying to feed us but we both keep on insisting that we're still stuffed. I honestly feel like I will never want to eat again.

I'm starting to wonder where Tyler has gotten to. He's been gone almost three hours. He must be having a major issue with the client. I want to message him and make sure everything is ok, but I don't want Angela and Penny to think I'm one of those clingy girls that can't stand to be away from their boyfriend for five minutes.

"I'm going to go pop Mia in the bath and then get her settled," Angela says. "Help yourselves to drinks and food, and if you get chilly, feel free to come on inside."

"Are you married, Penny?" I ask.

She shakes her head.

"No but I may as well be. I've been with Emily's dad since we were seventeen. We live as married, we just never got around to making it official," she says.

"Do you think you ever will?" I ask.

She shrugs.

"I mean never say never, right? But it's not something we talk about really. We're happy as we are," she says. "What about you and Tyler? Do you think you will get married to him one day?"

I hope so.

"I haven't really thought about it. We've only been seeing each other for a couple of months," I say.

"Oh, but he's smitten with you. I can see it in the way he looks at you. And you're just as bad," she says with a smile, which I return, my cheeks flushing slightly. "Hopefully you can keep his interest."

My smile turns to a frown.

"What do you mean by that?" I ask.

"Nothing," Penny says. "Sorry. I shouldn't have said anything."

"Oh, come on, spill," I say. "You can't say something like that and then just clam up."

"Well, it's just... he cheated on Chloe didn't he. I was just saying hopefully he won't do that to you as well," Penny says.

I can't imagine Tyler cheating on anyone. He's so genuine, so passionate. That would be damned hard to maintain if he had two women on the go. But why would Penny say it if it wasn't true.

"Oh, now I've ruined the night, haven't I? Me and my big mouth," Penny says.

"No, not at all," I say. "Let's just forget about it. We've all got a past, haven't we?"

Penny smiles and nods her head.

"Yeah, I guess we have," she says.

We move the topic of conversation back onto safer ground and by the time Angela joins us again, we're talking about the PTA at Emily's school and how they keep trying to get Penny to join but she couldn't think of anything worse to do with her evenings.

Another half hour passes, and Penny says it's time she was taking off. She calls a cab, and we say our goodbyes.

"I'm sorry," I say to Angela. "I thought Tyler would have been back by now."

"Don't worry," she says.

"Why don't I call a cab and I'll just message him and tell him to meet me at my place," I say.

"Honestly it's fine," Angela says. "It's only seven o'clock. Have a few more drinks. He'll turn up eventually."

I nod my agreement and Angela stands up.

"Should we go inside? It's getting a bit nippy out here," she says.

"Sure," I say.

I follow her inside, through the kitchen and into the living room where we sit down.

"Can I ask you something personal?" I say after a moment's pause, Penny's words still rattling around in my head.

Angela nods her head and sits forward to listen to me.

"Did Tyler cheat on his ex-wife?" I ask.

"Bloody Penny can't keep her trap shut," Angela says. "It all got a bit messy towards the end with those two. Tyler and Chloe, I mean, not Penny. Yeah, he cheated on her, that's why they got divorced. But it doesn't mean he'll do it to you."

I nod my head. I know it doesn't, but I would have preferred it if she had said Penny had it all wrong. She is slurring her words though and I wonder how much she really does know and how much she is embellishing because she's had a drink.

I can't help but think it's probably true though. Penny had no reason to make up a lie about Tyler and no way would his own sister play along with it. She thinks he cheated on his ex-wife and that tells me a lot. Also, it suddenly makes sense of what Camille said to me at work. At the time when I found out she was friends with Chloe, I assumed she was just trying to cause trouble between Tyler and me out of loyalty to Chloe. Now though, I suspect that she likely heard about Tyler cheating too and while it might have been a nice little bonus if she split us up, maybe she genuinely was warning me, so I didn't rush into anything and then get hurt. Maybe I should have thanked her instead of trying to think of a bitchy little comeback when she told me.

Angela has gone off to the bathroom and I'm sitting alone wondering whether or not I should confront Tyler about all of this. I decide quickly against it. It will only cause trouble. It will make life in the office damned awkward with Camille and worse, it could cause a rift in Tyler's family if he gets mad at Angela for telling me about him cheating and that's the last thing I want to do.

I decide I'm going to leave it all where it belongs – in the past. Like I said to Penny, we all have one, and we've all made mistakes and had moments we're not proud of. I'm going to take Tyler as I find him and not judge him on a past relationship. I have no idea of any of the circumstances surrounding Tyler cheating – and that's assuming that he did actually even cheat. They might have already been arguing and fighting and as good as done. Maybe she cheated on him first and he got revenge. Maybe she thought he was cheating and wouldn't believe him when he said he wasn't. There are so many ways it could have gone down and not one of them are really any of my business unless Tyler chooses to open up to me about that time in his life and tell me himself about it.

Angela comes back from the bathroom and starts talking to me about when her and Tyler were little and I let myself forget about everything else and just picture the two of them in her stories. I can't help but laugh at some of the antics the two of them got up to when they were little. They sound like they were a right handful but sweet with it. The sort of kids you can't stay mad at for too long.

Finally, Tyler reappears, and he joins us for a while, chatting and laughing along with us. It's so funny listening to him and Angela, how they have different versions of the same story, her version blaming Tyler for whatever trouble they had gotten into this time, and his version blaming her for it. It definitely makes me wonder how different their stories would be when it comes to Tyler and him cheating on Chloe.

After a while, Tyler asks me if I'm ready to go and I say that I'm ready whenever he is. I thank Angela for a lovely day, and she says we should do it again sometime. I readily agree and I really mean it. I have had a great time and I'd love to get together with them all again. We hug and then Tyler hugs Angela and thanks her for keeping me company whilst he was busy.

We leave the house and go back to Tyler's car. He pulls away from the house and we both wave to Angela as she watches us from the front step.

"You were gone ages," I say. "What happened? It wasn't Alex, was it?"

"Alex?" Tyler says, looking confused, but then he seems to remember who Alex is and he shakes his head. "No, it wasn't Alex. It was Malcolm Croft. You know the one? We're designing his summer house. He wants all of those colored pebbles for the gardens."

I nod my head.

"He doesn't seem like the demanding asshole type," I point out.

"He's not," Tyler says. "He had every right to call me, and he was entirely reasonable about the whole thing. More reasonable than I would have been in his position, I think. One of the contractors turned up with the samples of the pebbles for the garden as we had arranged. He chose one and a couple of hours later, the contractor returned with a truck full of them and dumped them all in his current garden. He wouldn't listen when Malcolm tried to tell him it was the wrong site, that the place they were for isn't even built yet he was just choosing them so I could get them quicker when the time came."

"Oh God, that sounds awfully messy," I say with a laugh.

"Oh, it was," Tyler says. "I hope your time was spent a lot better than mine."

"It was," I say. "Your sister and her friends and your parents are all so nice. And who could resist little Mia?"

"She's the best isn't she," he says.

I smile and nod my head. It's obvious he adores Mia. It makes me wonder why he doesn't want his own children, but I know I have had far too much to drink to even broach that subject right now and so I let it go. I suppose it's different being the favorite uncle and getting to do all the fun stuff and then hand the kids back when the more serious stuff comes into play.

13

SUMMER

It's the Monday after the barbecue and Tyler and I are back at work. We are having our lunch break. Instead of going out for lunch, Tyler slipped out earlier to grab us some sandwiches and we're eating them in his office. We finish eating and Tyler stands up.

"I'm going to the breakroom to grab a coffee. Do you want one?" he asks.

"Yes please," I say.

While he's gone, I sit and scroll through my Twitter feed on my cell phone. I jump slightly when Tyler's cell phone goes off, the sound of an incoming message, and the vibration through his desk scaring me for a second. The cell phone is right on the edge of the desk and as it vibrates, it moves closer to the edge, and I can see that it's going to fall so I reach out and pick it up to stop it from falling off the desk.

"What the hell are you doing?" Tyler demands from behind me.

He sounds super pissed off and I put both cell phones down and turn to face him. He isn't looking at me, he's looking at his cell phone. He crosses the office and sits down, putting the coffees on the desk and snatching the cell phone up.

"Excuse me?" I say, pissed off myself because of the way he has spoken to me.

"What were you doing with my cell phone?" he asks. The anger seems to be gone from his voice now, but he's still looking at me with a pissed off expression on his face.

"I was stopping it from vibrating itself onto the floor," I say. "It went off and the vibration sent it skittering across the desk. Why? What did you think I was doing?"

"Reading my messages," Tyler says with a shrug.

"Reading your messages? Why the hell would I want to do that? And what is so bad in there that this is your reaction?" I demand.

"There's nothing bad in there, I just need to know that I can trust you. I don't like the idea of being spied on, that's all. I mean you understand, don't you?" Tyler says.

"Oh, I understand alright," I say. "Don't worry. Next time, I'll let it fall on the floor and break."

"That's not what I meant," Tyler says.

"I couldn't give a fuck what you meant," I say. "I'm not going to get accused of spying on you again, so if it happens again, the cell phone falls." I reach out and pick up my coffee and my own cell phone and I stand up. "Thanks for the coffee. I'd best get back to my work."

"Summer wait," Tyler says before I'm even halfway across his office. I ignore him and I hear him getting up behind me. He rushes across the room and gets between me and the door. "Please. I overreacted and I'm sorry. I know you aren't like that. I just... yeah... I'm sorry. Don't leave. Please."

He looks like he really means it and my heart melts. I

suppose I get it. If it had been the other way around, I might have assumed the same thing myself and if I thought he was going through my cell phone, I might have reacted in much the same way.

"Ok," I say softly.

Tyler seems to sag slightly like the relief has deflated him momentarily. He puts his hands on my face, one on each cheek and kisses me. I kiss him back for a moment and then I pull back.

"Ok, that's enough," I smile. "This kind of thing is very much not a work Summer thing."

Tyler looks confused and I laugh.

"Forget it," I say. "I just mean if we keep kissing, we're going to get carried away and that's a big no-no for us here in the office remember."

He smiles then and we go back to our seats. As if to taunt us and remind us that it caused an argument between us, Tyler's cell phone goes off again. He picks it up and reads his message and types a quick reply, then he puts it back down. I notice he flips it on the way to his desk so that he can put it face down, something he has never done before.

I try to ignore it and I try to think of something to say that isn't related to the stupid goddamned cell phone. I can't think of anything, and I resort to talking about one of my designs for a client. Tyler listens and nods in all the right places, but I feel as though he's distracted and not really hearing me. And through the conversation, his cell phone goes off twice more and twice more he replies to whatever messages he's getting and puts the cell phone back face down.

"Bloody clients," he says, the third time his cell phone goes. "I can't even have lunch in peace."

I smile along with him, but I'm becoming increasingly suspicious that there is something going on here.

"Are you ok?" I say after a pause.

"Sure. Why wouldn't I be?" Tyler replies.

"I don't know," I say. "You just seem quiet today, like there's something on your mind. You can talk to me if there is, you know."

Tyler smiles and reaches up and strokes my cheek.

"Thank you," he says. "But there's really nothing for you to worry about. I'm fine."

His cell phone goes off again and this time, he drops it into his pocket when he's finished replying.

"Right," he says. "Sorry to dash off but I've just noticed the time and I have to get out to a client's site. Feel free to stay here and finish your coffee."

He kisses the top of my head as he passes me and then he's gone before I really have a chance to respond to him. I see his keys on his desk and sigh and grab them. I go to the office door with them. Tyler is still in sight, and I call his name. He glances back and I hold up his keys. He rolls his eyes and gives a half laugh.

"I'm so forgetful lately," he says. "What would I do without you huh?"

He takes the keys and he's off again and I still haven't had a chance to ask him anything about where he's going. I duck back into his office long enough to collect my cell phone off his desk and my coffee and then I go back to my own office. I may as well sit at my own desk to drink it as sit in Tyler's office on my own.

I try to push my paranoia to one side, but I can't. There is something going on with Tyler; something he is hiding from me. I have no idea what those messages were about or who they were from, but he most definitely didn't want me to see them and that in and of itself rings alarm bells for me.

And then he tried to make out that they were from a client. If that had been the case, he wouldn't have cared if I saw them. Hell, he probably would have read them out to me so we could both laugh at the client's audacity if he or she was giving Tyler grief.

I wish I could let this go. I really do. I so badly want to just be able to trust Tyler to talk to me about whatever he has going on when he's ready to. But I'm starting to think that time won't ever come, and I need to know for my own peace of mind what exactly he's up to. The strange behavior started on Saturday when he ducked out of Angela's barbecue. He had a perfectly plausible reason for the call and even for the home visit, but that wouldn't have taken almost four hours to sort out surely. I tried to ignore that fact at the time and just let it go but I can't anymore. It's eating away at me, and I have to know.

I turn to my computer and open up the client directory. I type the name Malcolm Croft into the search bar and his file pops up. I look at it quickly. He genuinely has had Tyler sourcing pebbles for his garden. What if the story Tyler told me is true? What if Malcolm is one of those unreasonable clients where it's easier just to do things their way than argue with them (assuming they have plenty of spending money of course)? Maybe he insisted that Tyler stay at his place until all of the pebbles were removed. But no. Like I said at the time, Malcolm doesn't seem like one of those asshole clients and when you've been doing this job as long as I have, you can smell the assholes from a mile off.

There's one way to find out for sure if Tyler was with Malcolm during the barbecue or not. I really don't want to do this, but I don't see what other options I have if I truly want my mind to put this to rest. As much as I hate myself for doing this, I know I have to, or I'm going to drive myself insane with the wondering.

I lift the receiver of my desk phone and type Malcolm Croft's number in. I listen to the phone ringing until it is answered with a rather gruff sounding hello.

"Hi Mr. Croft," I say. "This is Summer Malone from Clark and Wilkinson, the architect firm that is designing your summer house?"

"Hi Summer," he says, his voice sounding less gruff. It's probably now he knows this isn't a sales call.

"This is probably a long shot, but Tyler lost his keys on Saturday, and I was just wondering if he left them at your place?" I ask.

"My place?" Malcolm repeats. "Why would he have been at my place on a Saturday?"

I feel my heart sink, but I try one last time, hoping to jog a memory, even though I'm sure there isn't a memory of Tyler's visit because it didn't happen.

"He came out to sort out a mix up with your pebble delivery?" I ask.

"No, no. My pebbles came last week and they're fine," Malcom says.

"Oh," I say. "I'm so sorry Mr. Croft, I must have the wrong client. I think it's just a connection I made in my mind now with you and pebbles."

He laughs at that, and I'm glad. The last thing I want to do now is piss a client off. Especially one that isn't mine and I have no legitimate work-related reason to be talking to.

"My apologies for wasting your time Mr. Croft," I say. "Have a lovely day."

"You too, darling," he says, and the line goes dead.

I replace the receiver back on the telephone on auto

pilot. I sit staring at the telephone for a moment, looking at it as though it's somehow the telephone's fault that I have just possibly had my suspicions confirmed.

I hate to think badly of Tyler, and I so badly want to trust him, but the evidence is piling up now and it's getting harder and harder to ignore it and keep moving along on some sort of blind faith in Tyler.

When I think about it, three people have told me Tyler is a cheat or a player, both of which to me mean similar things. One of those people may or may not have had an agenda being that she was Chloe's friend. The other two though, if anything, they would be on Tyler's side surely, especially Angela. When a guy's sister tells you he's cheated on his ex-wife, you believe her.

So ok, he has a past. A not very nice past, but it has been and gone and it doesn't mean he will do the same thing to me. Maybe he learned from cheating on Chloe or maybe he only did it because they were over each other anyway.

Or maybe he is a serial cheater, and I'm fooling myself thinking I'm somehow special to him and he won't do the exact same thing to me. Isn't that how most cheaters get away with it? Because every woman that gets with him thinks she can somehow be the one to change him.

I sigh. I just don't know anymore. One thing I do know for sure is that whether Tyler is cheating on me or not, he lied to me. If it had just been the client's name, I could have given him the benefit of the doubt and thought he got two clients mixed up with each other. But he even told me what was meant to have happened and there's no way he would get that story wrong, and after such a massive fuck up, he wouldn't have gotten the wrong client's name either.

I sit and think. What could he have been doing that made him feel like he needed to lie to me if he isn't cheating on me? I come up with a blank. I can't think of a single thing that makes sense. If he was doing something personal that he didn't want to go into detail about, he could have just said that.

The more I think about it, the more agitated and yes, angry, I'm getting. It most definitely looks like Tyler has been taking me for a ride. I want to confront him, to scream and shout and demand that he tell me the truth. But I won't. At least not yet. Because everything I have is either an assumption or something circumstantial or someone else's word and until I have real, hard proof that something is going on, it will be all too easy for Tyler to lie his way out of this and make me look paranoid. And that will give him the head's up that I'm onto him and he will be even more careful about covering his tracks.

I'm not quite sure whether this is me deciding to give Tyler the benefit of the doubt until I'm sure one way or the other about what he's up to, or whether I'm just riding this thing out now until I get some concrete evidence of his wrong doings, but either way, I feel a bit better for having a plan, no matter how simple the plan may be. And the plan is simple – watch and wait – because if Tyler is cheating on me, at some point, he will make a mistake and I will catch him red handed so to speak.

And simple or not, any plan is better than just sitting debating the matter in my head until I want to scream in frustration because all I have are questions, questions and more questions and no satisfactory answers to them.

14

SUMMER

It's been a week since the barbecue and almost a week since I called Malcolm Croft. I'm no further forward in learning why Tyler lied to me about where he went during the barbecue, but it doesn't feel as though he's cheating on me. I know it could well just be wishful thinking on my part because I obviously don't want him to be cheating on me, but it feels like more than that.

He's been so attentive to me these last few days and we've had a lot – and I mean a lot – of red-hot sex. Neither of those feel like things that would be happening if Tyler had someone else on the side besides me. And besides, he's hardly been out of my sight all week. As far as I know, he hasn't had any on site meetings this week, and every lunch time, we've eaten together. We've also left the office together and ended up at either his place or my place. There surely just hasn't been time for him to be cheating on me.

Maybe he was seeing someone else before we got serious, and he went to tell her they were done last week. Maybe he really went to a client's property, and he did just get mixed up. Maybe I got mixed up. Maybe the client lied.

Maybe. Maybe. Maybe. Here I go again with all of the questions and none of the answers, and actually, feeling like Tyler isn't cheating on me makes the matter even more convoluted and all of the secrecy makes even less sense.

Still though, I know that I have to give him the benefit of the doubt, at least for now, because the more I think about it, the more sure I am that this is just me being paranoid.

"Last one," Tyler says, waving The Deathly Hallows Part Two DVD case at me. "Are you ready to have your mind blown?"

I laugh and nod my head. I have to admit I have really enjoyed these movies. I kind of thought that perhaps I was too old to appreciate them properly before I started watching them.

Tyler gets up and puts the DVD on and then he comes and sits back down beside me on my couch, and we snuggle up and start watching the movie. Now I have managed to push my misgivings to one side, I'm much happier and I have to say there are far worse ways to spend a Saturday morning than cuddled up with Tyler watching a fun movie. I got so into our Harry Potter movie marathon that Tyler actually brought the DVDs here, so we didn't have to stop watching them when we decided to spend last night at my place.

Just over two hours later, I lift my head up off Tyler's shoulder as the movie ends.

"Wow," I say. "I have to admit those were better than I thought they were going to be. Once the first one is out of the way, and I suppose the second one to some extent, they really are amazing."

Tyler picks up the remote control and turns the DVD player and the TV off. He puts it back down on the coffee table in front of the couch and then he smiles at me.

"But which is better? The books or the movies?" he says.

"Call me old fashioned, but the books. I loved the movies, but the books are always better than the movies," I say.

"And that is the right answer," Tyler says with a soft laugh.

"Oh cool," I say with a grin. "So, what do I win?"

"This," Tyler says, and he leans forward and kisses me softly on the lips.

I kiss him back and wrap my arms around his shoulders. He pushes his hands beneath my hoody and runs them over the bare skin of my back and then they come around to the front of my body and knead my breasts.

Our kiss turns from a soft and gentle kiss to a hungry, passionate kiss as Tyler's tongue darts into my mouth. I take my arms away from his shoulders and undo his jeans and push one hand into his boxer shorts. I grab his cock in my fist and begin to pump my hand up and down. Tyler moans into my mouth and his kneading of my breasts becomes more frantic.

I up the pace of my hand on his cock and he moves his mouth from mine for long enough to pull my hoody over my head and ditch it on the floor and then his mouth is on mine again and his hands are tugging at my sweatpants. I lift my ass from the couch and my sweatpants slide down. Tyler gets them to my knees and then he pulls one leg down, leaving the other one where it is in his desperation to be inside of me.

He pushes his jeans and boxers down to his mid thighs and then he takes my hand away from his cock and lays me on my back on the couch. He gets on top of me and plunges inside of me. His movements are slow at first, his thrusts long and teasing, his cock sliding in and out of me in an almost leisurely fashion.

The slow thrusts allow me to build up to an orgasm as my g-spot is tantalizingly rubbed time and time again. I dig my fingers into Tyler's shoulders through his t-shirt as I feel my orgasm slowly overtaking me.

My clit and pussy seem to explode with pleasure, which creeps up into my stomach and breasts, down into my thighs, making my skin tingle and my nerves pulse with pleasure. I moan out and whisper Tyler's name as he keeps moving slowly inside of me, keeping me in the throes of my orgasm.

The pleasure goes on and on until I feel myself starting to slowly come undone, I can barely breathe, and I can't think of anything except how amazing Tyler feels filling me up with his thrusts. I cling to Tyler, using his body as an anchor to keep myself from floating away on a red wave of ecstasy.

Tyler kisses my neck, and the tingling sensation starts there too, rushing down to meet the one coming up. I cling tighter, tighter. I can't even call out Tyler's name anymore because I can't get any air. I'm trying to breathe, my throat working, but nothing is coming in or out. I'm starting to feel dizzy, but rather than making me feel fearful, it makes me feel free, like I'm no longer tethered to my body, like I can experience a feeling of pleasure so pure it must be something in my soul rather than my pussy.

I put my head back and I can feel the tendons standing out on my neck. I don't know how much longer I can take this for, and I just have to trust that Tyler knows my body well enough to know when I can't take anymore. He is still filling me, sliding in and out at that delicious, torturous pace.

Tyler runs his fingernails lightly down my exposed throat making my skin burst out in goosebumps that chase his fingers up my neck and then back down it again. He puts his palm flat on the front of my throat, his fingers on one side of my neck, his thumb on the other. He squeezes gently.

For a moment, blind panic seizes me. I can't breathe at all now and my throat is being closed up. The last time he held my throat like this, it was only for a second and I loved it. This is like he's trying to strangle me and I'm not sure how I feel about it.

I try to ask Tyler what he's doing, tell him to stop. I grunt a sound and my eyes open, and his hand starts to go away. The second his grip loosens I miss it and I want it back, need it back, and I shake my head desperately until the pressure is back on my throat again.

This time, I don't feel panic. I feel lightheaded, dizzier by the second, but it feels amazing mixed with the pulsating pleasure of my climax. It is a thrill to know that if he wanted Tyler could squeeze the life out of me and kill me and giving myself to him in this way, showing him the ultimate trust is such a turn on that I think I might burst. Yes, I decided how I feel about it and it's a massive yes from me.

Finally, when I don't think I can take it a second longer, Tyler releases his grip on my throat and when he thrusts into me, he does it hard and fast and I'm released from the prison of pure pleasure and I coast down, feeling warm and alive and utterly sated.

I feel a weird sensation on my leg after that and I realize it's Tyler's cell phone, still in his jeans' pocket. He's getting a text message, but if he hears or feels the cell phone, he doesn't let it throw him off his stride. He's pounding into me, filling me, thrilling me once more.

When he hits his orgasm, I feel his cock thrumming

inside of me, a twitching feeling like it's undulating with his pleasure. He cries out as he spurts into me, a sound of pure, primal pleasure that sends a delicious shiver through me.

After Tyler climaxes and slips out of me, we lay in place clinging to each other until we have ourselves under control once more. When I feel like I'll be able to walk without my legs giving way beneath me, I sit up.

"I need to go to the bathroom," I say.

Tyler moves so that I can get up. I stand up and push my leg back into my loose sweatpant leg and I pull my sweatpants up. I grab my hoody off the floor and put it back on as I head for the bathroom. I quickly pee and wipe myself, flush, wash my hands and then I go back out to the living room.

Tyler has pulled his boxer shorts and jeans back up and he's holding his cell phone. He looks up as I come back into the room, and he locks his cell phone's screen and pushes it back into his pocket. I tell myself it's just a coincidence. He isn't doing it to hide it from me. He smiles at me as I sit back down beside him.

"Are we doing anything tonight?" Tyler asks.

"I thought maybe we could just stay here, and I'll cook, or we could order take out," I said. "But if you've had a better offer, feel free."

I keep my voice light, but I'm breaking inside. Is that what's happened? Has some other woman texted Tyler wanting to see him tonight.

"Don't be silly," he says. "What could be better than being with you."

He kisses me and I tell myself to relax.

"I just wanted to know whether to come back here later on or whether I would need to go home and change," he says. "I have to pop into town now."

"Oh, give me five minutes to change and I'll come with you," I say.

I haven't been to town for ages, and I wouldn't mind taking a walk. Plus, I think I will definitely cook something tonight instead of us getting takeout. I can get a few items for the meal I'm going to cook for us rather than making do with what's in the fridge and the cupboards.

"You don't have to do that," Tyler says. "You stay here and relax. I'll only be a couple of hours."

"No honestly, I want to," I say. "I need to grab some stuff and I could do with getting out of the apartment for a bit."

"Ok," he says with a smile.

I lean over and kiss him and then I go to my bedroom to get changed. I could really use a shower first, but I don't want to give Tyler any other reason to leave me behind. His smile when he agreed for me to go into town with him seemed fake to me and I could sense his reluctance to let me tag along with him. It's something to do with that text message he got, I just know it. I was wrong about his side chick wanting to see him tonight, but it looks like the skanky bitch wants to see him now. Ugh and to think we were making love while she was texting him.

If I ever see this bitch, I don't know whether I will be angry with her or whether I will just feel sorry for her. I mean imagine being desperate enough that you can't get your own man and have to have the scraps of someone else's. I bet he's texting her now saying that he can't get away after all. Well good. I hope she's crying.

I quickly get out of my sweatpants and hoody. I pull on a pair of panties and a bra and then I look in my closet. I don't want to wear anything too over the top just to go to the mall, but I also want to remind Tyler that I can scrub up ok and show him what he has.

I settle on a pair of three-quarter length tight jeans that I know show my ass off to perfection and a bright yellow tank top that makes my skin look tanned. I pull them on and nod to myself in the mirror. I quickly spray under my arms with deodorant and then I brush my hair, deciding to leave it down. I spritz myself with perfume and put a slick of lipstick on, then I go back to my wardrobe.

I really want to wear heels to make my legs look longer but I know I won't cope walking around the mall in heels, but I definitely don't want sneakers, so I compromise with a pair of flat sandals that have a little sunflower on them that matches my top. Ready to go, I go back into the living room.

"Ready," I say.

Tyler stands up and turns around to look at me and he smiles.

"You look gorgeous," he says.

"Oh, stop it," I say.

"No, you do," he says.

He comes to me and kisses me hard on the mouth, his hands cupping my face and I kiss him back and I can't help but question myself again. Would he be so attentive to me all of the time if he was seeing someone else? Would he really be this unable to keep his hands off me? I don't know and the constant questioning is getting too much for me. I shake it off and decide to just enjoy the moment. I pull back from the kiss and smile at Tyler.

"If you keep doing that, we'll never get into town," I say with a smile.

He makes a frustrated moaning sound as he releases me. I smile to myself as I pick up my purse. I go to the coffee table and pick my cell phone up and put it in the purse. I go to the door and take the key out and open the door and put it in the other side. Tyler steps out and I follow him. I close the door, lock it, and drop my keys into my purse which I then sling over my shoulder. Tyler takes my hand as we walk down the hallway and then down the stairs to the lobby.

"We'll take my car," he says.

I nod my head and let him lead me to his car. We get in and he drives us to the mall. We find a parking spot surprisingly easy for a Saturday morning.

"Should we grab some lunch first?" I say as we get out of the car and my stomach rumbles.

"Sure," Tyler says, looking at his watch.

"Since when did we eat by the clock?" I say laughing. "I thought we ate when we were hungry, slept when we were tired."

"And fucked when we were horny," Tyler says quietly.

I laugh and shake my head.

"We'd never stop," I say.

"That's true," he agrees. "And no, I'm not eating by my watch, I just happened to want to know what time it is."

We go to McDonalds for lunch where I get a McChicken sandwich with fries and a Diet Coke and Tyler gets a Big Mac meal with Fanta Orange. It was quiet when we first came in, but as we sit and eat, more and more people start coming in and I'm glad we beat the lunch time rush.

We chat about this and that as we eat, nothing particularly ground-breaking, although we do have a moment where we have a good laugh. A woman comes in with a tiny white poodle. The server tells her that animals aren't allowed and asks her to leave. She starts shouting and causing a scene, demanding a manager. The server goes into the back and returns with a woman.

The woman with the dog looks at the new woman and says she can't possibly be the manager because she's too young. After a bit of back and forth, she finally accepts that the woman is indeed the manager. The manager reiterates what the server told her, and the woman goes ape shit, saying that the dog is her service animal because she is blind. The manager is incredulous at this and points out that one, she could see how old the manager looked and two, the dog isn't on the ground, it's in her handbag and therefore not much use as a seeing eye dog. Realizing she is beat, the woman screeches and storms back out of the building, pausing to pull a handful of straws from the dispenser and throwing them on the ground.

"Well, that sure showed me," the manager says under her breath as she bends down and picks them up and drops them in the garbage.

"I bet she wishes she could put that awful woman in the garbage," I say, and Tyler nods his head in agreement. "I just don't get people like that, you know. It's bad enough when a toddler throws a tantrum because they can't have their own way, but when a grown woman does it it's just vile."

We finish up our meal and Tyler goes to the garbage can with our trash. He comes back and we leave the restaurant.

"Where should we go first then?" I ask.

Tyler glances at his watch again and then he looks quickly at me and then away.

"Actually, I thought we might as well each go our separate ways and do what we need to do then meet back at the car in say an hour and half? Will that give you long enough to do what you need to do?" he says.

"Well yes," I reply. "But why split up? It's not like we're in a hurry, is it?"

"Speak for yourself," Tyler says. He grins and moves closer so that he is whispering in my ear. "If my ass looked as good in my jeans as your ass looks in yours, believe me, you'd be in a hurry too."

I laugh and shake my head, but I don't really want us to split up all the same and I think Tyler knows it, even when he looks at his watch yet again.

"So, we'll meet back at the car at three?" he says.

I nod my head and he kisses my cheek and then he hurries off. If I'd known he was going to do this, I would have just walked down to the shop on the block over from mine for the stuff for dinner.

I'm once more torn about Tyler. On the one hand, he seemed pretty determined to get rid of me, and he was definitely checking his watch in a weirdly obsessive way, like he was going to be late to meet someone. At the same time, he seemed pretty convincing when he made the comment about my jeans, and he wasn't exactly worried about being seen with me if he is going to meet his bit on the side.

I make a spur of the moment decision. I need to put my mind at rest one way or the other and stop wondering about what's going on. I decide to follow Tyler. He is still in sight, a few shops down. I start to walk in the same direction as him, being sure to keep people between us so I'm harder to spot if he looks back. I also make a point of looking in shop windows so if he does happen to turn around and spot me, he is much less likely to notice that I'm following him.

He reaches the end of the section of the mall we are in. It branches off to the left and to the right and I see him choose the right-hand side. I up my pace a little bit because I don't want to lose him, but by the time I reach the end of the section, I'm already too late. I can't see him anywhere.

I stop in place and spin around in a small circle, ignoring the tutting from people who have to step around me. Nope. I've lost him. I wasn't that far behind him. He must have gone into one of the shops along here. Should I wait?

I decide I'll wait but I don't want it to be too obvious in case he sees me, so I go into the first clothing store I see and stand looking through the clothes nearest to the window where I can still see anyone coming or going from the nearby shops. He would have to be in one of the nearby ones. He wouldn't have had time to get to the other end of this strip.

I feel like I've been in here looking at this one rack of clothes for ages and I'm sure the store assistants must be starting to think I'm up to something a bit more nefarious than watching for my boyfriend. I would definitely be suspicious of someone standing at one rack of clothing for this long, especially in the doorway where they could make a quick getaway.

I decide to leave the store. I must have missed Tyler altogether and he did get to one of the further away stores. He must have been mingled in with the crowd and I didn't spot him when I reached the corner. Or maybe he realized he was going the wrong way and doubled back on himself without me seeing him. Whatever it is, I have to accept that I've failed in my mission to follow him. I'm just going to go and grab the few things I need for dinner and then go and sit in Starbucks with a latte until it's time for us to meet back up again. I might even treat myself to a new nail polish.

I am strolling along towards the indoor market area where I know they sell the freshest vegetables when I spot Tyler again. I duck behind a group of teenagers and peer around them. It's definitely him. He's just come out of a jewelry store.

Suddenly I feel so stupid. He was being a little bit secretive because he was buying me a gift. That has to be it. The text message was likely the store telling him whatever he had bought was ready for pick up and that's why he hadn't wanted me to tag along and then when I practically forced myself on him, why he was so insistent on us splitting up.

I make my mind up there and then to never ever doubt him again. But right as I make this decision, a woman appears, waving, and Tyler waves back at her. What the fuck is he playing at? She doesn't look a day over twenty. Gross.

I try to slow down my racing thoughts. I have literally just said I will never doubt Tyler again and here I am doing it again straight away. He only waved at her for god's sake. She could be one of his friends' daughters or something.

But no, that's not all he's doing. They are walking towards each other, and Tyler is opening his arms and the woman is stepping into them and embracing him. I feel sick but I swallow down the bile that rises into my throat. The group of teenagers I ducked behind have moved on now and I'm frozen to the spot, unable to move. If Tyler was to turn around now, he would be looking right at me, but he doesn't. He's too focused on his side chick.

He has released her from his hug now, but he's still touching her. He's holding her by her upper arms, holding her out and looking at her, drinking her in. Is he comparing her to me? Is he wondering why he is stuck with some old bird when he could have this younger model on his arm?

He finally releases her, and he holds out the small bag to her from the jewelry shop. She smiles at him and takes it and that's it. I have seen enough. More than enough. There's no way I can keep kidding myself into thinking she could be his friends' daughter. He clearly had arranged to meet her here and he bought her jewelry. To me, that rules that possibility out.

The spell that is holding me frozen on the spot breaks

and I turn around and hurry away from Tyler and his mistress. Mistress. Ha. She's barely old enough to be legal. I force myself to walk at a normal pace because the last thing I want now is to draw attention to myself and have Tyler notice me.

I wait until I've turned the corner to the main drag we came from and then I up my pace and before I know it, I'm running, my eyes blurred with tears, nausea rolling through my stomach. I make it outside of the mall before I double over, retching, and throw up in the bushes next to the entrance. A woman walking towards the mall stares at me in disgust and shakes her head. She must think I'm drunk or something. I wish that was all it was.

I stand up and wipe my mouth and then I start walking away from the mall, towards the curb to hail a cab. I can taste something bitter in my mouth and I don't know if it's the after taste of the bile I brought up or the after taste of my broken relationship. Maybe it's both.

I reach the curb, get into a cab and give him my address. Then I sit and stare out of the window, not really seeing anything, just trying not to cry. The journey seems to take forever, and I have to keep reminding myself none of what has happened is the cab driver's fault and not to start yelling at him to hurry up because I'm angry at Tyler.

Finally, he pulls up outside of my apartment building. I pay him and tell him to keep the change. He thanks me as I get out of the cab and then I close the door and he pulls away. I go to my building and let myself in the main door and then I go up the stairs to my apartment. I'm lucky enough not to bump into any of my neighbors because I can't stop the tears from coming now. They run down my face and drip off my chin. I reach up and wipe them away the first couple of times, but they just keep coming back and, in the end, I just leave them to drip off my face.

I let myself into my apartment, close the door, and then I lean back against it and slide down it until I'm sitting on the ground, my knees raised, and my arms wrapped around them. I let go then and I let myself sob until I find myself doing that hiccupping thing that people do when they have run out of tears, but they haven't run out of hurt.

I push myself up off the ground and go to the living room. I check the time. I'm supposed to be meeting Tyler in half an hour. While it would give me great pleasure to just stand him up and let him hang around waiting for me, wasting some of his time like he's wasted so much of mine, but I decide not to do it. Not because I'm being the bigger person, but because I think he will eventually show up here and I'm not ready to see him yet. Maybe I never will be. Although I know I'm going to have to see him at work, that's a day and half away and I can avoid him for that time at least.

I pick my purse back up from where I put it on the ground beside the couch I'm sitting on. I get my cell phone out and write out a text to Tyler.

"Don't contact me again, you cheating motherfucker. I hope she gives you herpes."

I delete it quickly before I can press send. I know if I send that, Tyler will start with the explanations and explain all about how I have gotten it wrong and I can't be dealing with that. I'm afraid that I will want to believe him so much that I will just allow myself to go along with his story and I can't do that anymore. I have done it once but never again. I write out a new text message.

"Sorry to ditch on you. Felt sick so I came home. Maybe best we don't see each other today."

I send that one and sigh and lean my head back against the couch back and close my eyes. I open them again because when they are closed, all I can see is her waving to Tyler and then Tyler hugging her.

My cell phone pings, pulling my attention to that instead. I know it's going to be Tyler and I know that I'm not going to respond to him no matter how much I might want to. I'm going to read his message though because I know it will torment me more not knowing what it says than it will ignoring it. I open the message and read it.

"Oh no, I hope you haven't caught some sort of bug. Get into bed and have a nice long rest and hopefully you will feel better after it. If you change your mind and you want some company or some chicken soup, let me know. Love you x."

My eyes fill with tears again. How can he be so sweet, so attentive, and be cheating on me at the same time. I don't get it. I only know that it hurts. I do decide to take part of his advice though and I go through to my bedroom, leaving my cell phone where it is so that I can't be tempted to use it.

I crawl into bed and pull the covers over me, trying to ignore the fact that it smells like him. I don't think I'll be able to sleep but snuggling under the covers feels nice and I close my eyes and let my tears come once more.

15

SUMMER

I was wrong about not being able to sleep. Apparently, I have turned into such a massive cliché right now that I actually cried myself to sleep. How pathetic is that? I look at my watch, surprised to see that it's after nine. Holy shit, I've slept for hours. I guess I'm in for a sleepless night tonight then.

I get up and go through to the bathroom where I take a shower and brush my teeth and then I come back to the bedroom and get into a pair of fleece pajamas and brush my hair. Just because I won't be able to sleep doesn't mean I can't let myself be comfortable.

I go and sit down on the couch and channel surf aimlessly for a while. I'm debating whether to bother making dinner seeing as I feel like I'll be sick if I eat anything but also knowing on a more rational level that eating something will probably make me feel a lot better, when I notice the light on my cell phone flashing to say I have messages.

I debate ignoring the messages, but now that I've seen that flashing light, it's annoying me not knowing what my messages say. Plus, it's always possible that there's a message from someone else other than Tyler like Rebecca or my mom or someone and I don't want to ignore my friends and family just because Tyler is an asshole.

I have seventeen missed calls and eight text messages all from Tyler. I figure by now he must know that I know, and this is him trying to dig his way out of the shit he has caused. I start reading through the text messages and see that actually, I'm wrong. It's not him begging for my forgiveness after all. He is still buying my being ill story and his texts start off asking if I managed to get any sleep and if I'm feeling any better. They then go through a similar vein, each one more insistent than the last saying that he is worried about me.

Another message pings in while I'm holding the cell phone. Maybe I'll reply and tell him I'd feel better if he would take the hint and fuck off. Maybe I'll tell him to go and boil his head. Or maybe I will just continue to ignore him. I open the text message.

"I'm really worried now. I need to make sure you're ok. I'm on my way over, x."

Oh great. That's all I need. I start to text back telling him not to come here but then he's going to ask why, and I no longer have the energy to lie to him about being ill or the energy to fight with him about what happened. I decide to just ignore the message and hope that he was just saying that to get a rise out of me. And even if he does turn up, I just won't open the door and he won't be able to get in. That convinces me he won't come. He must know that I have to let him in the main door and that if I'm not answering my text messages, I'm likely not going to answer that either.

All the same, I get up and go to the intercom and silence the buzzer. That will make it easier for me to ignore it if he does turn up. I go back to the living room and glance at my cell phone. There are no more messages or missed calls and I breathe a sigh of relief that he has finally taken the hint and is leaving me alone.

I keep watching the time and I finally allow myself to relax when enough time has passed that Tyler would have been here by now if he was really coming. I channel surf a bit more but I'm not in the mood to watch anything. I switch the TV back off and debate going back to bed. I know I won't sleep, but I can lay and read in comfort.

I stand up to head through to the bedroom and do just that when there's a knock on my front door. I start towards it. It must be one of my neighbors; no one else could have gotten into the building. I've reached the door between the living room and the hallway when the knock comes again, louder this time, and accompanied by a shout.

"Summer? Summer? Can you hear me?" the voice shouts.

It's Tyler. Fuck. Someone in one of the other apartments must have let him in. I back away from the door and debate ignoring him, but he's yelling again, and this time he's doing it through the letter box. I'm worried that he's going to disturb my neighbors and judging by the urgency in his voice, if I'm being honest, I'm worried he might kick the door in or call the police if I don't answer him, either of which I can do without.

With a begrudging sigh, I go to the door. I tell myself just to get rid of him. I have no intention of letting him bullshit me anymore. With that thought in the forefront of my mind, I pull the door open. I look at Tyler and all of my resolve falls away. Why does he have to be so damned hot? It makes everything so much more difficult.

"Oh, thank God. I've been so worried when you didn't

answer my texts or calls. I'm guessing you were sleeping?"
he says.

I feel a rush of warmth in the pit of my stomach. He
cares about me. He was worried. No, I tell myself. It doesn't
matter. It doesn't change what he has done. Just because he's
cheating on me doesn't mean he wants me to die, and he
was probably starting to think I had passed out or
something.

I just shrug one shoulder as an answer. I mean technically I was sleeping when he sent most of the texts and
when he called. I just don't let on that I was awake before he
came over here. I wonder if somewhere in my subconscious,
I didn't reply to his text messages because I wanted him to
come over after all, because there is a part of me that
needed to know he cares about me a bit. And of course,
because I want to see him as much as I try to tell myself that
I don't. It still doesn't change anything though. It doesn't
matter how hot he is or how much I love him or how much I
might want to see him, I can't be with someone who isn't
faithful to me. I just can't.

"Are you feeling any better?" he asks.

I nod my head. I don't trust myself to speak in case my
voice breaks. I just want him to go away. I'm not ready for
this at all.

"You still look a bit pale," he says. "But as long as you're
feeling better that's all that matters."

I nod my head again and he frowns slightly.

"So can I come in then?" he asks.

He gives me a big smile when he says it, but I can hear
that he's worried. His voice has a nervous quality to it that
I've never heard before. I don't know if it's because he
suspects I know what he's doing or if he is still genuinely
worried about me being ill.

I suppose to his mind, not knowing that I saw him with his side chick this afternoon, I'm acting a bit strangely not speaking and not letting him in. I clear my throat and hope that my voice comes out sounding normal. I'm going to tell him I don't have the energy for visitors right now and that I'm just going to have an early night. But then I'll have to see him again and have it out with him before work on Monday. Fuck it. I might as well get it over with now.

"Sure," I say, standing back from the door.

Tyler steps in and peers at me as he passes me, that worried look still on his face. I ignore the worried look and I don't say anything else. He goes through to the living room, and I close my door and then I follow him. He's sitting where I was sitting on the couch, so I sit down next to him on the other side of the couch.

I can already feel myself relenting. It's being so close to Tyler and the concern he's showing for me. I can't just brush this all under the rug though. It's much too big for that. I can give him one last chance to admit it though and although that will be hard to hear, maybe I can start to forgive him if he's honest with me and promises me he'll end things with her and never ever do this again.

"So, town this afternoon was a waste of time. I felt sick before I got anything I needed," I say. I force myself to smile. "Please tell me you got what you went for, and it wasn't an all round bust."

"Yeah, I did," Tyler says. "I got a new pair of jeans which I just spotted and liked so I bought them. And I got what I actually went for too so that's a bonus. What was it you needed that you didn't get?"

"It was just some stuff for dinner tonight but obviously with being sick earlier I wouldn't have eaten it anyways so maybe it wasn't the worst thing that could happen before I bought it all," I say. "Did you bump into anyone you know?"

"Why would you ask that?" Tyler says.

He's looking at me with a look of suspicion now and I realize I probably wasn't exactly subtle with the way I worded that. I think fast and cover myself.

"Oh, just I saw Danny from accounts, and I was just thinking if he saw us both separately at the same place, imagine the gossip we'd be going into work to on Monday," I say.

Tyler laughs softly.

"Yeah, it would be horrendous," he says. "But no, I didn't see Danny. I didn't see anyone. I was alone all afternoon."

He says the last part too quickly and he looks down into his lap instead of at me as he says it. I have given him chance after chance to come clean and he is still lying to me, and I snap.

"You are such a liar," I say. Tyler's head snaps up quickly and he frowns at me. "You can look at me like that all you like. I saw you, Tyler."

"Saw me what?" he says, but I can tell by the resignation in his voice that he knows exactly what I saw.

"I saw you with her. Your bit on the side. Fucking hell Tyler, it wouldn't be so bad, but she doesn't look a day over twenty," I shout.

"I can explain..." Tyler says.

"Oh really," I say. "What you're just friends with her, is that it? Then why wouldn't you tell me about her? Sure, I'd tease you for being friends with a barely twenty-year-old but surely that would have been better than this."

"She's not twenty," Tyler says. "She's fifteen."

"Fifteen? Jesus," I say, but Tyler hasn't finished.

"And she's my daughter," he adds on.

"Your... what?" I ask

"She's fifteen. Her name is Daisy and she's my daughter," Tyler says.

"I don't understand," I say.

This was the last thing I was expecting. The possibility of it hadn't even crossed my mind. How the hell could Tyler have a child he just never mentioned before? How hadn't she come up even once with Angela or his parents at the barbecue? I have so many questions yet the shock of all of this renders me silent. Tyler puts his hand on mine, and I look at him.

"Can I try to explain?" he says quietly.

I nod my head. I can't say I'm happy he's kept this from me, but at least he's not cheating on me. After jumping to the complete wrong conclusion, I definitely owe him the chance to explain. I probably owe him a huge apology too, but I just can't think straight enough for that yet. I want to hear this explanation first.

"Before I married Chloe, I slept around a bit. I got a girl pregnant, although I had no idea about that until around a month ago when Daisy contacted me and said she thought I might be her dad. I remembered her mom when she gave me details of who she was, and I knew it was possible that I was indeed her dad, so I provided the DNA sample she requested, and it came back a match.

"I asked Daisy if we could meet up and try and have some sort of relationship, but she said no and I respected that, but I told her if she ever changed her mind, she only had to say the word. She texted me while we were at the barbecue. I maybe should have said I was busy, but I really wanted to meet her, and I felt like if I said that, she would never ask again.

"We hit it off and we've been meeting up regularly since. I'm sorry I didn't tell you," Tyler finishes.

"I still don't get why you didn't just tell me. I mean you can't have thought I'd be pissed off because you slept with someone fifteen years before we met," I say.

Tyler laughs softly.

"No, I didn't think that," he confirms. He is serious again when he goes on. "I wanted to tell you, really, I did. But I kept thinking about how much you hate the idea of having kids and I didn't want to lose you, but I didn't want Daisy to not be a part of my life either. I somehow thought I could keep you both this way I guess."

Again, I have a ton of questions, but I decide to start with the obvious one.

"I don't understand why you think I am so against the idea of having children," I say. "I love children. I thought you would have seen that by the way I was with Mia."

"Oh yeah, I wasn't implying you weren't great with Mia, but that doesn't mean you want kids of your own does it," he asks.

"Well, no not necessarily I guess, but I still don't understand how you came to the conclusion that I don't want children," I say.

"Remember your pregnancy scare?" Tyler says. I nod my head. It's not really something I could forget. "Well, that's what made me think you didn't want kids. You were so nervous waiting for the result and then when you saw you weren't pregnant, you were so relieved. I went along with not wanting kids because if I have you that's all that really matters to me."

"First it wasn't because I didn't ever want kids," I say. "I was nervous because we were still so new together and at that stage, a baby changes everything. I was afraid if I was pregnant, I would lose you because as much as I love you, I couldn't have given up my child. I was also equally afraid that we would stay together only because of the baby and nothing else. I thought you didn't want kids either."

He smirks at me. "You just said you love me. In the present tense. Does that mean there's still a chance for us?" Tyler says.

I nod my head.

"Yes, of course there is. But no more sneaking around and lying. I can't be in a relationship with something that thinks they need to lie to me," I say. "And if you can forgive me for jumping to the wrong conclusion."

"Agreed no more lies. I am sorry for being sneaky and not just telling you the truth. It seems so stupid now. But why did you assume that Daisy was someone I was cheating on you with?" Tyler asks. "I mean fair enough after I lied about seeing her. But if you just saw me with her, what made you assume the worst of me?"

"I didn't want to think the worst of you," I say. I decide to just tell him everything. If we are to have any future together, I need to be honest with him as well. I see that now. "After you left the barbecue, everyone got kind of drunk, and Penny ended up telling me that you cheated on your ex-wife. Now that threw me a bit, I'll be honest, but I decided that we all have a past, and I wasn't going to judge you on past mistakes. It kept bugging me though and I ended up asking Angela if there was any truth to it. She said it was true, but she was quick to point out that you'd learned your lesson and it didn't mean that you would cheat on me too. I knew she was right, and I told myself to let it go.

"I really meant to do that too, but then you were acting weird, like you were hiding something from me, and Penny isn't the only person who warned me you like to get around.

I decided to put my mind at rest and call Malcolm and find out if you were really there that Saturday. Don't worry, I covered myself. I said you'd lost some keys and I was just checking if you'd lost them there and when he said you hadn't been there, I said I must have made a mistake and I made a joke about pebbles being involved and me associating Malcolm with pebbles. He wasn't suspicious.

"I knew though that I needed more proof before I confronted you or you would lie your way out of it, so I didn't say anything about it. I was starting to think I was crazy to even suspect such a thing until today when it was so obvious you didn't want me to come to town with you and then even after you relented, you blew me off once we got there. I decided to follow you and see for myself what was going on. So, knowing all of that can you see why I thought you were sleeping with Daisy?"

"I guess so," Tyler says. "But I have to be honest with you Summer. I don't like how you just believed such terrible stuff about me. And I don't really like how you were sneaking around behind my back trying to catch me."

"I know," I say. "I'm sorry. I was just so paranoid."

"That day in my office when you had my cell phone. You were going through it weren't you?" Tyler says.

"Actually, no," I reply. "I really was telling you the truth that it vibrated towards the edge of the desk, and I thought it was going to fall and smash."

"Would you have been tempted to look at the message if I hadn't come in when I did?" he challenges me.

I think for a moment and then I shrug one shoulder.

"I don't know," I say. "I want to say no of course not, but honestly, I don't think anyone can know for sure what they'd do in that situation until they are in it."

"Fair enough," Tyler says. "Well, I guess it's time I told

you the truth about what happened with Chloe and me."

I shake my head.

"You don't have to do that," I say. "Honestly. I believe that you're not cheating on me and that's all that matters. The past is the past and if you cheated on Chloe, that's none of my business."

"But I didn't cheat on Chloe," he says. "She cheated on me. I have found it so difficult to trust anyone since we got divorced because of that and then the first time I do, you accuse me of cheating on you. You have no idea how much that hurts me, Summer. I would never cheat on anyone because I know just how shitty it feels to be the one being cheated on."

"I'm so sorry. I didn't..." I start.

Tyler shakes his head.

"It's ok. I'm not saying it to make you feel bad or apologize. I just want you to understand that no matter what happens, I would never, ever cheat on you," he says. He goes quiet for a minute and then he looks up at me. "Do you believe me? About Chloe?"

I think for a moment and then I nod my head. I don't understand how it all fits together, how Angela got it backwards, but I do believe Tyler. I always should have.

"I do and you don't have to explain anything if you don't want to, but I am curious as to why Angela would lie like that," I say.

"She doesn't realize she is lying," Tyler tells me. "I had been working late a lot, working weekends, you know what it's like." I nod my head. I do know what it's like. He goes on. "Chloe wasn't happy about it. She said she understood my business was important to me blah blah blah but at the same time, she still wanted me to spend more time with her. I knew she had a point and that I wasn't being fair to her.

Never being available for her, and I would have hated that if it was the other way around and she kept on choosing work over me every time, so I decided to finish early one Friday afternoon, turn my cell phone off and spend all weekend with her, just the two of us.

"I didn't tell Chloe. I wanted to surprise her, so I finished work at lunchtime on Friday and went home. I thought she was out when she wasn't in the living room or the kitchen, so I went upstairs to take a shower. And I found her fucking some other guy in our bed."

"Oh my God," I say. "That's awful. You must have been heart broken."

"I was. But I was angry too and I wasn't going to let Chloe play the victim. Yes, I had been neglecting her a bit, but it was for our future. It's not like I was out drinking with the boys every weekend. I was working for fuck's sake," Tyler says. "I told her to pack her shit and get out and that she'd hear from my lawyer about a divorce.

"That should have been the end of it but with Chloe, nothing is ever simple or easy. She decided she didn't like me standing up for myself and so she started to tell everyone that I was the one who had cheated on her. I know it sounds crazy that everyone, even my own sister and parents believed her, but Chloe was just someone people gravitated towards, someone they liked and trusted. She could be so charming when she wanted to be and playing the victim was her speciality.

"I lost a lot of friends over it because a lot of our friends were mutual friends and even if the guys didn't really care if I had cheated on Chloe, their girlfriends and wives did and it got to the point where I didn't want to cause trouble in other people's relationships, so I stopped even trying," I say. "And Angela. Angela is a girl's girl. She is one of those people who believe women regardless of what the actual evidence might say. So, she believed Chloe and no amount of me telling her otherwise would sway her. She didn't want to fall out with me over it though and eventually, we just agreed to disagree and not mention it again."

"Wow," I say. "Chloe sounds like a right bitch."

"Yeah. I didn't see it at first obviously, but you're right, she was," I say. "But now I'm just glad to be out of that relationship and I've made new friends, real friends who can't be swayed into thinking I am some sort of villain. So, it's all good. And now I have you. Right?"

"Right," I agree.

Tyler leans in to kiss me and I move towards him, but at the last minute, he pulls away.

"Wait," he says. "Are you really sick or was that just something you said to get away from me?"

"A bit of both," I admit. "But it wasn't a bug. I just felt sick at the thought of you with someone else. And I've showered and brushed my teeth since then."

He laughs softly.

"Good to know," he says, and then he kisses me, and I feel as though everything is right in the world again. Everything that is except for one thing. I pull back from the kiss.

"You're not going to tell Angela I told you what she told me are you? Just I really liked her, and I don't want there to be any animosity between us," I say. "And she only answered my questions. I was the one who brought it up."

Tyler shakes his head.

"My lips are sealed. Let's just put all of this behind us," he says.

He kisses me and I nod my agreement as we kiss. I genuinely don't think I could be happier than I am right now.

16

TYLER

As I kiss Summer, I think about how close I came to losing her today. The thought of losing her makes me hold her tighter. I never ever want to risk losing her again. Especially not over a misunderstanding. It was a little bit ironic that I almost lost her because of something I was doing to hide the thing that I thought would make me lose her, when actually that wouldn't have bothered her.

I still can't believe she thought I was cheating on her, but at the same time, I suppose I have to admit that it made sense from her point of view. She had no idea that someone cheating on me had ripped my life apart, so she had no reason to think I was so against cheating. And then add that to the lies and the secrecy and the fact my own sister can't see the truth of what happened with Chloe and me and feels the need to do the sisterhood thing and warn anyone who might get close to me that I'm a cheater, and yeah, I can definitely see why Summer got the wrong end of the stick.

The one good thing to come out of it though is it has brought us closer in that neither of us want to lie to each other or hide things from each other anymore and I think that can only be a good thing. I will do everything in my power to make sure I never lose Summer, but if I do, at least this way, I will know it was my own dumb fault and not a misunderstanding if anything does go wrong between us.

Summer moans low in her throat as I kiss her neck. Her moan pulls me out of my head and back into the moment and I decide that's where I want to stay. I don't want to dwell on the past and keep thinking about almost losing Summer. I want to think about the here and now, and appreciate the fact that Summer is in my arms as well as in my head.

I slide to the ground off the couch and move to face Summer. I smile up at her and she smiles back at me, her eyes full of lust. She lifts her ass before I even get hold of her waist band ready to peel her clothes off of her. I love how eager she is for my touch, and I feel a jolt of desire flood me. I pull her pajama bottoms off and throw them to one side and then I pull her forward, so she's perched on the edge of the couch.

I push her knees apart and crawl between them and then I move my face closer to her. I run my tongue through her lips from her clit to her pussy and back again. She shivers, her body shaking slightly beneath me. I lick her again, teasing her and savoring the salty taste of her. I stop teasing her and concentrate on licking her clit. I press down on it with my tongue and move it from side to side. Summer moans and presses herself against my face.

I suck her clit into my mouth, and she moans again. I suck on it, stretching it and tugging it. I nibble gently on it and Summer writhes beneath me, her feet coming off the floor. She makes a whimpering sound that spurs me on, and I suck her clit again. Finally, I release her clit from my mouth and go back to licking it. I lick and lick until I know she is more than ready for her climax and then I run my tongue backwards through her slit and to her pussy.

I gently lick around her opening and then I push my tongue inside of her and move my head back and forth, thrusting into her with my tongue. She cries out in pleasure, and she takes my head in her hands, holding onto my hair and tugging it. The stinging feeling in my scalp is nice and it shows me how much Summer is loving this, which spurs me on to make her feel every bit of her orgasm.

As I move my tongue in and out of her pussy, I bring my hand up her thigh and across her stomach and then down to her slit. I find her clit with two fingers and massage it as I tongue fuck her. I feel her clit pulsing beneath my touch and I can feel her pussy starting to twitch and I know she is just seconds away from coming.

I up the pace of my fingers on her clit and I find her g-spot with my tongue and press on it with the tip of my tongue. Summer doesn't just moan; she screams in pleasure as she comes. I feel her juices coating my face and I pull my tongue out of her. I lock my mouth over her pussy and suck, drinking in her juices.

She tastes amazing, salty, sweet, musky. I could drink her in all day, but my cock has other ideas. It's rock hard, straining against my jeans. The need to be inside of Summer is all consuming.

I move my face away from her pussy and give her clit one more going over until she is gasping and panting and then I take my hand away. While she's coasting down from her orgasm, I quickly get out of my clothes. When I finish stripping, I sit back on my knees again and see Summer watching me with a hungry looking grin on her face.

I take her hands in my hands and pull her off the couch, so she ends up sitting across me, straddling my thighs. I lift her pajama top up as she raises her arms. I take it over her head and throw it aside and then we look at each other, taking in each other's nakedness. Summer looks amazing, her flushed pink skin that becomes paler as it reaches her breasts, her darker nipples, a layer of shiny sweat on her chest.

I reach up and take her breasts in my hands and squeeze them gently. I take one of her nipples in my fingers and release the other breast then I lean forward and take her other nipple into my mouth. I roll one between my fingers and my thumb and I suck on the other one. I intend to tease Summer for as long as I can bear it, but she has other ideas.

Summer lifts herself slightly and then I feel her grab my cock. The next thing I know, she is lowering herself onto me and my cock is slipping inside of her pussy. I moan and flick my tongue over her nipple one last time and then I release her breasts and put my arms around her, drawing her close. I kiss her hard on the mouth, my cock inside of her but both of us remain still while we kiss. She clenches around me, and I can't stand the wait any longer.

I take my mouth from hers and begin to move inside of her. She moves up and down in time with my movements and I fill her all the way up, stretching her tight little pussy, making her call out my name as I fill her right to the top and bump against her cervix.

She throws her head back and it makes her chest move forward and with each thrust, her nipples tickle my chest sending delicious little shivers through me. I keep thrusting and she moves her head back down, pulling me tightly against her and wrapping her legs around my waist. I keep pumping into her, and the new angle increases the friction and I know I can't last much longer.

Summer whispers my name and clings more tightly to

me as she orgasms, her pussy tightening around my cock. I thrust through her tightness, and I let myself go, pounding into her faster and faster until I freeze, motionless as I come hard, thinking of making a baby with her makes my dick harder.

It's my turn to cling to Summer and I bury my face in her neck as I spurt into her a second time. I slip out of her, and we hold each other while we get our breaths back. Summer leaves her legs wrapped around me, and it feels amazing to be all wrapped up in her limbs this way. I never want this to end, but inevitably, I know it must. We can't sit here forever.

After a few minutes, my breathing has returned to normal, and my heart doesn't feel like it's trying to burst free of my chest anymore. Summer lifts her head up from where it rested on my shoulder and smiles at me. She leans forward and kisses me, a tender, loving kiss that makes me tighten my hold on her for a second.

"I don't want to get up, but I have a cramp in my calf," Summer whispers in my ear.

I half laugh but I know how painful a cramp can be and so I come up onto my knees and lift her up with me and sit her back down on the couch. She smiles as I lower myself back down and massage her calves for her.

"Thank you," she says after a minute or two. "It's gone now."

"That's good," I say. "Because I still have one little secret left to share with you."

"Oh," Summer says. "And what's that then?"

I smile at her and then I reach out for my discarded jeans and pull them back towards me. I push my hand into my pocket and find the small box. I don't pull it out immediately, I just sit holding it while I look up at Summer.

"It's something I bought in town today," I tell her.

Was that really only today? Was it only today I nearly lost her? It feels like forever ago, the horrible gut-wrenching moments erased by the deliciousness of the sex we have just had.

"Ok," she says, dragging the K out.

"It's something for you actually," I say.

"Well give me it and stop keeping me in suspense," Summer laughs.

"All in good time," I say to her. "You see, before you can have it, I have to ask you a question. And you can only have it if you answer the question the right way."

I take my hand back out of my pocket, content in the knowledge I can grab the box easily when – please be when and not if – I need it.

"I already told you the books were better than the movies," Summer says.

I laugh and shake my head.

"Not that. I mean that was important, but this is even more so," I say, enjoying teasing her.

Summer interlaces her fingers and turns them backwards and pushes them outwards, cracking all of her knuckles. She moves her head from side to side, her neck cracking at both sides.

"Oh my God do you have to do that?" I say laughing.

"Sure, I do. I have to be ready," Summer smiles. "And now I am. Hit me with it."

God I love this girl. I smile at Summer and then I reach up and take one of her hands in mine. I stay on my knees, and I stop smiling, wanting this moment to be serious so she doesn't think I'm joking or anything.

"Summer Malone, I have loved you from the moment I set eyes on you, even if it did take me a while to admit that to myself. I want to spend forever with you. I can't imagine my life without you in it every single day," I say. "So, here's the question. Will you marry me?"

Summer looks at me in shock for a second and then her eyes fill with tears, and she nods her head.

"Yes," she says. She sniffles a bit. "Yes, of course I will."

I come up and pull her into my arms and we kiss. Our kiss tastes of Summer's salty tears and I reach up and wipe them away with my thumbs as I kiss her. I pull back from the kiss and smile at her.

"That was the right answer," I say.

Summer smiles back at me and I get up and sit on the couch beside her. I lean down and pull the small blue velvet box from my jeans pocket. I open it and hold it out to show Summer. Her hands go to her mouth, and she squeaks and then more tears flow.

The ring is a yellow gold band with a dazzling one carat diamond set in the center of a circle of smaller diamonds.

"It's absolutely beautiful," she says.

"A beautiful ring for the most beautiful girl in the world," I say.

I take it out of the box and hold it out and Summer gives me her left hand. I smile and push it onto her engagement finger. It's a perfect fit and I breathe a sigh of relief, glad that I guessed it about right when I was trying to show the assistant in the jewelry store the width of Summer's finger.

She holds her hand out in front of her, her head tilted to one side and admires her ring. The tears are running freely down her face again and once more, I reach up and brush them away.

"Are you happy?" I ask after a few minutes have passed and Summer has mostly stopped crying.

"Happy?" she says with a soft laugh. "That's an understatement. You know when we talked earlier and got everything out in the open?" I nod my head and she smiles and goes on. "When we finished that talk and we were still together and stronger than ever at the end of it, I thought to myself that I was the happiest I had ever been. And now not even an hour later I am even happier than I was then."

"Then that's going to be my mission," I say. "To only ever make you happier than you are at any given moment and to never ever hurt you or make you feel sad."

She puts her hand on my cheek and looks me deeply in the eyes. She smiles.

"I love you more than life itself," she says.

"You're my everything, I love you so much," I tell her.

EPILOGUE

Summer

Three Months Later

A lot has happened over the last three months, but I think the most important things are my moving in with Tyler and me finally meeting Daisy. Daisy is such a sweet kid and we hit it off straight away. She has finally told her mom that she's looked her dad up and Tyler and I have started to talk to Daisy's mom and organize things between us now that Daisy wants to see her dad on a regular basis.

She is coming to spend the next school holiday break with us, and she'll be staying for a full week. When Tyler asked me if it was ok, I told him I loved the idea but that we couldn't expect Daisy to stay in one of the guest rooms, that she is family and deserves her own room. Tyler agreed and that weekend we went into town and got a load of things to convert a guest room into Daisy's own room.

I have just finished putting the finishing touches to the

room and I stand in the doorway and look in. What was once a characterless room that looked like something out of a Travel Lodge with its neutral colors and boring furniture, now looks like something that I hope Daisy will love.

Three of the walls are now painted yellow and the fourth wall, the feature wall, is papered with a wallpaper with a beautiful daisy pattern on it as a tribute to our Daisy. The floor is white oak wood, and it has a big, fluffy white rug in the center of it.

Daisy's bed is up a ladder and beneath it is a couch where she can sit and watch the giant TV that is hung on the opposite wall. I have also sourced a wardrobe and a chest of drawers that are white and match the room, and I have made a bookshelf to match and filled it with books that I hope Daisy will love. Some of them are my own teen favorites and some of them are some of the YA books I read and love now. Some of them are recommendations from the bookstore assistants when I told them what I was doing. And of course, there's a full box set of Harry Potter books for her to read.

I have just made her bed with pretty yellow and white bedding, hung her light-shade up, and the room is ready for her. I hear Tyler coming up the stairs. I have just called him to say the room is ready and to come and take a look and see what he thinks. He comes up behind me and wraps his arms around my waist. I lean back against him and put my hands on top of his arms.

"Well? What do you think?" I ask him.

"It's perfect," Tyler says. "Daisy is going to absolutely love it."

"Are you sure?" I ask, nervous suddenly in case she hates it.

"Of course, I'm sure. She's getting her own room with a

TV the size of a cinema screen and a shelving unit filled with more books than a library has. What more could she possibly want?" Tyler reassures me.

"Yeah, you're right. She's going to love it," I say. "And I'm going to do everything in my power to make her feel welcome here."

"I know you will," Tyler said. "And I will be doing the same. I'd love to get to the point where she drops in because she wants to you know?"

I nod my head. I do know and I feel exactly the same myself. We stay in place for a minute looking at the room, each of us lost in our own thoughts. After a moment, Tyler kisses my neck and I turn in his arms and kiss him on the mouth then rest my head on his shoulder. After holding each other for a while, I pull back and smile at Tyler.

"The room next to ours is going to be the next one to get a makeover I think," I say.

Tyler smiles and nods his head.

"Ok. What are you thinking? An at-home office space or a reading room or what?" he asks.

"Actually, I was thinking more like a nursery," I say with a smile.

It takes Tyler a moment to register the meaning of my words and then his eyes open wider.

"Wait. Are you saying you're..." he starts then trails off and looks at me questioningly.

"Pregnant?" I finish for him. "Yes!"

We grin at each other and then Tyler picks me up and swings me around in a circle. He sets me back down and we kiss again. And just like that, Tyler has done it again. I didn't think I could be happier than I was the moment he proposed to me but seeing his reaction to hearing I'm carrying his child; well, I am by far the happiest I have ever been.

The End

Chapter One
Savannah

I smiled secretly at the stares from a few of my colleagues as I carried the deliveries outside to my van. It was stinging cold but that was not an excuse not to dress well. Wearing my favorite skin tight jeans and high heeled boots, I felt like a million dollars.

Which was a good thing because my bank account was close to zero. Ethan, my six-year-old son, and I were surviving on the little money I'd saved back in Rogers and now, this job at the grocery store.

"Be careful out there, Savannah," Heather said, with a wave.

I grinned. "I will." While a lot of people only saw the disadvantages of my job, for me, it was perfect. I could pick my hours, which meant that when Ethan started his new school next week, I would be able to pick him up and drop him off.

I only had two deliveries but both were up in the mountains. I packed up the two deliveries in my minivan or rather my Aunt May's, and went to the driver's side. Sliding into the driver's seat, I said a silent thank you to my Aunt May. She was my mother's younger sister and my favorite relative.

I felt a familiar stinging in my eyes and pushed the feeling back down. I had promised myself not to cry again. I'd cried enough. Aunt May would not like it. After typing the first address into maps on my phone, I turned the ignition key and the van roared to life.

Ten minutes later, I was out of town and headed up the twisting road up the mountain. Thank God it was wide and even though the weather had been terrible, today it was mild.

My phone rang from the dashboard. A glance at the screen and my heart skipped a beat. It was my sister Ivy.

Ethan.

My chest tightened as I pulled over to the side of the road. I grabbed the phone and touched the screen to answer.

"Hey Ivy." My voice was deceivingly casual, hiding the fear coursing through me. I resisted the urge to blurt out if Ethan was okay.

"Hi," Ivy said cheerfully.

I squeezed my eyes shut with a surge of relief. She would not be this cheerful if there was anything wrong.

"I'm home today and I thought I would check up on you," she said.

"We spoke last night," I reminded her, though she didn't need any reminding. "I'm good, busy at work. How are the kids?"

"Good, they're upstairs in the games room." Ivy's house was huge but she and her husband ran their own law firm in Rogers, Montana.

"Great," I continued. "I'll call you guys in the evening, okay?"

"Are you sure you're okay?" she asked, "I can send you something to tide you over."

"I'm fine, thanks." I hated to ask for help from my family and she was already doing enough keeping Ethan while I settled into our new lives here in Paradise.

We hung up and I continued my drive. Google maps told me to take the next left. I thanked God for technology. I was fine with a voice on my phone telling me which direction to go, but if you gave me a physical map, I was lost.

I took another left turn and followed the driveway that cut through a well taken care of lawn. Coming to a stop in front of a neat single-family home, I cut the engine and went to the back to grab the crate. I carried it to the house and gently deposited it at the front door.

Before I could ring the bell, heavy footsteps sounded and a second later, the door swung open.

"Hello. You must be the new delivery lady," an elderly woman said, a smile on her face.

"I am," I said, smiling back. "Do you want me to carry these in for you?" The instructions were to leave the delivery at the front door but there was no way I was leaving the heavy crate for her to carry.

"Yes please, that would be lovely," she said, holding the door open for me.

I lifted the crate and stepped into the house. I waited for her to lead the way into the kitchen.

"My name's Dorothy," she said, "and my husband's name is Rory." Her gait was slow as she led the way through an open plan space to the kitchen beyond.

"I'm Savannah," I told her.

"You must be new in town," she said, coming to a stop in

front of the kitchen counter. She patted the space she wanted me to place the crate.

"I am but not so new. My Aunt May lived in Paradise and I came to visit her over the years. I've moved into her cottage."

"I knew May. She was a lovely woman," Dorothy said. "It's a small world. I always say, be kind to everyone you meet, you never know who they might be."

"Very true." I could see that she wanted to talk and I felt bad as I inched away from the kitchen. I really needed to get a move on since my next delivery was quite a distance away. "It was nice to meet you Dorothy. I'll see you next time."

My heels made a clicking noise as she followed me to the front door. "It was lovely to meet you too. Are you headed to Cameron's? Like us, he gets his deliveries done twice a week."

"Yes, I think that's him. How far is it to his house?" I opened the front door.

"Twenty minutes if the weather is good," she said. "Pass our regards. He's got a heart of gold, that Cameron."

"I will," I called out cheerfully as I made my way to my van.

I loved how people in small towns looked out for one another. It was one of the reasons why I'd decided to move into the cottage Aunt May left for me, rather than sell it or rent it out.

Dorothy's estimation was correct and in twenty minutes, I had reached my destination.

"Wow," I said aloud when I stopped the van in front of the two story, gorgeous, rustic house. My gaze swept over the landscaping which looked as if it had come straight from a postcard.

The views. If I lived in that home, I would have my

groceries delivered too, as well as anything else that I needed. I would never leave it unless I absolutely had to. I gingerly got out of the van and went around to get the delivery.

I took my time walking to the front door, enjoying the views and the absolute peace that surrounded me. The house itself had windows which covered entire walls. The owner had brought the natural surroundings into the interior of the house. If by some miracle I ever became rich, that was the kind of house I'd live in.

I rang the bell twice but there was no answer. I deposited the crate on the ground. The temptation to look around was too great to resist and I walked around the house, following a gravel path. The garden surrounded the house, all the way to the back.

Beyond the neat grass were woods and just as I was about to turn back, I heard a soft but distinctive sound of someone chopping wood. I followed it, cursing under my breath when the heel of my shoe sank into the grass with every step I took.

The noise took me through to the woods until I came to an opening which looked like an open-air woodwork station. That's when I saw him. He had to be Cameron. Tall, broad-shouldered and deeply tanned.

My eyes followed the ripple of his arms as he raised the axe and brought it down with a loud thud. He was shirtless and clearly a man who spent his time outdoors, and not basking in the sun. Working. I imagined tracing each of those cut lines with my tongue.

An ache rolled through me and settled between my legs.

God. I'd not felt that way about a man, let alone a stranger, in a long time. He must have sensed my presence or heard my quick breathing, because he turned around abruptly.

He stood staring at me, axe in his hand, and a frown etched across his masculine face, as if at any moment he would swing that axe at me. If Dorothy had not mentioned he had a good heart, I would have turned around and ran to my van as fast as my heels would let me. My legs carried me closer. I realized I was waiting for him to say something.

His tightly muscled, broad chest gave off vibes of great strength and protection. It made me instantly think of resting my head against it, even if just for a moment, but when I moved my gaze up to his face and his icy blue eyes, I almost gasped. There was no warmth or kindness there. Just a barren space of terrible coldness.

"What do you want?" he asked abruptly, the frown on his face intensifying.

For a few seconds, I couldn't speak. A sudden chill hit my core. I couldn't believe his rudeness. No hello or any form of politeness. He couldn't be the good-hearted Cameron that Dorothy had referred to. There was nothing good-hearted about the ruggedly handsome man glaring at me.

"I brought your order from the grocery store," I said automatically.

"Leave it at the front door," he instructed coldly, and turned his back to me. I watched dumb-founded as he raised his axe in the air and continued chopping as if I wasn't fucking there.

For a few seconds I was so stunned by the way he had so rudely dealt with and dismissed me I just stood there staring at him. Even though I wanted to say something, I couldn't. He wouldn't hear my voice above the noise of the axe meeting wood, anyway.

Grinding my teeth, I turned away and made my way back to the front of the house. My breathing returned to normal when I entered the van. What was the matter with him? And why did he live here all alone? I answered the last question myself. With that kind of attitude, who would want to live with him?

What a first impression!

I moved my hand to the ignition key, but I was shaking too much to turn it. A fresh wave of anger went through me. If I was honest, I would have admitted it wasn't just the way he treated me that had affected me so much. It was the way I had responded to him that bothered me, but I wasn't being honest right then.

I turned all my focus to fuming at him.

He wasn't going to speak to me like that. How dare he? That was not the right way to treat people. Maybe no one had ever told him that. Well, that was about to change right now. I got out of the van again, propelled by righteous anger and indignation.

I marched back to the woods wishing I'd worn sneakers as my progress was slower than I liked. The sound of chopping wood had gone and it was silent, except for the sounds of insects and nature.

He had obviously heard my clumsy footsteps because he stood staring at me. The axe was now leaning against the trunk of a tree.

"Maybe no one has ever told you this, but you are a rude human being," I said.

His gaze seared me, moving down my body before returning to my face. A hint of amusement pulled at the corners of his mouth, incensing me further. "You're right. Nobody has ever told me I'm rude, but then again, I've never had someone walk onto my property and stand there, gawking at me, saying nothing either."

He had a deep, authoritative voice that distracted me from my anger for a second. "I was not gawking." Maybe I had been. The man was super hot, after all, but I wasn't about to admit that. As a matter of fact, my cheeks flushed when I remembered the insane way my body had reacted to him.

"Don't you have any more deliveries to make?" he mocked, "Or are you paid to stare at random men you come across in the woods?"

I pointed a finger at him. "You—" But I was at a loss for words. I hated his guts, but he was right. I *had* been staring at him, and still was. In my defense, he honestly was the most physically tempting male I'd ever come across in my whole life.

I tore my gaze from the intriguing V line that ran down until it disappeared down the low waistband of his jeans. I shook my head. In my state there was no getting the better of him. Embarrassed and still deeply furious with him and myself, I whirled around, and without another word, marched to my van.

This time for good.

Chapter Two
Cameron

I craved a cup of coffee at the end of the shift and not just any coffee. I wanted the kind that Joe's coffee house in town made. I hated going into town and rarely did, but good coffee beckoned. I had just done a shift, hiking with visitors. It was not too bad. None of them had wandered off and gotten lost.

As I parked my Jeep in front of the coffee house my gaze moved to the grocery store next door. I'd thought of that woman more than I liked. She'd even invaded my dreams. Savannah. I'd found out her name from Dorothy when I passed by to check if there was anything they needed.

Just remembering how she had stood up to me to let me know how rude I was, made me smile. I pushed her out of my mind and crossed the road to Joe's. I grabbed the door at the same time as someone from the inside yanked it open.

The next thing I knew, hot liquid was splashed all over my jacket. Thankfully, my field jacket was thick and other than looking unsightly, it didn't get through to my skin.

"Oh my God, I'm so sorry," a familiar voice gasped.

I shifted my gaze from the dripping mess of my clothes to Savannah's absolutely horrified face. Her hand was slapped over the mouth that I had been face-fucking in my dream. She was trouble with a capital T and I didn't want no trouble in my life at the moment. I wanted no strings. Of any kind.

"It's fine." I shook off the excess and side-stepped her to enter the coffee house.

I strolled to the counter while everything in me demanded I have a conversation with the woman who had been invading my thoughts for longer than I cared. But for what purpose? I reminded myself the only kind of female I was interested in was one I could have sex with and immediately forget about.

To accomplish this successfully, she had to be from another town. Someone who I would never see again. As sexy and delectable as she was, Savannah simply did not fit into that criteria. Dorothy had already mentioned that Savannah was the late May's daughter, and she had moved into town permanently. Savannah wasn't right for me, not even for a quick roll in the hay.

"Hi Liz," I greeted the dark-haired woman behind the counter. She was Joe's wife and they ran the coffee house together. Before them, Joe's father, Joe Senior, had run the coffee house.

Liz smiled at me. "Well, well, well. It's nice to see you again, stranger. You disappear in those mountains for too long. What can I get you? The usual?"

"Yes please."

"Let me buy that for you, please?" Savannah urged, sidling up next to me.

Remembering she had spilled half her coffee, I said to Liz, "And her coffee to go as well."

"Oh please, don't make me feel worse. I should be buying the coffee," Savannah cried frantically.

"Don't worry about it," I muttered curtly, not even looking in her direction.

"I'm so sorry. I was... distracted."

"It's fine."

Blessed silence. Not for long, though.

"Are you headed to work?" she persisted.

I hated small talk, but for some reason, I found myself turning towards her and responding to her question. "I'm coming off work."

"We haven't properly introduced ourselves," she mumbled, a smile trembling on to her luscious lips and her hand sticking out towards me. "I'm Savannah Hayes, just moved into town."

I considered ignoring the hand, but that uncertain smile got to me. I took the peace offering she held out, but as soon as our fingers brushed, sparks shot up my arm. Fuck, what the hell was that! That had never happened to me before.

No woman had ever affected me so viscerally. I could see she had felt it too. She snatched her hand back as if she had been bitten by a snake.

"Cameron Elliott," I said, blood and heat rushing to my cock.

"It's nice to meet you," she said, her eyes flitting from my face to my chest. Her cheeks were flushed and she seemed and she looked as if she wanted the ground to open up and swallow her whole.

I didn't need anyone to tell me the intense attraction was mutual. Savannah Hayes wanted me just as much as I wanted her. Not that, that improved the situation one bit. I was glad when Liz brought our drinks. I grabbed mine, gave her a twenty-dollar bill and turned to leave.

"Have a nice day," I called over my shoulder.

She couldn't accuse me of being rude after that, could she. In my truck, I was embarrassed to find that my cock had swelled even more. The more I dwelled on her, the more I grew.

I drove home with thoughts of a naked Savannah in my mind.

No matter what I did, I couldn't stop thinking about her. I could picture her even though I'd looked at her for less than thirty seconds. Her red hair had been covered in a beanie and she had worn those tight jeans accentuating the curve of her ass and thighs.

I pictured myself pulling her jeans down over those curvy, thick hips and grew harder. Savannah had a body that made you want to toss her on a bed and ravish her. I found myself wondering if she would do my delivery again.

And that was where I drew the line.

It was stupid to fantasize about her. I needed to completely stop thinking about her. There was no future there. She was a good girl and all I ever want ever again is bad girls. Fuck em and leave em, kind of girls.

I got home and went outside to chop firewood in an effort to get her out of my mind. Bad decision. I kept visualizing her in those jeans that molded her body just right.

***

I finished chopping wood for the day and headed back to the house. I usually worked four days a week from Monday to Thursday and I looked forward to the three days of downtime. Heading straight up to my bedroom for a shower. It was a big house. I could still remember the first time my family saw the house.

They couldn't believe it was for one person, especially my mother. She kept walking into every room musing at the size of it. At the end of it, she had commented she couldn't live in a house this big. She lived alone with Cassie, my youngest sister, and she already thought that my old childhood home was too big for them.

As I stepped into the shower an image of Savannah popped into my head. It was so long since a woman did that. And just like that Amanda rushed into my being.

My chest constricted as the familiar pain spread from a core point to the rest of my chest. It was true what they said, the pain of grief faded over time but it never went away. It has been five years now since I lost her and it still hurt deeply. With a sigh, I stood under the hot rivulets of water and allowed my mind to empty. Experience had taught me to push the sadness away before it invaded my mind and took root.

Slowly, slowly, I turned my mind to other things, until I was once again a functioning human being. No one would be able to tell the difference.

I got out of the shower and was picking out clean clothes

to wear from my walk-in closet, when the doorbell rang. I frowned, wondering who it could be. Grocery delivery was the day after tomorrow. Probably someone else who had lost their way.

I wrapped the towel around my middle and went downstairs. I opened the door and Savannah stood there, looking like a Christmas gift that had been delivered early. She held a cake box in her hands. Her eyes moved down to my bare chest, then below to my lower region and to my shock, my cock visibly jerked.

That had never fucking happened before. Her eyes widened as she raised them up to my face.

"Hello," I said as calmly as I could, as though my erection was not causing a tent in front of my towel.

"Hi." Her eyes dropped to my cock again.

I suppressed a grin. Her discomfort and obvious reaction was fun to watch. She roused herself and held out the cake. "I brought this for you as a measure of my apology. I'm sorry for pouring coffee all over you and ruining your obviously expensive jacket."

The only thing I remembered about that incident was how hot she looked. I shrugged. "Thanks for the cake but it's completely unnecessary. I have more jackets than I need."

"I made it myself," she put in hopefully, a small glint of pride coming into her eyes.

I raised my eyebrows.

"It will make me feel better if you take it," she said, almost pleading.

I nodded and put my hand out, ready take it without touching her skin, but instead of letting go, she held onto the box.

"Do you want me to take it to the kitchen for you?" she asked, staring pointedly at my naked chest.

I'd forgotten I was nearly naked. "Sure thanks. I'll go get dressed, then we can have some together."

As she made her way to the kitchen, I sprinted up the stairs. I whistled as I dressed. It surprised me how happy I was to have some company. But not just any company. Her company as I actually preferred spending hours upon hours alone.

I dressed in record time, grabbing some jogging pants and a t-shirt. Back downstairs, I found that Savannah had found the coffee maker and was making us some.

"I hope you don't mind, but I didn't want cake without something to wash it down with."

"Not at all. Would you like me to hang that up for you?" I nodded towards her jacket.

She smiled and unzipped her jacket. "Okay. Since it looks like I've more or less invited myself in."

My eyes were glued on her chest when she took off the jacket. She was wearing skin tight jeans like the other day and a low-cut spaghetti strap top that was showing a whole lot of cleavage. She had full, perfect breasts and her skin was like cream, smooth and silky. She looked good enough to eat and I could feel the familiar stirring in my cock for her.

I distracted myself by fetching mugs and side plates for the cake.

"Where can I get a knife?" Savannah asked.

I directed her to the right drawer, while staring at her shapely ass. I'd never seen a woman so perfectly made for my hands and mouth.

The moment that thought formed, guilt quickly followed it. How could I think that about another woman? Amanda had been perfect for me. I turned away from the sight of her. But Amanda was gone. Lost forever and

Savannah was here. I mourned my dead wife for so long and maybe I just wanted a little comfort for me, for a while.

"How long have you lived here?" Savannah asked, breaking into my thoughts. She'd settled down at the island with our coffee and two slices of cake.

"Five years," I said slowly. Had it really been that long? Where had the years gone? Even as I asked the question I knew very well where the years had gone. I'd been buried in grief unable to even contemplate that one day, I would feel alive again.

Without realizing it, the darkness had slowly lifted. In last few months I had a lot of not great, but good days. Days when I felt content to be alive. Days where I could tolerate being around other people.

"Dorothy told me that you are a park ranger?" Savannah commented, as I took my seat next to her.

"I am," I replied as I became aware of her floral scent. It reminded me of sunshine and summer. So she had asked about me too.

"It sounds like an interesting job." She fidgeted in her chair and then reached for the fork. Her arm brushed against her mug, sending it sliding across the island. She muttered a string of curses.

I quickly got up and hurried to the counter to grab a kitchen cloth.

"I'm sorry," she said, trying to stem the flow of coffee down the island.

"It's fine. It doesn't matter. There's more coffee."

She grabbed the towel from me and moped it all up, moving back and forth until the surface was dry.

Savannah sat on the chair with her back to the island sinking her teeth into her bottom lower lip. An irresistible urge to see her happy and laughing came over me. I moved to her and placed a hand on her knee. A fairly innocent gesture, but it stopped being innocent when she looked at me with her large softly brown eyes. I could feel myself drowning in the velvety depths.

"I'm so clumsy," she whispered.

"No, you're not." Without conscious thought, I moved between her legs until her face was a couple of inches away from mine. "It was an accident and can happen to anyone."

Her gaze dropped to my mouth and I knew she was thinking about kissing me. That's all I needed. I crushed my mouth to hers and she draped her arm around my neck and pulled me to her.

I slid my hand to the back of her head and a tiny moan escaped her lips. She parted her lips and I slid my tongue into her mouth. She had a coffee taste in her mouth and beyond that, a strawberry one, as though she had sucked on one before entering the house. I bit and sucked her lips until they were swollen.

Every time she moaned into my mouth, the fire in my blood increased, almost consuming me. I felt as horny as a fucking teenager. I moved my hand from her knee to her chest, cupping her full breast, her stiff nipple grazing the palm of my hand.

She let out a loud moan, but suddenly grew still.

I understood immediately, backed away and caught the look of horror in her eyes. It was as if icy cold water had been poured over her... and me. Without saying a word, she swung her legs to the side and slid off the stool unsteadily.

"I'm sorry I have to go," she gasped.

I didn't say anything. Not that it would have mattered anyway, she was already halfway out of the kitchen. She grabbed her jacket and without looking back, disappeared through the door.

I raked my fingers through my hair.

Fuck! What had I been thinking? I didn't even contemplate going after her. What was I going to say? Sorry for kissing you? Sorry I couldn't control myself around you?

I was an idiot. I had allowed her to light a dangerous fire inside me.

I listened to the quick taps of her shoes until the front door opened and shut with a soft click. I looked at the slices of cake on the plate. Chocolate. So she made it herself. I collected some icing on my finger and put it on my tongue.

Delicious.

Still, it was not sweeter than her mouth.

But that was taboo. Or was it?

Chapter Three
Savannah

"I just listened to the news. There'll be a storm today," Heather said. "Be careful out there."

"I will," I told her. My biggest problem was not the weather. I'd been dreading this day since yesterday when I left Cameron's. I shook my head free of that memory and carried the crates to the minivan, one at a time.

I settled in the driver's seat and inhaled deeply before turning the ignition key. My insides were shaking and as I started to drive, memories of that kiss invaded my thoughts and I couldn't shake them off.

What had been wrong with me? How would I have kissed a stranger? It didn't matter how attractive he was. Sane women did not go around kissing men they did not know. What kind of woman must he think I was?

I had done a lot of stupid things in my life, including getting married to Finn. The only thing that made me not regret the marriage was Ethan. I loved my little boy with all of my heart and he was the only reason I got up every morning.

Heather had not been wrong. The weather was not great. A light snow was falling and the wind was picking up but it wasn't too bad. I drove slowly and carefully, grateful that my Aunt May's van was sturdy enough to navigate the slippery roads.

I had a few deliveries to make along the way to Dorothy's and by the time I got there, snow had started falling in earnest. I hurried out of the minivan and went to the back to grab her delivery.

She must have been watching out for me at the window because by the time I got to the front door, it was already open.

"Hi Dorothy," I said. "Can I come in?"

"Yes of course my dear," she said. "It's terrible out there. I wasn't sure you were going to come."

"It's not too bad," I told her. "I'll be done in a few hours." I carried the crate to the kitchen and found an older man, I assumed was her husband stirring the contents of a pot.

"This is Rory, my husband," Dorothy said.

Rory smiled and nodded at me, then he continued what he'd been doing.

"Stay with us until the storm is over," Dorothy said.

I was touched by the concern in her voice. "I'll be just fine. Besides, Cameron's place is not too far off from here. Plus, my minivan is made for this weather," I said with a smile to reassure her.

It really was cold I thought as I entered the warmth of the minivan. I couldn't wait to finish my deliveries and head back to the cottage. I had two more days to get it in order before Ethan came home from my sister's place.

The closer I got to Cameron's place the more that stupid kiss haunted me. Except that it was not stupid. It was the hottest kiss I had ever shared with anybody. Cameron kissed as if he was dying of thirst and I was his oasis.

I couldn't forget how my body had come alive at the touch of his lips or the way his hand had cradled my head to hold it in place. My panties had been completely soaked by the time I fled the house and that night I had barely slept and when I did, I had dreams, erotic dreams that left me feeling unfulfilled in the morning.

I swallowed hard as Cameron's house came into view. I turned off the engine and inhaled deeply before reluctantly leaving the safety of the van. I was going to apologize to him and then hopefully, with my dignity intact, leave.

Just as Dorothy had done, Cameron had the door open when I got there. I saw him and my breath hitched.

"Hello," I said and tried not to look at him, but it was impossible not to. Our fingers brushed as he took the crate from me. Immediately our gazes locked. I could have bet my last dollar that Cameron was thinking about that kiss too.

"This is not good weather to be out in Savannah," he said.

"I know but I'll be done soon," I told him. "You are my last delivery." I followed him into the house staring at the muscles on his shoulders as he carried the crate through to the kitchen. He dumped it on the counter and then moved to the coffee maker.

I hoped he didn't think I was going to stay for coffee. It was embarrassing enough that I had to see him again without making it worse by spending more time in his company.

"Make yourself comfortable," he said. "This storm is going to be here awhile."

I shook my head. "I can't stay. I have to go but before I do I want to talk to you about something." I folded my hands into fists and forced myself to continue.

Cameron moved closer to where I stood. I wished I could take a step back but I couldn't without looking like a coward. I raised my gaze to meet his eyes. "I wanted to apologize."

A puzzled look came over his features. God he was handsome. Concentrate.

"Apologize for what?" he asked.

My heart pounded so hard I was sure he could hear it. I tapped my thigh with my left hand. "I shouldn't have lead you on the last time I was here."

Cameron's features relaxed and a hint of a smile pulled at the corners of his mouth. He cocked his head to one side and contemplated me. "I kissed you, Savannah. And I must say that I enjoyed it. I was actually hoping we could do it again."

My jaw fell open. Before I could say or do anything Cameron took a step forward and wrapped his strong muscular arms around me.

I should have stopped him but instead I looked up into his eyes. Big mistake. I felt as if I was falling in the icy blueness of his eyes.

"We should get rid of the coat. It's hot in here."

He gave me a few seconds to respond, but when I didn't, he removed his hands from my waist and began to unbutton my jacket. I needed to say something. But I couldn't bring my mouth to move. On the last button, he looked at me as if giving me one last chance to say no.

Again, I did not respond because my body was dying to feel his hands on me. I was helpless to say anything. I wanted this so badly. I hadn't been touched or held by a man in almost two years.

Unfortunately my ex-husband had been a terrible lover so I didn't think I was missing out too much. At least, until I laid eyes on Cameron.

Cameron peeled off my jacket and helped me out of it. Then he draped it over a chair and ran his callused hands over my bare arms while his eyes hungrily raked over my body.

I'd worn a halter dress that I had no business wearing with my cup size. But I loved halter dresses. I found them cute and to be honest I think there was a part of me that had been hoping Cameron would get to see it. That he would find me irresistible. Foolish, I know.

"You look beautiful," he said, his voice thick with desire.

I felt beautiful.

Cameron pulled me close, crushing my breasts against his chest. My nipples came alive, aching and longing for his touch. He brought his mouth to me and brushed his lips against my mouth.

I inhaled his manly scent and with a moan I closed my eyes and draped my arms around his neck.

I parted my lips inviting him into my mouth. He groaned and depend the kiss then without warning he dropped his hands to my hips and lifted me, placing me gently on the kitchen counter.

"God, you're so sweet," he muttered in between desperate kisses to my lips that left me wanting more.

Cameron ran his hands over my thighs, pushing my dress farther up and all the while our lips were locked on each other. My chest rose and fell with every breath I took.

His hands moved all the way up past my belly to my breasts. He cupped them and rubbed my nipples with his thumbs over the material of my dress. A moan escaped my mouth and at that point I didn't care about anything except getting rid of the deep ache between my legs.

"I need to taste you, Savannah," Cameron snarled suddenly, as if he no longer bear the wait.

His words went straight to my pussy. I was so aroused my whole body felt as if it had been lit on fire. Cameron stared at me, waiting for an answer.

The rational side of me tried to kick in. I should stop him, but I pushed that voice away. No, not this time. I wanted this man so badly. Just this once, I told myself. It had been so long. I deserved one moment of passion. Of forgetting all my responsibilities and having a bit of fun.

"Yes, yes, I want you to taste me," I whispered feverishly.

Cameron groaned and shoved the rest of my dress up. "Spread your thighs and show me your pussy," he ordered.

Pre-order the book here:
Surprise Proposal

ABOUT THE AUTHOR

Thank you so much for reading!
If you have enjoyed the book and would like to leave a
precious review for me, please kindly do so here:

Flirting With The CEO

Please click on the link below to receive info about my latest
releases and giveaways.
NEVER MISS A THING

Or
come and say hello here:

ALSO BY IONA ROSE

Made in the USA
Middletown, DE
19 January 2023